SUNRISE SONG

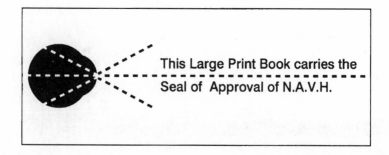

This Large Print Book carries the
Seal of Approval of N.A.V.H.

SUNRISE SONG

Catherine Palmer

Thorndike Press • Waterville, Maine

Published in 2005 by arrangement with
Tyndale House Publishers, Inc.

Thorndike Press® Large Print Christian Romance.

The tree indicium is a trademark of Thorndike Press.

The text of this Large Print edition is unabridged.
Other aspects of the book may vary from the original edition.

Set in 16 pt. Plantin by Elena Picard.

Printed in the United States on permanent paper.

Library of Congress Cataloging-in-Publication Data

Palmer, Catherine, 1956–
    Sunrise song / by Catherine Palmer.
        p. cm. — (Thorndike Press large print Christian romance)
    ISBN 0-7862-7642-8 (lg. print : hc : alk. paper)
    1. Americans — Kenya — Fiction. 2. Women zoologists
— Fiction. 3. Wildlife refuges — Fiction. 4. African
elephant — Fiction. 5. Businessmen — Fiction. 6. Kenya
— Fiction. 7. Large type books. I. Title. II. Thorndike
Press large print Christian romance series.
PS3566.A495S86 2005
813'.54—dc22   2005004876

For Janice Owens Duffy
in loving memory of her daughter
Kristin Lynn Duffy

National Association for Visually Handicapped
------------------------ *serving the partially seeing*

As the Founder/CEO of NAVH, the only national health agency solely devoted to those who, although not totally blind, have an eye disease which could lead to serious visual impairment, I am pleased to recognize Thorndike Press⋆ as one of the leading publishers in the large print field.

Founded in 1954 in San Francisco to prepare large print textbooks for partially seeing children, NAVH became the pioneer and standard setting agency in the preparation of large type.

Today, those publishers who meet our standards carry the prestigious "Seal of Approval" indicating high quality large print. We are delighted that Thorndike Press is one of the publishers whose titles meet these standards. We are also pleased to recognize the significant contribution Thorndike Press is making in this important and growing field.

Lorraine H. Marchi, L.H.D.
Founder/CEO
NAVH

⋆ Thorndike Press encompasses the following imprints: Thorndike, Wheeler, Walker and Large Print Press.

When elephants fight,
it is the grass that weeps.

SWAHILI PROVERB

ONE

"She's chillier than the ice on Kilimanjaro," Clive Willetts snorted. The lanky British pilot banked the small aircraft and glanced at his boss, the new owner of the flying safari company. "Not to say I don't like Dr. Thornton, sir. It's just that she can be touchy at times. She doesn't like people intruding."

"And I suppose she'd classify my little visit as an intrusion?"

"More than likely."

Rogan McCullough slid back his starched white cuff and studied his watch. Three separate dials indicated time zones around the world. Here in Kenya, it was ten o'clock in the morning.

His flight from London had been delayed twice, putting him four hours late into Nairobi. After sending his suitcases ahead to his hotel with the limousine, he had boarded one of the two sleek and well-equipped Catalina PBY 5As owned by Air-Tours Safaris. During this short flight over central Kenya in clear weather, Rogan wondered at his chances of selling a cranky, eccentric scientist on his newest brainstorm.

He gave the watch an absentminded tap as he stared out the side window. Far beneath the plane rolled verdant hills covered in a tangle of vines, eucalyptus, and Nandi flame trees. Small villages occupied clearings, their thatched huts dark against the bright red-orange soil. Then, as though a confectioner had neatly sliced away the middle of a green-iced sheet cake, the fertile highlands stopped. The land fell sharply, and a great barren yellow plain stretched far in the distance until it reached the rise of the distant escarpment.

"The Great Rift Valley," Clive explained, as if sensing his boss's interest in the abrupt change. "It runs from the Mediterranean Sea most of the way along the east coast of Africa. Strangest thing you'll ever see. It's a fault — as though the continent tried to split in two a few million years back. The whole Rift Valley is full of unusual land formations."

Rogan nodded, well aware of the unusual configuration. Despite his preoccupation with business, he had always had a keen interest in natural sciences. As a small boy, he had collected rocks and fallen birds' nests. At his boarding school, his room had been littered with pieces of driftwood, feathers, and pressed leaves. Even as an adult, he'd chosen to include climbing and caving among his pastimes. He kept a record of the mountains he wanted to scale. Through the years, he had checked them off one by one.

Now, seeing this land he'd always dreamed about, Rogan felt something uncomfortable stir inside his chest. He recognized it immediately, though he had never put a name to it. Nature, the magnificence of the earth's wonders, always brought up this prickling curl of awareness. It was a touch, a voice, a sense of something . . . someone . . . higher and greater and more intelligent than himself.

God, he thought, and just as quickly he pushed away the certainty of a creator. He didn't doubt the existence of a higher power, but he felt sure that such a being could not be interested in the minutia of human existence. Rogan's own life was abundant proof of that.

Unwilling to continue in this train of thought, he shifted his attention to the British pilot, whose skimpy blond mustache wandered across his upper lip like an uncertain centipede. "You mentioned formations," he said. "Volcanoes?"

"Quite right," the pilot confirmed. "Some of them are still active. And there are lakes full of pink flamingos. Caves lined with thousands of bats. Craggy black lava flows. Soda-rimmed marshes. Snowcapped mountains. And escarpments."

He let the plane drop and glide along the sheer edge of the valley.

"Can anything live down there?" Rogan asked as his gaze traced the razor-sharp cliffs and the wide plain between.

"The place is a regular Garden of Eden, sir. Zebra. Gazelle. Antelope. Cheetah. Elephant."

"People?"

"Unsociable sorts. The Maasai have the run of the place. They're a fierce, primitive lot who still carry spears and don't think too highly of modern civilization. And, of course, there's Dr. Fiona Thornton."

"Ah, yes," Rogan said. "Dr. Thornton." He conjured up the image he'd formed of the woman who ran the Rift Valley Elephant Project. He pictured her as a mixture of his high school English teacher and his great-aunt Rose.

In the weeks spent planning his trip, he'd come to imagine Dr. Thornton as a short, buxom woman with steel gray hair and a thunderous voice. She would wear a khaki dress left over from some World War II women's corps, thick support stockings in a pale shade that skin had never considered turning, and heavy black lace-up boots. Her stern face would wither him from the shade of a pith helmet as her pinched lips formed the answer she would snap at his request. *Absolutely not.*

Unable to suppress a grin, he shook his head. *Sorry, Dr. Thornton,* he thought, *but I'm afraid you've met your match.*

Rogan leaned against the headrest and closed his eyes. As a matter of fact, he was looking forward to the challenge of outwitting the old battle-ax with as much anticipation as he felt for a boardroom confrontation at McCullough Enterprises. His persuasive style and bullheaded stubbornness had built the company into a billion-dollar operation, after all. And he intended to reverse the sagging revenues of Air-Tours by applying the same determination.

"If you'll excuse my frankness, sir," Clive spoke up, "you look bushed. Jet lag will catch up with a man, no matter how strong he is. I'd suggest you get a little rest. When your father owned Air-Tours, he used to stretch out in the lounge back there and take a nap. We've got a well-stocked bar, a library of old maps and books, and a clean rest room. Your father always said the rumble of the engines did him more good than a hundred-dollar massage."

"I'm fine. Really."

The pilot smiled, showing a set of uneven teeth beneath the wispy mustache. "Your father learned the hard way too. But after he'd been coming to Kenya for a few years, he once told me that Africa was the only place where he could really rest. Africa was where he could let go. He said it was the only place he knew of where he was really himself —"

"If you don't mind," Rogan interrupted, "I'd rather not talk right now, Clive. I need to review some figures."

"Yes, sir." The pilot gave him a sideways glance and clamped his mouth shut.

Rogan flipped the gold clasps on his leather briefcase and extracted a file. Air-Tours. The company had shown a steep decline in the past five years. He intended to rectify that. In many ways, resolving financial difficulties was his specialty. Oh, he enjoyed the media operations of McCullough Enterprises, and he liked working with the journalists and ad men he employed. Their bright-eyed enthusiasm kept him pushing for innovation long after his own fiscal goals had been met.

But Rogan truly excelled in the revival of companies on the brink of financial extinction. This was how he'd gotten his start. And the prospect of bringing some of his father's smaller businesses back to life helped ease the sting of the pitiful legacy he'd inherited. Rogan was well aware that the collection of flagging industries and the small lump sum — a tiny percentage of John McCullough's vast estate — were little more than conscience money. They were his father's way of acknowledging to the world that once, among all his other accomplishments, he'd produced a son.

After the senior McCullough's recent death, the rest of the estate had been parceled out among ex-wives, educational institutions, and charities bearing his name. Rogan didn't really care that he'd been left the financially weak companies, he told himself. He looked on them as a challenge. Something to keep him going.

From his office in New York, he had examined the books and records of Air-Tours and the other companies. He had made calls. Set up contacts. Investigated and instigated programs. In just three months, the pizza chain was showing a spark of life, and the hotels were preparing for face-lifts. Now he had his sights set on the tiny flying safari company.

Rows of numbers swam before his eyes as Rogan stared at his father's signature scrawled across a balance sheet. *John McCullough*. The ink flourishes personified the man. They suggested extravagance. Wealth. Show. Pomp. Scandal. Clive Willetts's recounting of talks with the tycoon didn't fit the picture his son held of him. Rogan rubbed a finger across his temple.

He didn't want to think about his father. When the memories intruded, he felt six years old again. Six years old and hiding behind the stair rail watching his parents hurl accusations and Ming Dynasty vases at each other. Six years old and trembling as his mother screeched and wept and hung on to his father's coattails. Six years old and frozen inside as he stood at the iron gate of an ivy-covered boarding school and stared at the settling puff of dust from his father's Mercedes as it roared off.

Rogan slammed down the briefcase lid. Clive lifted one eyebrow.

"About Dr. Thornton," Rogan said irritably. "What's she most likely to respond

16

to? Money? Publicity?"

Clive sniffed. "Well, Dr. Thornton isn't your average sort of person, if you know what I mean. She's more than a little eccentric. Not the kind of woman who'll give you the time of day . . . unless you're an elephant."

"Surely she's in need of funding or new supplies. I've heard these research projects are always in the hole."

"Could be. I wouldn't doubt it."

"You told me she gives you tips on where the elephants are so you can fly tourists over them. You must know something about her. How does she operate? What drives her?"

"She's never said a word to me about herself, mind you. Just talks about elephants. She grew up in Kenya as I did. But we didn't know each other in those days. My father farmed near the coast, and we stayed fairly isolated. She was born in Nairobi to an American father and an English mother. There were four children in all — three girls and a boy. I've met them, of course, but they're all living in different places now. Tillie's an agroforester in Mali. Jessica owns an old house on Zanzibar Island. Grant is an anthropologist. He lives here in Kenya, but he stays out in the bush most of the time. Their father is a professor at the University of Nairobi — still teaching, I think. The mother was a painter, but she died a long time ago."

"How?"

Clive shrugged. "No idea. Anyway, after university, Fiona Thornton came back to Kenya and met a woman studying lions in the Amboseli Game Park. Dr. Howard sponsored her, saw that she got her doctorate, and helped her get research grants. Since then, Dr. Thornton has studied elephants. Elephants are her passion. It's like I've tried to tell you, sir; she doesn't have much interest in humans. When she does actually decide to say something, it might be only two or three words . . . if you're lucky. Odd thing about Dr. Thornton, though. The Africans who work with her call her Matalai Shamsi. It means Princess Sunrise."

Rogan shook his head, declining to respond as the plane banked steeply and began its descent into the Great Rift Valley.

Fiona Thornton stared at the neat column of figures for a full minute. She lifted her head. "Three calves this month," she said.

Sentero eyed her, his face impassive.

She tapped her pen on the metal folding table. "I want to find the M family this afternoon. Moira was in estrus in —" she scanned the papers in her hand — "in April. During the long rains, I saw her in consort with the old bull James. At the time, he was definitely in musth. Moira's had the full twenty-two-month gestation, and I've noticed other signs of impending delivery."

"Yesterday she was restless." Sentero's voice was deep, his English enunciation clear.

"She seemed out of sync with the others, don't you think?"

The African nodded, then stiffened and lifted his focus, as if he could see through the tent's olive canvas roof.

"What is it?" Fiona had come to rely on her Maasai assistant's keen senses. He often heard and saw things much sooner than she did.

"Airplane."

"It won't land here. It's probably going to one of the Mara lodges."

Sentero shrugged. "It will come here."

At that moment Fiona heard the distinct rumble of the plane's engines. She chewed the inside of her lip for a moment, then brushed a hand across her forehead. Talking to a visitor . . . a stranger . . . was the last thing she wanted to do. Standing, she replaced her records in a metal file box and locked it.

"I didn't order any supplies from Nairobi. Did you?" she asked.

Sentero shook his head. Framed in the opening of the tent flap, his tall, sinewy body stood dark against the brilliant African sunshine. He was a sinister-looking man with a face chiseled by time into sharp angles and harsh planes. His eyes, small and almost black, glittered with a canny sparkle.

Sentero always wore traditional Maasai garb — draped layers of bloodred cloths, some plaid, some checked, all smelling of woodsmoke. Three bead necklaces circled his throat, one a choker with a central button of mother-of-pearl, the other two dangling down his bare chest. His ears, each lobe pierced and stretched to form a two-inch hole, sported beaded bands of red, yellow, white, and blue. Occasionally Sentero plugged the hole of one earlobe with an old black plastic film canister filled with tobacco. Chewing tobacco was his only vice.

"Start the Land Rover," Fiona said as

the plane's engines roared over her camp. The tent trembled. Vervet monkeys shrieked in the acacia trees overhead. Her cat leapt down from his perch on the wardrobe and darted under the bed. She grabbed her jacket and camera. "I'll tell Mama Hannah to ward them off, whoever they are."

Sentero flashed his only smile of the morning, snatched his iron-tipped spear from beside the tent pole, and strode out. Fiona knelt at the foot of the small camp cot. Flicking on her flashlight, she swept its beam through the dust until she caught the cat's green eyes.

"Sukari, are you afraid?" With small kissing noises, she gently patted the tent's canvas floor. She snapped off the light. "Come on, sweet one. That was just an old airplane. I won't let it hurt you."

Sukari crept forward until he butted Fiona's cheek. She stroked beneath his chin, smiling at the deep, satisfied purr. The spotless white cat was nearly blind, the casualty of a close encounter with a spitting cobra. Fiona stroked between his ears and nestled her nose against his furry neck.

"Now, be a good boy," she whispered. "Sentero and I are going to see if Moira's had her calf. I'll zip you into the tent, so mind your manners and don't chew on my philodendron."

The airplane slipped over the tops of yellow-trunked acacia trees. Like great green umbrellas, their canopies provided a measure of shade in the otherwise scorching heat. Rogan took in the pitiful little camp scattered at the edge of a nearly dry streambed. Several scraggly, patched, and faded tents, olive in color and nearly camouflaged, rested in the shadows like bedraggled bag ladies. A thatch-roofed shed of some sort emitted a thin wisp of blue smoke. Like an aging, rusty King Pelinor, a Land Rover with a dented fender guarded the camp's entrance.

He made mental notes about the needed upgrade. New tents, of course. At least ten of them — the deluxe model, with room for two beds and a table. An expanded campfire area. A dining room with a connecting kitchen. Bath and shower rooms.

The plane descended toward a humped dark mountain shaped like an elephant's sloping back. Then it swung around, touched down, and taxied across a stretch of uneven ground.

"I know you're a pilot yourself, sir,"

Clive commented. "In Africa you'll want to watch out for antbear holes when you're landing. Those things can ruin the landing gear. Your wheel goes in and *boom*, that's it."

"What's going on there?" Rogan grabbed the chrome door handle before the plane had come to a stop. Just across the riverbed a tall figure strode across the clearing. "Who is that?"

"It's Dr. Thornton, sir. And it looks like she's making for her car. She's leaving."

"Not if I can help it." Rogan flung open the door and swung down from the plane. Loosening his tie, he set off through thigh-high golden grass. Behind him the plane's propellers wound down with a deep, air-cutting *thunk-thunk*. A rich smell of heat and soil and fragrant grasses hung thick in the air. It clung to him as he walked, filtered through his hair and onto his skin as if alive and seeking.

Rogan scrambled down the stream bank and splashed through the broad trickle of water, a damp sediment seeping into his shoes. He hurried on, irritation making inroads into his careful composure. The woman ignored him and marched toward the Land Rover as if she'd never even heard the plane come in.

"Dr. Thornton," he barked.

She stopped. For a moment she seemed to disappear, her body camouflaged among the slender acacia trunks. Her clothing, a pale green shirt and tan slacks, melted into the surroundings. She made no sound. And then she turned her head.

Rogan's first realization was that Dr. Fiona Thornton was no battle-ax. Great-aunt Rose and his high school English teacher vanished into thin air.

This woman had hair the color of a flaming sunset. Red-gold. Rippling over her shoulders in a tangled swath. A pair of hazel eyes, thick lashed and as wary as those of a lioness, scrutinized him. Accustomed to painted lips and powdered cheeks, he was startled to realize that her face was bare. Yet color infused it with life — cheeks and nose blushed by the sun, faint freckles beneath a ruddy tan and lips almost too full.

He cleared his throat. With one hand extended, he walked toward her. "Dr. Thornton, I presume?" He smiled, hoping to melt her a little.

"Yes." She spoke only the single word, but her voice had a husky quality that resonated in the marrow of his bones. She made no move to grasp his hand. Coolly she assessed him. With an unpainted fingernail, she tapped the camera that dangled against one curved hip.

"Dr. Thornton, my name is Rogan McCullough. I'm sure you've heard of McCullough Enterprises, New York." When she didn't respond, he leaned toward her and coaxed her fingers from the camera strap. He expected a cold-fish handshake. He was wrong.

Their hands clasped as if they had silently agreed to engage in a duel of elemental arm wrestling. He stared into her eyes. Camouflage eyes, green and brown, mottled with bits of gray and yellow. He sensed that she hid inside them, revealing as little as possible of herself.

"I have a proposal for you, Dr. Thornton," Rogan continued. "It's one I think you'll like very much. May we talk?"

"Sentero," she snapped suddenly, jerking away her gaze — and her hand. She spoke in Swahili. *"Ngoja kidogo, tafadhali."*

The African cut the Land Rover's engine and emerged from the vehicle. He moved leopardlike across the clearing, his spear held against one bare brown thigh and pointing at the intruder.

Rogan swung around and assessed the Maasai. His heart began to race as he re-

25

alized that this was no New York board-room. This was Africa. This was an eccentric woman and her savage guard. A man with dangling earlobes and snakelike black eyes was advancing on him, weapon menacing. Here the rules were different.

"Excuse me, but what does he have in mind with that spear?" Rogan asked.

Dr. Thornton's lips twitched, and her mouth formed a wry smile. "Don't worry," she said as the African's path took him safely to one side. "I've told Sentero to wait until we're finished."

"Does he really need the spear? Wouldn't a gun be more efficient?"

She glanced at Sentero, then stepped back and ran her eyes down her visitor. "You, on the other hand, are perfectly equipped for the African bush," she said. "A gray business suit? A navy tie? Please."

"My flight into Nairobi was late. I didn't have time to change."

"Wool?"

"It's February. Winter in New York." Retaking the offensive, he gestured toward a pair of faded canvas camp chairs beside the fire ring. "Could we sit down, Dr. Thornton? I'd really like to —"

"What is it you want, Mr. McCullough? I'm very busy today." Aware he had disturbed her, interrupted her routine, Rogan made up his mind to be as civil as possible.

"May we?" He held out a hand to indicate the chairs as he gently cupped her elbow. The touch — the warmth of her sun-heated skin against his palm — sent an unexpected current up his arm. With effort, he dismissed it. This was business, after all.

As if in an effort to escape him, the woman pulled away and took a chair.

"Now, Dr. Thornton," he began, seating himself across from her. He leaned forward, focusing on her face as he spoke. "As the new owner of Air-Tours Safaris, I've been studying ways to make my company viable. When I was in New York —"

"Tea, *toto?*" A small African woman spoke as she emerged from the shadows of a nearby tent. "And perhaps some chocolate biscuits for your guest?"

"No thank you, Mama Hannah," Dr. Thornton said. "Mr. McCullough won't be staying long."

The elderly lady nodded, her head swathed in a brightly colored scarf and her small dark feet clad in a pair of neon yellow flip-flops. "I could cook some rice pudding. Or a sausage."

At this, the scientist's face broke into a

warm smile. She reached out and took Mama Hannah's hand. "I'd love a sausage for dinner. But Sentero and I are going out in a moment to check on the M family. We won't be back until sunset."

"I will cook a sausage for you at sunset." She glanced at Rogan. Dark, birdlike eyes scanned him up and down. "You are hot. Your feet are wet. You have no peace. 'Change your ways. . . . Live in harmony and peace. Then the God of love and peace will be with you.' "

With this final word, she turned and headed back into the tent. Rogan gaped after her, aware that he was sweating inside his wool suit, and his feet were damp from sloshing through the stream. And as for peace . . .

"As I was saying," he began again, cutting off his own thoughts. "When I was in New York inspecting the Air-Tours records, I spoke with Clive Willetts by telephone. He mentioned that you had been a big help to him. He told me about your camp and your elephant research projects. And that was when I began to see a future for this place."

"I have no trouble seeing the future, Mr. McCullough. I've worked with the Rift Valley elephants for more than ten years, and I intend to continue working with them for the rest of my life. I have only one goal, and that's to ensure the survival of the African elephant in the wild."

"Exactly my point. And that's where Air-Tours comes in. I have the resources to help you accomplish your goal."

"What resources are those?"

"As you may know, Air-Tours caters to wealthy individuals. We work with highly influential people. People who make a difference in their world. I'm proposing to bring them here, Dr. Thornton. To the Rift Valley. You can show them what you're doing. Show them the life of the African elephant and why that life deserves preservation. You're a brilliant woman. You have a lot of creative energy. People will flock to learn from you. Think about it. You could hold seminars. You could touch people with the stories of your elephants."

"What on *earth* are you talking about?"

Bemused, Rogan studied her. This woman showed none of the enthusiasm he'd seen in other potential clients, who usually swallowed his speeches as though they were strawberry ice cream. In fact, she looked as if she'd just eaten a dill pickle.

"I'm suggesting," he said, "that I can introduce you to the kinds of wealthy, influential people who are always looking for charitable foundations to support. With the cooperation of Air-Tours Safaris, you could have a major impact on wildlife awareness."

"Mr. McCullough, I appreciate your interest in the elephants, but we really have nothing to discuss."

"What do you mean?"

"I'm not interested in your plan, Mr. McCullough. Air-Tours is failing, so you want to lure rich tourists with promises of 'getting close to the animals.' You want to bring planeloads of loud, trash-littering, gum-chewing people here to complain about the poor roads and the lack of hot water and electricity. They'll squeal over the lions and scream at the sight of a snake. They'll try to pet the vervet monkeys and feed bananas to my elephants."

"*Your* elephants?"

"*My* elephants. And if you think I intend to allow —"

"Dr. Thornton, please." He struggled to keep from revealing his annoyance at her unreasonable reticence. "I'm genuinely puzzled by your lack of understanding here. These are the people who can support your project. These are the people who have the money to make the difference between a healthy budget and a skimpy one. They matter to your elephants. I have a vision here, Dr. Thornton."

"I have a vision here too."

"Don't you see what I'm offering you? I propose to provide you with new, comfortable tents. I'll expand the camp area, clear some of those trees —"

"My acacias?" Her voice shook. "You'll do nothing of the sort."

"I'll build you a brand-new water pump," he continued. "Don't you understand? I'll bring in generators. You'll be able to see at night. You'll be able to work and study as late as you want."

"I don't want generators. They smell. They belch diesel smoke."

"New Land Rovers, Dr. Thornton. Think about that. I'll buy you three or four of them if you want. And how about a water hole? I could build a big concrete water hole for you. The elephants would be able to come right up to the camp and drink."

"And what's going to keep them from walking in here, knocking your tents flat, and smashing your generators? Elephants have no interest in human boundaries, Mr. McCullough."

"I'll hire guards. This could be a completely self-contained enterprise. I'll put in a kitchen for staff and visitors, and I'll bring in a professional chef."

"All that, and a big trash pile for the elephants to forage through, no doubt. Look, Mr. McCullough, I've found plastic bags, gloves, medicine bottles, pieces of metal, and all sorts of wrappings and containers in elephant droppings. And it's due solely to the rubbish the tourists leave behind."

"I'd build a fence."

"Nothing can keep elephants away but an electric fence. They walk right through iron and wood and even concrete without the slightest hesitation. My elephants have died after eating shards of broken glass from human garbage pits. *Died.*"

Her face went soft all of a sudden. The chilly veil over her eyes lifted, and Rogan saw in them a deep, unbearable pain. Dr. Thornton lowered her head and sagged in the chair. He stared at the top of her head, at the wild red-gold tumble that even at a distance smelled of rainwater and fresh air. She was breathing deeply, and with each breath came the slightest shudder.

"I'm sorry," he said. "About your elephants. About . . . about the glass."

For a long time she didn't look at him.

"I didn't know elephants would eat

trash," he tried again. "I wasn't aware of that."

"We've had a drought," she whispered. "The December rains failed. The grass is almost all dead or eaten away. But even in the rainy season, elephants raid the lodge garbage pits. Once they acquire a taste for bananas, mangoes, pineapples —"

"Forbidden fruit."

She lifted her head. "Elephants don't know what's good for them and what isn't. They're not like humans."

"Not all humans know what's good for them either."

"I know what's good for *me*, Mr. McCullough. The Rift Valley Elephant Project is my life. I don't want changes. I won't allow anything different, anything disturbing."

"Change can be a good thing," he countered. "Look, I have a certain measure of influence to accomplish the things I feel are important, such as wildlife conservation. There's a sense of satisfaction in that."

"In other words, power."

He shrugged. "You could call it that."

"I don't need power. I have peace."

"Peace?"

She spread her long, tanned arms. "I'm

33

out here with God and the animals. What more could I possibly need?"

"You need empowerment, Dr. Thornton. You need financial support. You need people to provide that support."

"The last things I'll ever need are power and money. I need people least of all. As I told you, I have the elephants. I have my camp and my research. That's all I require."

"You need what I have to offer, Dr. Thornton. And so do your elephants."

"I'll be blunt, Mr. McCullough; I don't need you," she said, standing. Her eyes flashed with warning. "I don't need you, and I don't want you."

"Just let me outline my proposal, Dr. Thornton," he tried, in as gentle a voice as he could muster. "On paper. Let me explain in detail what I can do for you. Let me bring in one group of tourists. We'll show them your work. Just a test run. A trial."

"Absolutely not," she snapped.

Before he could respond, she pivoted and motioned to Sentero. The African was on his feet instantly. He loped toward the Land Rover, spear glinting in the noon sun. In moments, they had climbed into the vehicle and were pulling out of camp.

"How did it turn out, Mr. McCullough?" Clive Willetts asked, coming up beside Rogan. "Did you talk her into it?"

Rising, Rogan smiled. "Not exactly."

"Well, I warned you. She doesn't like to talk. I've never seen anyone who could stand up to Dr. Thornton."

Rogan loosened his tie and unbuttoned the collar of his shirt as he studied the vanishing Land Rover.

"Let's start back to Nairobi," the pilot said. "There's no shame in losing a match with someone as stubborn as Dr. Thornton."

"Losing? Hardly, Clive. In fact, I'd say the battle has only just begun."

Slinging his suit coat over one shoulder, Rogan set out across the grassland toward the airplane.

TWO

Like a slow and silent periscope, Fiona rose through the Land Rover's roof hatch. Binoculars to her eyes, she scanned the group of great gray animals near the water hole. Concerned about the M group, Fiona and Sentero had been studying them each afternoon of the three days that had passed since Rogan McCullough's visit. A huge female with large curved tusks scooped dry, red dirt into the tip of her trunk and blew it over her head. The dust settled on her back and ears in a fine, talcumlike powder.

A smaller female with a deep slit in her left ear rubbed her head against the larger animal. A young male lay stretched out on his side in the stubbly grass. A second calf slumped near the first. Beside the babies, a half-grown female hung her head, her trunk flaccid and almost touching the ground.

The dust-bathed matriarch of the herd eyed Fiona for a moment. Then she draped her trunk over one tusk. Her eyes shut. Her breathing deepened.

"They're napping," Fiona whispered.

"Is Moira there?" Pen in hand, Sentero flipped through a notebook. "I don't see her."

Fiona studied the forest of wrinkled gray legs and, above them, the muted landscape of sloping gray backs. One of the elephants stirred and swished her trunk at the flies. "She's behind Margaret."

"Has she had her calf?"

"No, I don't think so. She's restless again this afternoon, though. She keeps waving her trunk and swinging her front foot. Look at Madeline! She's so fat. Could she be pregnant? She's awfully young — only thirteen."

"You show no record of her estrus on this chart."

"It's possible I might have missed it. She was hardly more than a calf, and she was always acting so silly during that rainy season. Once that year I lost the M group for two weeks. They vanished altogether."

Sentero rose through the hatch and lifted his own binoculars. "Yes, Madeline is very fat. I think she is pregnant."

Fiona studied the small, brown eyes of her assistant. He regarded her gravely. In silence, they communicated their fears.

Then Fiona sighed. "Why did the rains

have to fail?" she breathed. "Why now?"

Sentero shrugged. *"Shauri la Mungu,"* he said. "The will of God."

Fiona let the binoculars dangle. She propped her elbows on the warm metal roof and studied the dozing elephants. A fly landed on her arm. She watched it for a moment as it cleaned its long front legs, rubbing them together over and over. Its bulbous red eyes gazed blankly. The fly uncurled its proboscis and tested Fiona's skin. Finding nothing of interest, it buzzed away.

"Do you really think a drought is God's will?" she asked her assistant. "Something so destructive? so terrible?"

"All things are in the hands of God."

Pondering this, Fiona watched a white egret skim the surface of the pathetic water hole. Landing on skinny legs, it picked a path across the geometrically cracked and dried mud. Then, with a quick hop, it settled on Moira's back. The elephant shook her head, her ears rustling with irritation. The egret lifted its long neck for a moment, but when Moira slumped again, the bird tiptoed up the elephant's neck and began to peck for ticks.

"What about evil?" Fiona said softly. "If God is good, then where does evil come from? Mama Hannah would say the drought is Satan's work."

"Even Satan is under the hand of God."

Raised at the skirts of the wise African woman who had been like a mother to the four Thornton children, Fiona knew Scripture backward and forward, and she lived with a strong sense of the presence of God. Mama Hannah had taught her to believe. But belief was not enough, as the elderly woman reminded her.

Surrender remained the essential part of the Christian walk — and Fiona couldn't bring herself to bow in submission to a God who permitted Satan to rule the earth. She had met evil and known him. Once . . . long ago . . . she had seen his bloodred face and heard the thundering echo of his voice. She would never forget, and therefore, she could never surrender.

"If Satan is under God's dominion," she said to Sentero, "God must be very weak. Satan does whatever he wants."

The African was silent for a moment. Finally, he let out a sigh. "Satan is ruler of this world, Dr. Thornton, but not of the human heart. We have charge of our hearts. Unless we surrender them to God."

"You've been listening to Mama Hannah."

He grunted. "She is wise, that old woman. It's good she came to visit us."

Fiona could not agree more. It was a delight to have the dear woman in her camp — despite Mama Hannah's quirks and her propensity for quoting Bible verses left and right. Letting out a breath, Fiona studied the long grass, so dry it was almost silver as it ruffled in the breeze. In the distance a faint rumble shimmered across the sky. Fiona lifted her head. A plane?

Her thoughts lurched immediately to a man she wanted only to forget. Rogan McCullough.

A strange name, Rogan. *Rogue*. Like an angry rogue bull whose tusk had broken off, leaving an unbearably painful raw stump. Like a bull in musth, when the male drive was so strong the elephant plunged through his territory challenging every other male for the right to mate. Like the elephant she had named Jesse James, whose gang of militant bulls must have experienced something so terrifying in their young lives that they hated the sight and smell of humans. When Fiona came upon one or another of them, they tore up bushes and trumpeted their fury at her. One, Billy the Kid, had gouged a large hole in her Land Rover door. Another had trampled a village outside the park. Though hunting was illegal in Kenya, the Maasai had speared the elephant to death.

Fiona shook her head. Rogan McCullough wasn't like that, was he? He was no rogue. He wore a silly wool suit in the middle of Africa. He proposed ridiculous ideas like building concrete water holes and chopping down the acacia trees.

After all, where did he live? The city. She pictured him in his antiseptic world, surrounded by a clutter of clean-shaven executives with shiny black shoes and pasty white hands, soft from the lack of manual labor. He probably had one of those sleek apartments filled with chrome and glass. Sanitary. Efficient.

At the water hole, a small herd of Thomson's gazelles emerged from the grass. Glancing warily about, they tiptoed to the shore. Some kept watch, black noses lifted to the wind and white tails flicking anxiously. Others spread spindly legs and lowered their heads to drink. The elephants took no notice.

Rogan McCullough, Fiona decided, had absolutely no sense of her world. He thought he could bring a gaggle of noisy tourists and expect her to show them the real Africa. This Africa. This quiet, sleepy, dangerous, burning land. These magnificent beasts who strode the plains, whose family units, bond groups, and clans were so complex she had struggled for years to sort them out.

How wrong Rogan was. He knew nothing. He understood nothing. She crossed her arms, willing away the memory of the man whose blue eyes had pinned her every time he spoke. Sentero, Mama Hannah, and the other Africans she knew rarely met her gaze. It wasn't polite to stare.

But Rogan McCullough stared. And he talked — badgering her out of her detached composure. She was a scientist, after all. And yet, under this man's baiting she had spouted off about "her" elephants and "her" acacias. As if Africa could ever belong to any human. She had come close to tears telling him about the elephant who had died from eating glass. And she had sensed things . . . feelings . . . she didn't want.

Though she knew it was ridiculous, her thoughts had returned to him often in the past three days. Memories of his light brown hair, his tall, solid physique, and his blue eyes had drifted in and out of her thoughts. It was his mouth that annoyed her the most. If only he'd had hard, pencil-thin lips, she could have forgotten him. If only he hadn't said those few sensible things, his mouth moving over the words —

She slapped the roof of the Land Rover. "Sentero, let's move on."

The Thomson's gazelles bolted from the water hole, their brown bodies vanishing into the grass with a flash of black stripes and white tails. The elephants stirred and shook their heads. Their great wrinkled eyelids slid apart, and they stared at her like irritable great-aunts wakened early from their afternoon naps.

"Dr. Thornton." Sentero glanced at the digital watch on his left arm. "You disturbed the elephants and frightened away the Tommies. Now our reading of their sleeping time will be inaccurate."

"Oh, skip it for today," she said. "Let's find the R group. I want to see how Rosamond is handling that bullet wound."

As she slumped into the seat, a puff of dust clouded around her legs, then settled to the floor. She shooed a fly and blew at the glass on her binoculars. "Rain," she said. "Why won't it rain?"

Rogan ran one finger down the sleek mounted ivory tusks on the table in his executive suite. "Yes." He spoke into the black telephone receiver. "Dr. John Thornton of the University of Nairobi. The anthropology department. This is the third time I've been transferred. Is Dr. Thornton there?"

"Are you his student?" a starchy voice returned.

"No, I'm not his student. I'm a visitor from the United States, and I'd like to talk to him."

"Dr. Thornton has requested that he be contacted only by students in his advanced classes. He's working on an important project."

Rogan jammed a thumb onto the tip of one tusk. "Madam, I'm becoming impatient here. I need to speak to Dr. Thornton about his daughter and the Rift Valley Elephant Project."

"I'm sorry, sir. Dr. Thornton does not like to be disturbed."

At the click on the other end of the line, Rogan banged down the receiver. "How on earth is a man supposed to get any information around here?"

He jerked aside the heavy gray silk curtains hanging behind the tusks and stared out at the city of Nairobi. Several skyscrapers dominated the center of the metropolis. Two of them were round towers, one topped by a strange, upside-down rotating cone. Others were tall, glass-windowed office buildings, hotels, and apartments. A few older structures left over from the British colonial era elbowed for space, their half-timbered or stone facades oddly quaint among the modern monuments to progress.

On the streets below Rogan's luxury hotel suite, honking cars sped around bougainvillea-covered roundabouts. Traffic lights flashed green, yellow, red. People stopped at street corners to chat or buy a newspaper. Indian women in bright silk saris . . . African businessmen in sleek polyester suits . . . an elderly British couple tottering arm in arm toward a sidewalk café.

Rogan dropped the curtain into place and picked up his list. Sliding a gold pen from his breast pocket, he drew a black line across "Call Dr. John Thornton. Find out Fiona's background and what might influence her."

He raked a hand through his hair. In the three days he'd been in Nairobi, he'd had no luck at all. He couldn't contact Dr. Thornton. The daughter obviously had inherited her reticence from her father. Her brother, Grant, yet another "Dr. Thornton," was out in the bush working on . . . yes, an "important project." Were they all alike, these Thorntons? The wildlife federation's director had no new information about Fiona Thornton. He couldn't comment on her financial status, he informed Rogan. The Ministry of Tourism had been no help at all.

Rogan knew he should forget her. He had the names of three other researchers. But their work wasn't nearly as appealing. One was studying rock hyraxes — little rodentlike animals that resembled prairie dogs and were almost as shy. Another researcher was into termites. And the third studied crocodiles in Lake Turkana in the blistering desert heat of the Northern Frontier District.

Tossing the notebook on the table, he jabbed his intercom button.

"Yes, Mr. McCullough?"

"Ginger, come in here, please."

"Yes, Mr. McCullough."

In a moment the huge, brass-studded carved door of the room opened. A thin blonde in a tight yellow suit and high heels clattered into the room. Her hair, trimmed close around her head, was spiky stiff with mousse and spray. She always reminded

Rogan of an old photograph, sepia toned, with the lip and eye color painted on but the true dull brown-gray tints showing through.

"Ginger, where's Clive? Clive Willetts?"

His secretary flipped through the notebook in her hand. Her inch-long fingernails traced a line down the page. They were crimson today, he noticed. One had a diamond stud in a hole drilled through the nail. It always made him feel a little sick to look at that nail.

"He said he'd be at the airport this morning inspecting the planes," she told Rogan, her voice nasal. "He has a group of tourists flying out tomorrow."

"Call him. I'll take him to lunch." He tugged a suit coat onto his shoulders. Ginger sped to assist, her red nails scrabbling at the fabric. He shooed her away. "On second thought, never mind. Cancel that. I'd rather not talk to him this morning after all. Anything from Megamedia?"

"No, sir. I'll let you know the minute they phone. I'm expecting a call any moment."

"Ginger, please. I need your attention here. I've tried to explain this. It's *night* in New York. The middle of the night. Nobody's going to phone until this evening at the earliest."

"Yes, Mr. McCullough. I keep forgetting." She gnawed on one red lip.

Immediately he felt bad. He sighed. "What's happening with the interview with Jackson Ayodo? That idea I had to promote Air-Tours in cooperation with the national museum. Have you set up a meeting?"

"Mr. Ayodo isn't available this morning, sir. I've been trying to contact him since eight-thirty."

"All right, never mind." He turned away. "You can go back to your office now, Ginger. I have some things to take care of here."

"Yes, sir."

He watched her clatter across the inlaid wood floor, her high heels clicking and her ankles looking as if they might collapse at any moment. Why had he been so short with her? She was obviously doing her best, and he knew it had been hard for her to leave New York for two weeks. A makeshift office in a hotel room in a foreign country certainly wasn't what she was accustomed to.

But the sight of those long nails and that spiky hair had made him think of the contrast with Fiona. And the thought of Fiona irritated him. He had to admit, it wasn't just the fact that she'd turned down his offer cold. Nor the fact that no one could give him any insight into her.

It was Fiona herself.

He thought about the women he knew. How elegant and sleek they were compared with her. The women in his circle knew how to dress. They wore suits of linen, silk, or wool in shades of taupe and beige and black. Necklaces of gold circled their necks. Shimmering stockings covered their legs.

Then there was Fiona. From an objective standpoint, the woman was frankly unappealing. Wasn't she? Her eyes were strange. Camouflaged eyes, haunting him. And she had freckles. Freckles! The women he knew would have had them lasered off — or at least would have covered them with a thick coating of makeup and powder. Not to mention that mass of fiery hair. Fiona didn't even seem aware that she *had* hair. Uncombed, unparted, unpermed, undyed, unfrosted, unsprayed, unanythinged hair. Masses and masses of thick, coarse, red hair. Hair he'd wanted to touch so badly he could hardly stand it.

He slammed his fist onto the table,

strode into his bedroom, and grabbed his briefcase. He had to forget her. Forget Fiona Thornton and her ridiculous elephants.

She didn't know what she had turned down. He could have brought her fame, recognition, in-depth articles in national magazines, and spots on late-night talk shows. He'd been willing to spend his money to equip her with brand-new Land Rovers, tents, a complete staff. She was crazy, that was all. Completely nuts.

He would talk to the crocodile man. And the termite man.

He hurled the briefcase onto the bed. He didn't want crocodiles or termites. He wanted elephants. He wanted Fiona Thornton. And she needed him, whether she knew it or not. Even if she didn't need the recognition and the improvements he was offering, she needed something else. She needed his money.

"Ginger!" he bellowed, striding back into the main room of his suite.

The carved door flew open. "Yes, Mr. McCullough!"

"Ginger, come here." He pulled out his wallet and thumbed off a wad of bills. "Take this. I want you to get me some clothes."

"Yes, sir. A new suit? Something in navy? A . . . a striped tie?"

He stared at her, struck by how little she understood him. No one understood him. He wasn't sure he understood himself.

"Never mind, Ginger." He took the bills from her pale fingers and headed for the door.

"Mr. McCullough, Mr. McCullough!" She hobbled after him. "Where are you going? What if someone calls? What shall I tell them, Mr. McCullough?"

"Tell them I've gone shopping."

Fiona downshifted the Land Rover into first gear and ground up the steep slope of the ravine. Dust spun a fine red cloud. Pebbles pinged against the metal chassis. Mama Hannah, who had come along to see the elephants, gripped the dashboard, her lips moving in silent prayer.

"Sentero, I want you to contact the Wildlife Federation when you're in Nairobi," Fiona shouted over the roar of the engine. "Tell Mr. Ngozi the situation looks critical."

"Shall I also phone the Ministry of Wildlife?"

"Yes. I want to be sure they know this park is in a severe drought, and the impact on the animals may be catastrophic."

As the Land Rover topped the hill, a low thornbush scraped the undercarriage. Fiona grappled with the unwieldy stick shift. Only after the vehicle leapt forward did she lean back against the hot seat. A tingle of satisfaction at what she had observed trickled deep inside her. But it was satisfaction tinged with fear.

Madeline, one of the lovely young females in the M group, had given birth the day before. Her calf, a floppy, pink-eared male, had been nursing avidly all afternoon. This was Madeline's first baby, and she seemed a little unsure of herself. But her older sister, Mallory, and her mother, Megan, along with Matilda and even Margaret, the grande dame, had fawned over the tiny elephant.

If the baby stumbled, Mallory rushed to lift him, her trunk gingerly nudging his backside. Margaret, huge and matronly, made certain the calf always stayed in the cool shade of someone's shadow. And if he wandered out of the inner circle of protective legs, she rumbled until someone went to fetch him.

It had been a happy scene, Fiona thought as she steered the Land Rover onto the rutted track that led to camp. So happy that she and Sentero had cheered, and Mama Hannah had voiced praises to God for this wonderful little miracle. A miracle, yes, but oh so tenuous.

The elephants were thinner than they should be at this time of year. Their shoulders and hipbones showed beneath the skin, and they had begun to look like sagging gray tents left too long in the weather. They were listless. Testing the brittle grass with their trunks, they kicked at dry roots in frustration. Newly weaned calves, already looking weak and lethargic, foraged beneath their mothers for bits of dropped grass.

Fiona had thought about traveling to Nairobi herself to speak to the authorities. But she liked neither the long drive nor the crowded city. In fact, she couldn't remember the last time she'd been there.

It was strange that she had even considered it. And all the more strange because her nagging thoughts of Rogan McCullough coalesced into a new shape. She would go to Nairobi, she began to imagine, and she would see him.

She pictured herself strolling down Kimathi Avenue. He would notice her from a distance and lift a hand in greeting. "Well, hello, Dr. Thornton. What a pleasant surprise."

Fiona shook her head. This was ridiculous. The chances of running into Rogan McCullough in a city the size of Nairobi were almost nonexistent. Even more ludicrous was the idea that he would greet her with any sort of enthusiasm. In fact, he would probably turn and head the other way.

She wasn't going to Nairobi. Sentero had planned his trip for weeks, and he could take care of official business just as efficiently as she could. Better, perhaps.

"Look," Sentero was saying, his long sinewy arm pointing to the sky. "The plane returns."

"Which plane?" Fiona almost drove the Land Rover straight into an antbear hole. She swerved and fought to regain control of the wheel. Then she craned her neck to study the gray-blue sky.

Mama Hannah glanced at her, the tiniest of smiles lighting her small brown face. "You are driving carelessly today, *toto*."

"Sorry. I'm . . . I'm thinking about the drought."

"Yes, of course."

"It's one of the planes of Bwana Willetts," Sentero said. "But perhaps he's flying to the Mara Lodge."

"Do you think so?" She couldn't yet see

the plane, and it annoyed her to think it might speed past before she had a chance to look. That, in turn, annoyed her further. She had never given much thought to Clive Willetts and his Air-Tours safaris. Now here she was, trying to study the sky as avidly as she had scrutinized Madeline's newborn calf.

Both Sentero and Mama Hannah remained silent, though Fiona knew they could see right through her. It bothered her to be so readable. She had worked hard to level her emotions, to make herself inscrutable. And yet the Africans she knew had little trouble discerning her every humor.

"Here is a plate of mangoes, *toto*," Mama Hannah would say, using the word for a small child. "It will cheer you from this sadness. 'Weeping may go on all night, but joy comes with the morning.' " Or Sentero would tell her, "Sukari is hiding under the bed, *memsahib,* where he always hides when you are angry."

How did Mama Hannah and Sentero know these things? She studied the Maasai man for a moment. His small dark eyes scanned the horizon, darting like a pair of hummingbirds up and down, side to side. She knew his thin nose detected smells with more accuracy than hers did. His dark ears with their beaded, elongated lobes heard at levels she couldn't hear. He was more a child of this raw land than she could ever be. Did that give him the right to see into her heart and mind?

"Tell me, Sentero, what did you think of the bwana *mkubwa,* Mr. McCullough?" she asked, using a phrase of esteem for Rogan.

The Maasai never looked at her. "That man walks where he pleases and takes no notice of the world."

"And you, Mama Hannah? What did you think of him?"

"He moves always straight ahead," she said.

"That's for sure," Fiona conceded. "Well, I guess he's moved straight off to London or New York by now."

"Perhaps," Mama Hannah said. "Or perhaps not."

As Fiona emerged from the Land Rover, she immediately spotted her visitor, and her stomach clenched.

He stepped toward her, extending his hand. "Dr. Thornton, good afternoon."

"Mr. McCullough." She couldn't keep the surprise out of her voice. "I didn't expect to see you again."

The man's hand felt warm and hard as she shook it. It was slightly calloused, unyielding, with the strength she had sensed often in animals but rarely in humans. As always when it had been months — or even years — since she had engaged in the greeting ritual, Fiona was struck by the sensation of human touch. A part of her rebelled against the contact. Another part, some deep inner recess, responded.

Rogan was holding her, willing her with the grip of his hand. His eyes, blue as the African sky, probed. She wanted to turn away from them. They beckoned, as if searching for some hidden weakness, an Achilles' heel she had learned to shield.

"I've come with a new proposal for you," he said.

There it was, the arrow shot from the bow. How should she respond? Protect herself, guard the elephants whose lives God had given into her charge? She studied the man's face, an even face. This Rogan McCullough was handsome, though he looked nothing like the Greek statues she'd studied in college or the male models who posed in clothing magazines. Piercing eyes, their irises white-flecked and rimmed in navy, were set beneath a brow faintly etched with two parallel lines. Battle scars from the pressures of big business, she supposed. His nose was straight, classic. High cheekbones, sheer planes of smooth skin, and a strong chin balanced his face.

His hair couldn't seem to decide how to behave. Light brown with hints of gold on top, it had been willed into place, combed off his forehead and parted on the side. But in the slight breeze, the careful side part was quickly mussed, the strands sifting this way and that. From there his hair disobediently tumbled over the tops of his ears and down his neck. As though the man had forgotten he even had hair in back, it had grown long and thick, an unkempt ruffle that spilled over his collar.

All this Fiona could accept. It was his mouth — as in their first meeting — that tilted her off balance. Rogan McCullough was tall, and when she stared straight ahead, her eyes met his mouth. She wanted that mouth to be grim, rigid perhaps. But the crooked lift of his smile formed a shallow dimple in his right cheek. His teeth were strong, white, even. And his lips seemed to summon her, even when they said nothing.

She gave an exaggerated shrug. "Mr. McCullough, as I told you, I'm not the least bit interested in —"

"I think you'll find —"

"Really, I don't —"

"*Toto.*" Mama Hannah interrupted with such command that Fiona clamped her mouth shut. Beside the old woman, Sentero had jammed his spear shaft into the ground. His eyes, small and very dark, glittered.

"Yes, Mama Hannah?" Fiona asked.

Mama Hannah replied in the cultured, schoolbook Swahili she used only to communicate matters of great importance. *"Wapiganapo tembo, nyasi huumia."*

Fiona's eyes darted from Mama Hannah's to the businessman. She thought for a moment, weighing the words her beloved mentor had spoken. *"Ndiyo,"* she whispered finally. "Yes. I understand."

"Who is that woman?" Rogan asked as Mama Hannah and Sentero walked away together. "What did she say?"

"Mama Hannah is my mother."

"Your *mother?*"

Fiona elected not to explain further. "Mama Hannah reminded me of an old Swahili proverb: 'When elephants fight, it is the grass that weeps.' "

Rogan's eyes followed the pair until they disappeared behind the thatched-roof kitchen. "I guess in this case you and I are the fighting elephants. But what did she mean about the grass? What suffers if you and I happen to have a few differences of opinion?"

"Mama Hannah thinks the elephants are the weeping grass. So tell me what you have to say, Mr. McCullough. I will listen to your proposal. For my elephants' sake."

Their eyes met and locked. Fiona studied the blue depths of his and wondered whether Rogan McCullough would ever be able to look beyond his safari company and see the real needs of the wildlife.

At least he'd made some changes in one respect. The navy tie and wool business suit were gone. The starched white shirt and shiny leather shoes were nowhere in sight. Even the carefully shaven jaw now sported the shadow of a beard.

In place of the big-city uniform, Rogan had donned a cotton, khaki-colored safari suit. Epaulets on the shoulders. Large, square, pleated pockets on the chest. A D-ring belt. Trousers with knife-sharp creases down the front. And suede, crepe-soled safari boots. Though it was true that he had purchased the finest in tourist-style safari wear, Fiona couldn't deny that he looked much more comfort-

60

able than he had the first time they had met. In a way he had become more visible, as if he had shed one of his impenetrable layers.

She noted with some surprise that Rogan's shoulders were broad — massive even. Dark, crisp hair curled from the V neck of the safari jacket. More dark hair brushed down his arms. He looked more earthy, more masculine, to her. And yet the outfit, with its muted color and gentle lines, also had softened him somehow.

"May I call you Fiona?" he asked. "It's very unusual. Fiona."

The sound of her name spoken in his deep voice made her mouth go suddenly dry. She nodded.

For a moment she considered the camp chairs around the cold fire ring. If she offered him a seat, she knew he would start in on her again about wanting his tourists to overrun her tidy world. But if she turned him away, he would leave.

"Would you take a seat?" she asked.

"Thanks."

Settling into a camp chair, she decided she might like to study this Rogan McCullough a little longer. Perhaps one day she would write a thesis on human beings. New York businessmen, maybe.

She imagined herself sitting for hours in a bustling office, notebook propped on her knees. *"McCullough reviews morning agenda with secretary,"* she would pen. *"47 minutes. Blue eyes sharp and focused. McCullough plans strategic attack on next business conquest. 23.8 minutes. Deliberate tone of voice. Face set with determination. Straightens tie."* Perhaps she would even put a little monitor on him to record his blood pressure and heart rate. Or a radio collar, so she could track him through the concrete jungle.

"Fiona?" Rogan was asking. From the large leather attaché case beside him, a file had emerged. "Would you like to hear my proposal?"

"All right."

He flipped open the file and scanned through typed pages with careful rows of figures marching down them.

"I sense, Fiona," he began in a voice that had a stilted, more studied timbre, "that, like myself, you are a well-organized, efficient, logical person. I sense that you maintain an orderly existence. That you have a deep devotion to your chosen pursuit. That you would do anything to prevent its demise."

"Go on," she said, wondering what he was getting at.

"I also sense that you're a woman of foresight. You see potential for the future. You have ambition. Goals. Dreams, we might call them."

"And if I do?" She felt more hesitant now.

He held his breath for a moment, as if ready to plunge, to take a stab in the dark. She waited for the second arrow, aimed straight at her Achilles' heel.

"Fiona," he said, studying her eyes for the first sign of reaction, "the Rift Valley Elephant Project is in financial difficulty. Your funding has always been inadequate to accomplish the purposes you have in mind. And now, with the fiscal year only half over, the project is in trouble. Donations have slacked off due to national recession, economic hardships, worldwide tensions. Kenya is in a period of severe drought. Your dreams are turning to ashes. Your hopes for the future of the African elephant are growing dim. Am I right, Fiona?"

How did he know these things? Where had he gotten his data? "I'm listening," she said.

"I'm here to present you with the solution. It's not an easy solution. Problems of this magnitude are never resolved simply.

Sacrifice is often required. I trust you are aware of that, Fiona. But because I believe in the Rift Valley Elephant Project, because I'm committed to the future of the African elephant, I'm prepared to supplement your funding to the tune of a half-million U.S. dollars."

A gasp hung in the back of Fiona's throat.

"Examine these figures, if you will." Rogan held up a spreadsheet. "McCullough Enterprises, which is primarily a publishing entity, has always contributed generously to various organizations and causes. You'll see here our yearly contributions. And you'll find that we're broad in our support of worthy projects such as yours. I'm willing to add the Rift Valley Elephant Project to this list. Now, Fiona, I'm a businessman. And though you don't like to see yourself as one, you're a businesswoman. We're both concerned about generating enough money to keep our dreams alive. Am I correct, Fiona?"

She couldn't bring herself to answer.

"Dreams can't come true without financial support," he continued. "Your dream is to keep the Rift Valley Elephant Project alive, to help the African elephant thrive, and to keep it safe from extinction. My dream is to run a profitable flying safari business. Why don't we help each other, Fiona? I've flown to your camp today, alone, to speak frankly with you. I've come to make you an offer. An offer of half a million dollars."

Fiona moistened her lips. She glanced toward Mama Hannah, who was setting out the dinner. The elderly woman worked silently, her neon flip-flops noiseless in the dust. Fiona knew Mama Hannah had heard every word, and she wondered what the African woman was thinking.

"I'll draw up papers," Rogan went on, "papers solidifying the pledge of McCullough Enterprises in support of the Rift Valley Elephant Project. And I ask your cooperation in this."

"What kind of cooperation?"

"I've realized I was hasty when we talked the other day. You have a better understanding of your camp and the needs of the elephants than I do, of course. You know the elephants, and you sense the danger that threatens them. I'm only just beginning to see that, but I do care about their future, Fiona."

At his words, his quiet, deep-voiced expression of sympathy, something inside her escaped. She struggled to shut it away again, but it refused to be ignored.

"I'm prepared to incorporate your suggestions into the revitalization of this project," he said. "I'm prepared to hear and respond to your needs. I see us as a team. You need me, and I need you. If we work together, our efforts will bear fruit. My safari company will grow. The elephants will benefit from increased exposure, because visitors will become advocates for them. The visitors will benefit by expanding their worldview. What do you say, Fiona? Do we have a package here? Do we have an understanding?"

Fiona wanted to run from his intensity. His blue eyes cut into her, and she suddenly understood what he was trying to do. He was trying to touch her. He wanted to reach inside her and bend her to his will.

She studied the orange fingers of sunset that wove across the pink sky. The acacia trees, black in silhouette, stretched thorny arms heavenward. Monkeys settled on branches, their tails curling down and swaying in the slight breeze. A dove cooed. A cricket began to chirp.

Somewhere in the distance an elephant rumbled. It was a low, vibrating sound, almost inaudible. Margaret, perhaps, calling the others to gather near her for safety.

The new baby would suckle in contentment. Moira would grunt and rub her chin on Megan's back. Madeline would drape her trunk across her tusks, and her head would droop. Great, wrinkled eyelids would close.

"No, Mr. McCullough," Fiona said softly. "We don't have an understanding. But perhaps you would like to stay for dinner?"

THREE

Rogan stared at Fiona. He couldn't believe what had just transpired. This woman, sitting here in a broken-down, faded camp chair, preparing to eat heaven-knew-what for supper, had just turned down half a million dollars. It was unthinkable.

"So you aren't going to go along with my proposal," he stated.

"I said we didn't have an *understanding*," Fiona replied. "You haven't understood from the very beginning. You don't know who I am. You don't know what I do. You don't know why I do it."

"I think I understand you perfectly." Angry now, he stood and leaned toward her. "You drive that junk pile of a Land Rover out into the middle of the African bush and sit around watching elephants all day — that's what you do. And I do know why. It's because you'd rather stay hidden out here with your elephants than face reality. You're afraid of people who might be a little different from you. As a matter of fact, I think you're afraid of people *period*.

You prefer elephants to people. You're afraid to let my tourists come, just like you're afraid of me."

"I'm not afraid of you, Rogan McCullough." Her eyes blazed as she shot out of her chair. "Africa is my home. The elephants are my life. *This* is the real world, not some artificial megalopolis of steel and concrete and glass. Here people can be themselves."

He started to retort then thought better of it. Instead, he ran his eyes over her face, her amazing hair. But she wore faded T-shirts and ragged jeans every day. Who was this woman, and what made her tick?

"Maybe I really don't understand you. You're beautiful. You have a sharp mind that would let you hold your own anywhere. And yet you live out here in the boondocks talking to natives and elephants, for heaven's sake."

"Yes, it is for heaven's sake." She was breathing heavily, frustration etched in her face. "I do this because God put these helpless creatures out here, and if no one comes to their rescue, they'll die."

"God? What does He care about elephants?"

She hesitated a moment. "I'm not sure He cares. He's allowed a lot of terrible things to happen to them."

"If God doesn't care, then why do you?"

"Because . . . because they need me."

Rogan regarded her, his mouth dry, his stomach quivering with something he couldn't explain. "If God put the elephants out here," he said, "did He put you here too? And me?"

"I don't know." She shifted from one foot to the other. "God is in this place. He's a part of everything that happens. I have no doubt of that. I want . . . I wish He would step in and take control of His creation. But He doesn't. He lets these destructive things happen."

Rogan had never believed that God was involved with His creation at all. But Fiona seemed so sure of it, completely convinced. "Maybe He's not doing anything because He wants you to do it," he said. "You and me."

As they stared at each other, neither speaking, he watched her face transform. The traces of anger vanished. Fascination took its place. The green in her eyes softened. Their dark pupils widened, opening to him.

Neither moved.

Finally, she breathed in. "What are you trying to tell me? What are you . . . doing?"

"I'm trying to get through to you, Fiona. I'm trying to make you see —" He stopped speaking. It was as if he suddenly drew back from himself, as if a part of him slipped a mile away to study the situation. His body felt light, floating. He saw the tall man and the slender woman. He saw the way he had spoken to her. He heard echoes of the unfamiliar sound of anger in his voice. And he saw from the way he was looking at her that he wanted to touch her, to connect, to form a bridge between them. As if she could lead him somewhere, to a place he needed to go.

"I'm trying to . . . to explain," he said, stumbling uncharacteristically.

"Yes?"

"What I'm trying to say is that . . . that I'd be pleased to stay for dinner."

Fiona and Rogan sat under the stars sipping the last of their coffee. They had been silent through most of the meal, yet Fiona knew that if she continued to say nothing, Rogan would never understand why she had taken such a determined position against his proposals. He would continue to see her as a reclusive eccentric and not as she really was.

She cleared her throat. "I want you to

understand, Mr. McCullough, that I'm not completely isolated here in the Rift Valley. Sentero, my research assistant, is wonderful company. Mama Hannah is as fine a companion as I could ever hope for. I have a close relationship with the Maasai tribespeople who make their homes in the area surrounding the park. I've been known to dine in the lodge at Lake Naivasha. I do most of my shopping in the towns of Naivasha or Narok. Over the years I've had several foreign research assistants who have lived right in this camp with me. I have an extra tent down by the stream. It's not as though I'm a hermit."

Rogan surveyed her from across the white-clothed wooden table. In the evening breeze, a tendril of hair lifted and floated across her lips. "May I?" he asked, reaching across the table and sweeping it away with a fingertip. "Did you know you have an unusual accent?" he asked. "I can't tell if it's British or American."

Disconcerted by his touch, Fiona continued her explanation without responding to his comment. "I have a wireless radio I can switch on when I want the news from Nairobi. I have a transmitter to call for help if I need it. Not that I ever have. Once a month or so, the Wildlife Federation packages my mail and sends it to the lodge."

"Mail? It's hard to imagine you writing chatty letters to friends. Or sending perfume-scented envelopes to a man somewhere."

"I'm a researcher, Mr. McCullough. I correspond with my university supporters. I write papers for the foundations that fund the elephant project. I subscribe to various scholarly journals."

"I wish you'd call me Rogan."

She looked away.

"I mean, it is my name."

"A group of ladies from a church in Tennessee have been writing to me for years," she said. "They hold craft bazaars and bake sales, and then they send their proceeds to support my work. They see it as a mission — as though they're joining me in protecting God's creation. In return, I mail them photographs of the elephants. One woman sends me magazines when she's finished with them — *Good Housekeeping*, *Vogue*."

Rogan's eyebrows lifted. "*Good Housekeeping*?"

She settled her coffee cup in its saucer. "It's not as though I've never considered living in a normal house. I grew up in one.

73

I once lived with gardens and flowers and goldfish and bicycles. When I was very young, I used to dream that my life would go on the same way forever. I thought I'd live with my mother and father . . ."

Her voice trailed off, and she stared at her cup.

"What happened?"

She lifted her head, feeling the pain of things she could never speak about. "I suppose you've noticed that not *all* our dreams come true. Circumstances change. We change. God had a different plan for my life. And I'm happy with it."

"Are you?"

"Yes, I am." She felt that she'd said it a bit too defensively.

Rogan cleared his throat. "If you're such a normal, average woman, why is it the people around here call you Princess Sunrise? That sounds a little ethereal to me."

Taken aback, she sat up straight. "Where did you hear about that name?"

"Clive Willetts."

This topic of conversation could lead to an area she didn't want to cover, so she decided to simplify. "It's my hair. The Africans say it's the color of sunrise. I like to wear blue or green clothes so I can blend into the landscape and not startle the elephants. One or two of the men have mentioned that from a distance I look like the sun just coming up over the land. You have to understand; Africans are an imaginative people."

He mused for a moment. "Well, they are different. I'll have to backtrack on what I'd been thinking about your eating arrangements. You've got quite a cook there. Tell me more about Mama Hannah. I didn't realize a native could —"

"Listen," she interrupted, once again reminded of how far he was from understanding her world. "Mama Hannah is a native in the sense that she's indigenous to Kenya. She's not a native in the sense of being primitive, uncivilized, or in any way some stereotypical savage out of a Tarzan movie. Mama Hannah belongs to the Kikuyu tribe. She's intelligent, witty, and insightful. For years, she worked for my family in Nairobi. She's never been a servant, but she lives a life of Christian service. I've never known anyone as committed to Christ as she is. It's humbling. When we Thornton children grew up, she began to travel back and forth among us, spending months, even years with one or the other of us. I would trust Mama Hannah with my life."

"I didn't mean to offend," Rogan said. "I was just curious about her cooking."

"That's something new." Fiona had to grin. "When she came out here, Mama Hannah decided she wanted to give it a try. I had a few cookbooks, and she read them all, front to back. When she can't find an ingredient, she substitutes. It's been interesting, to say the least."

As though the sound of her name had evoked the little woman, Mama Hannah stepped out of the darkness and began to clear the table. Her dark hands worked swiftly, scooping up knives, forks and spoons, stacking plates, scraping food into a small tin. Fiona could see that she was smiling.

"*Toto*, what will you be wishing for dinner tomorrow?" she asked.

"Perhaps a roast," Fiona suggested. "Potatoes in a cheese sauce. A salad with vinaigrette dressing."

"A soup?"

"Chicken, please."

"And for dessert?"

"A pie will do. Chocolate, I think."

"Very good, *toto*. And now will you take tea beside the fire?"

"Not tonight, thank you, Mama Hannah. Mr. McCullough is going soon."

The elderly woman padded away, her arms loaded with clinking plates.

Rogan stared after her. "Vinaigrette dressing? Chocolate pie? Maybe I'll stay."

"Oh, she never cooks what I suggest," Fiona said, waving away the notion. "Every evening we go through the same ritual, and the following night Mama Hannah has cooked something entirely different. 'You requested chicken,' she'll say, serving up a marvelous coq au vin. 'And an oxtail soup.' Dessert is always a surprise. If I suggest pie, I'm more likely to get pudding."

"Doesn't she know? Doesn't she understand?"

"Of course she understands. But she's very creative. Once she settles into the kitchen, her imagination runs wild. It's been a delightful problem."

"I guess so," Rogan said. "My secretary keeps a computer file of dinners I've given, lists of guests, and the meals served. I like to juggle it and never have the same food or combination of people twice. But with Mama Hannah, you would never be sure."

"That's the fun of it," Fiona said. "Well, it's getting dark. You won't be able to see the antbear holes in the airstrip much longer."

"I suppose that means you want me to leave."

"No, no," she said, wanting to be polite. Then she realized how it sounded. "Of course, I . . . well, you said you'd be going."

"You mentioned that you have a radio. Mind if I listen to the weather report before I take off?"

As Rogan moved to sit near the fire ring, Fiona walked to her tent. She lifted the wireless from the desk where her cat lay sleeping. Stroking the top of Sukari's head, she whispered reassurances that she would return soon.

As she made her way across the dark clearing, she saw Sentero piling brush and firewood in the center of the ring of stones. Rogan was talking, his voice too deep for her to make out words from a distance. The African smiled and nodded, as though he were pleased at the conversation.

Fiona stopped in the darkness a few feet behind the camp chairs. Hugging the radio against her chest, she studied the back of Rogan McCullough's head. The brown hair falling over the edge of his collar gave him a look of gentleness. She could hardly imagine he was the same man who lived in a huge city full of noisy traffic, a man who negotiated hard-nosed business deals and who could casually drop half a million dollars on this cause or that.

From this view he didn't seem driven or forceful at all. His big shoulders stretched far beyond the confining width of the canvas chair back. He had relaxed one elbow on the armrest, his weight shifting the flimsy chair to a precarious angle. It didn't occur to Fiona to worry that the chair might collapse and send him sprawling. He was as solid as a rock. Immovable. It seemed, in fact, that the man was supporting the chair rather than the other way around. If the chair suddenly splintered, Rogan would simply remain, one elbow poised as if still resting on the invisible arm.

"So why do you live out here?" Rogan was asking Sentero. "If you've got a wife and seven children, seems like they'd need you around. Don't you want to live in your village?"

"Please try to understand the way of my people, bwana. I am the youngest son of fourteen children from three wives. When my father died, his cattle were divided among the older sons. My inheritance was only two goats, but my father had given me something just as valuable. He sent me to school and, later, to university. Because I have this good job with Dr. Thornton, I now own many cattle. Once every month I go on the bus from Naivasha to visit my wife and our children. I have paid for my three sons to go to school. One of them is studying at the university in Nairobi."

"But don't you get lonely out here? This place is so far away from everything."

"You don't understand, bwana. This place is in the middle of everything. Here we have our camp. We have our very fine kitchen. Here we have the stream, the Land Rover, the monkeys, the elephants. Here we have the quiet nights and the warm days. This is all we need."

Rogan lapsed into silence, and Fiona took her place in a chair nearby. Sentero was right, she realized as he wandered away. This camp was in the middle of everything. Closing her eyes, she listened to the night sounds: the hum of an insect, the rustle of leaves in the acacias, the grunt of a lion far out on the plain.

"I always imagined that New York was the center of life," Rogan remarked. "Trucks honking, sirens wailing, music pulsing from open windows until the wee hours of morning. The city is where decisions are made, deals are done, money is exchanged. Ideas become reality."

"Movers move," Fiona said, "and shakers shake. The earth trembles beneath the heavy, progressive footsteps of industry and business."

"That's right. I'm having trouble seeing how a little ragtag camp in the middle of nowhere could be the center of anything."

"The radio," Fiona said, setting the metal box in Rogan's lap. "Your world is ready to speak to you."

Leaning back in her chair, Fiona gazed at the vast plains that stretched beyond her camp. The African evening had melted away into night, and a blazing fire licked the edges of the white stones. Fiona could feel the heat as she sat staring into the flames, her hands folded in her lap, her eyes unfocused.

"In world news tonight, tensions continue in the Middle East," a voice announced as soon as Rogan turned on the radio. "A Pentagon spokesperson reiterated that the U.S. will not tolerate terrorism. . . . The British prime minister has refused to comment on the crisis in Northern Ireland. . . . South Africa today was the scene of more bloodshed. . . . Another attempted coup in Argentina has left hundreds dead and perhaps as many as three thousand homeless in fires. . . . Experts on global warming have warned that the situation is . . ."

Rogan shifted. His chair sagged in the opposite direction. "I've always listened to the news," he said in a low voice. "My business is the news." He gave a harsh laugh. "Sometimes *I'm* even the news. But tonight . . . out here in the silence . . ." He paused. "The announcer sounds like an angel of doom."

"And in local news," the radio spoke up, "the murder of a woman in the Shauri Moyo area of Nairobi . . ."

"Affair of the heart," Fiona whispered.

Rogan turned the volume down. "What?"

"Shauri Moyo. The name of that section of Nairobi where the woman was murdered means 'affair of the heart.' "

They both fell silent as the radio blared on. "A fire broke out in a downtown section of Thika this morning. Police believe arson is the cause. . . . In the Muthaiga district, a child was struck and killed by a passing motorist. . . ."

Rogan rolled the station dial. "Don't they have a weather report somewhere?"

Fiona said nothing. She picked up a stick and prodded the fire, and a shower of sparks shot into the black sky. The radio crackled as Rogan searched the airwaves. A pop tune faded in, its beat artificial and raucous in the night. It quickly died. The monotones of a talk show intensified, then ebbed. Another spot of music. Rogan left it on.

"Mind if I spend the night in your extra tent?" he asked. "I'd rather fly out in the morning."

She considered for a moment. "I guess not. I haven't had guests there in a while, though. Shake out your sleeping bag before you get in."

Neither of them moved for a long time. The fire began to die, the logs mellowing into glowing orange husks. The music continued, something soft and classical. A chill crept around Fiona's arms and slid up the insides of her sleeves. She shut her eyes.

Mama Hannah walked across the dark stage of her semiconscious mind . . . she of the soft skin the color of coffee and bright brown eyes with crinkles at the corners. Mama Hannah, whose mouth spoke words of faith and hope and the eternal love of God. Mama Hannah, who wore the wonderful faded yellow dress with a blue belt tied at her waist. A patterned nylon scarf tied over her head with a small knot at her neck that hid tight black curls salted with white. Somehow Mama Hannah had freckles too. She and Fiona often sat in front of the mirror, where they would compare. And laugh.

"Come, *toto*," Mama Hannah was saying. "We'll sing our song. 'Two fingers, two thumbs, two arms, two legs, one head, stand up, turn round, sit down, keep moving. . . .' Dance, *toto*. Dance, Fiona . . ."

"Fiona?"

She jumped at the touch. One warm hand covering her arm, Rogan leaned toward her. Somehow he had moved his chair nearer the fire, and now he sat beside her. Close. Too close.

"I asked if you'd like to dance."

"No, I don't . . . really . . ." She sucked down a breath as his hand slipped over hers. "I don't dance."

"I don't either," he said with a low chuckle, weaving their fingers. "But you look cold. And alone."

Before she could pull away, he reached up with his free hand and drew her head down onto his shoulder. Fiona felt as if she were still in her dreamworld, half asleep and half awake. Somehow a man's collar had gotten crumpled under her cheek. A man's rounded muscle pressed against her jaw. He smelled of . . . of what? Not Africa, surely. No, this was the scent of spice and something else, something unbearably compelling.

It was as though she had developed an extraordinary sense of smell. The crisp starch in his new shirt drifted into her nose and mingled with the earthy scent of red dust that had settled in his hair during the afternoon. And there was shampoo, something masculine. Soap.

His fingers squeezed hers, and she could feel the strength and warmth emanating from them. "May I put my arm around you, Fiona?" he asked. "You're shivering."

She realized she was trembling, but it wasn't from the cold. But how could she permit him to do this? She hadn't touched another person so intimately since . . . she couldn't remember when.

Before she could give her permission, he slipped his arm behind her, his hand resting on her shoulder. "Your hair is brighter than the fire," he observed. "I've never seen hair like this."

"My mother," she whispered. "She gave it to me."

"Every woman should be so lucky." He

smiled, and she began to fear she might crumble into pieces. He caught a handful of her hair and lifted it slowly. Then, like a lava flow, it slid and tumbled down her back. "It's soft."

"My father used to tell me it was as coarse as a horse's tail."

"I breed Arabians, Fiona. This is no horse's tail."

"I should . . . I should be going. I usually have breakfast at dawn, and it's getting very late."

"Stay."

"Really, I —"

"Stay with me, Fiona. I'm enjoying this. You feel soft in my arms. And you're so beautiful."

As his head lowered and his lips moved toward hers, she stiffened. "Well," she said, standing suddenly. "It certainly has gotten late, and I do believe the fire's out. Your tent is down by the stream. But don't worry, the animals have all finished drinking for the evening. If you hear thumps and bumps in the morning, it's just the monkeys playing on your roof. You'll find blankets in the metal trunk at the foot of the cot. Good night, Mr. McCullough."

She swung away, her hair bouncing behind as her legs ate up the distance to her tent. Collapsing onto her cot, Fiona covered her face with her hands and tried to breathe. And then she realized something that had never occurred to her in all the years in this camp. She knew suddenly that she was indeed in the middle of Africa. Alone. And now very much unsettled by one stubborn businessman.

Curled into a ball on her cot, Fiona pulled a blanket over her head. She hadn't been able to sleep in the hour that had passed since she left the campfire. Hadn't even changed out of her khaki pants and T-shirt. Sukari draped his body over her feet and began giving himself a bath. The whole bed trembled at his ministrations. She was tempted to spill the cat over the side and send him to his basket. She would never get any rest at this rate.

Pressing her fingertips against her lips, she tasted them. How they burned. When she closed her eyes, she saw Rogan's face moving closer, his breath warm on her skin, his mouth so close to hers. She felt his hands in her hair, squeezing and lifting. His words slipped through her bones like hot syrup. *Beautiful . . . so beautiful . . .*

She sat up and nudged the cat. "Sukari, please. Haven't you finished by now?"

The cat licked the back of her hand, his rough tongue dryly scraping her skin. Sorry she'd been short with him, she bent and nuzzled her nose in his rich fur. Now this cat was real. This cat understood her. He didn't send her world into chaos. This cat could be relied on.

Rogan McCullough could not.

The man understood nothing. Perhaps he had sidled up beside her and whispered flattery simply to get her to change her mind about his tourists. It was possible, wasn't it? She had learned long ago that, unlike cats who were both predictable and reliable, people could not be trusted.

Now that she thought of it, she realized that at his age, Rogan was probably married, with two or three children. At the least he would have a girlfriend in New York. Maybe he'd been married and divorced a time or two. Perhaps he had a mistress in every city. Wasn't that the sort of thing high-powered businessmen did?

Fiona pictured Rogan with someone chic and ultramodern. She would have short hair and polished nails and negotiate her own clever deals. Fiona thought of the ads she had seen in the magazines from

America. No doubt Rogan wanted a woman who might have stepped from the pages of *Vogue*.

She flopped backward onto the pillow and let out her breath in a rush. Why should she care what Rogan McCullough wanted in a woman? She was over thirty. She had established herself educationally and professionally as a dedicated and accomplished scientific researcher. She did not need any man to come along and snuggle up to her for any reason.

Throwing back the blanket, she buried Sukari in a tumble of wool. Then she lifted the hems of her khakis and slid her feet into her boots. Grabbing a flashlight from the file cabinet, she unzipped her tent door and stepped outside.

The cat meowed, but she didn't hear him.

"Mr. McCullough," she called, rapping the flashlight on a tent pole. "Mr. McCullough, this is Dr. Thornton. I have something to say to you."

She waited for a moment but heard nothing from the inside of the tent. Standing on tiptoe, she peered through a tiny tear in the canvas. The interior of the tent was completely dark.

"Mr. McCullough, are you in there? Rogan?"

The door flap swung back. Rogan stepped out into the moonlight, wearing nothing but his khaki trousers.

"Yes, ma'am?"

Fiona nearly dropped the flashlight. She didn't know why she'd expected to find him just as she'd left him. Even pajamas would have been better than this. Her father had always worn a nice set of plaid flannels. But then she really hadn't stopped to consider what Rogan might be wearing, had she? She hadn't even planned exactly what she would say to him. She had merely acted on impulse, something she never did unless faced with a charging elephant or some other life-threatening situation.

"I guess you realize it's after midnight, Fiona," Rogan was saying. "I thought you needed your sleep. Breakfast at dawn and all?"

"Well, I just . . . I . . ."

Amusement twitching his lips, he raised one arm, cocking it on the tent pole. "I'll have to admit," he said when she was unable to continue, "I'm glad to see you here tonight. I was thinking about you."

"Mr. McCullough, please." She found

her breath. "I came to tell you that I'm not the least bit interested in . . . well, in anything you have to offer. I was trying to tell you at dinner that I'm content with the life I've made for myself out here, and I don't want anything to complicate it. You might as well know up front that I will not be swayed from my position. You made a generous offer to the elephant project, and I thank you for that. But I just can't go along with being overrun by tourists. I'm content with a solitary life. And, as I said, I really don't think you understand what I'm trying to accomplish here in the —"

"Is that what you sleep in?"

"I beg your pardon?"

"This." He plucked the sleeve of her T-shirt.

"No. And it's hardly your business."

"Just curious." He grinned, as if enjoying the flush that rose to her cheeks. "Come closer," he said, taking her arm. "There's something I think I should tell you."

"I'm the one who came to talk to you."

He lifted a hand and tucked a ribbon of red-gold hair behind her ear. "What did you really come here for? This is the middle of the night. Or couldn't your speech about how happy you are as a single woman wait until morning?"

"But I came here to tell you —"

"Because tonight, when I was lying in my tent, I got to thinking about the way it felt when I put my arm around you just like this." He drew her into an embrace. "And I was wondering if maybe you'd been thinking about it too."

Yes, she thought. But she shook her head. "No. Of course not."

"Are you sure, Fiona?" He pulled her closer. "How long has it been?"

"Really, please, I —"

"How long since a man kissed you?" he asked. "How long since you let anyone hold you close?"

Forever! she wanted to shout. *It's been forever.* But she couldn't speak.

"Fiona," he said in a low voice. "I've decided you're right about how little I understand. So I think I'll stay a few more days. Then you can teach me everything about you that I don't know. How does that sound?"

She opened her mouth, but his fingertips covered it. And then he was straightening, setting her away from him.

"Until tomorrow," he said with a smile. "Good night, Princess Sunrise."

FOUR

Fiona sat on the edge of her camp cot and stared down at the wool socks on her feet. She wiggled her toes and watched the socks lump up and down. At least she had control of her limbs. Now.

What had happened? She'd made up her mind to tell Rogan McCullough one thing: that she wasn't the least bit interested in anything he had to offer. Not his offer of new Land Rovers. Not his half-million dollars. Not his warm arm around her shoulders.

Instead, he had told her that he would be staying at the camp for several days. Worse, he'd held her close and whispered in her ear. And she'd liked it! Liked it? She couldn't stop thinking about this man.

Her mind, normally absorbed with data and statistics, reeled with unstoppable thoughts that zinged back and forth like ricocheting bullets. And she hated bullets — despised them and everything they had meant in her life.

Not that she hadn't ever thought about

men. Oh, there had been a time when she had dreamed of a large house with a garden full of roses and a husband coming home for tea. She had imagined plump pink babies, their tiny fingers sticky with jam. She had pictured herself in someone's arms. He would hold her as gently as a china cup; he would treasure her and protect her. Like a handsome prince in a fairy tale, he would rise to her defense and make certain they lived happily ever after.

But, of course, these things hadn't happened to her. And she had concluded they didn't really happen to anyone. Tillie, Jessica, and Grant said they were happily married, but Fiona had not visited her siblings in years, so how could she know for sure? And Rogan McCullough, with his persuasive arguments and big-city lifestyle, was certainly no prince.

O God, she lifted up in a sudden welling of prayer, *Creator of the universe, hear my prayer! Take away this man and these thoughts. I have work to do. You put me here to care for Your creations, so keep me from distractions. Help me to . . .*

Fiona paused. She had never been any good at praying. Not like Mama Hannah was. When the old woman bowed her head and spoke to God, it was as though she were addressing a friend — not some distant, inattentive being. Mama Hannah's prayers were filled with praise. She acknowledged God as her Lord and master. Jesus Christ was her Savior, and she was humble before Him. But there was also a comfortable air about her prayers, as though God were inside her, listening and caring about everything she said.

Fiona addressed God as if He were one of her professors — someone she honored and revered but could never tell about her personal life, her dreams and fears and deepest desires. She believed in God and she respected Him, but He was outside her.

Mama Hannah had told Fiona many times that Jesus stood at the door of her heart and knocked. But Fiona was unwilling to let Him come all the way in. He could stand there, toe in the open doorway, while she did the work He had given her — caring for the elephants. She would be the best person she could for Him. She would read her Bible and try to understand Him. She would listen to Him and do His will. She would even acknowledge Jesus as God, as ruler of the universe, but she wouldn't let Him come in.

"I don't . . . don't trust You," she ground

out, clenching her fists. "You won't keep evil away, and You should. You have the power, God. You ought to exercise it. These animals shouldn't suffer so. And people . . . people shouldn't have to suffer either. Not when You could prevent it."

Now God had permitted this annoying Rogan McCullough into her life, and she wasn't about to open the door of her heart to him either. Not even a smidgen. He was disrupting everything — and certainly he wasn't behaving anything like a prince or a gentleman. Of course, a gentleman who treasured her like a teacup would never penetrate the high stone wall she had built to protect herself. It would take someone bold, someone as determined to get in as she was determined to keep him out. It would take a stubborn, single-minded, driven sort of a . . .

She jumped off the edge of the cot and grabbed a pencil from her desk. With a flick of her wrist, the propane lantern hissed into a bright blue glow. She tugged on her chair and sat down. Jerking open a file drawer, she dumped a manila envelope full of photographs onto the desktop.

Now, she thought. *Enough of princes and teacups. Back to the real me.* Rogan might hold her close, but she knew who she was.

She had withstood charging bull elephants. Surely she could withstand one blue-eyed man.

Fiona began sifting through the pile of photos. There was only one thing to do about the situation — show Rogan that she was right and he was wrong. And the M family would help her do just that. First thing in the morning, she would drive Rogan out in search of Margaret and the others. In the space of two or three hours, she would explain her work. As logically as if she were writing a thesis, she would outline why his plan would be a disaster. Then she would point him in the direction of his airplane and send him away for good.

Opening her laptop, she decided this was worth the use of her precious battery. She began to type, jotting down the points of her argument. The tumult of emotions inside her settled as she flipped through card files and analytical data. She searched notebooks, careful mosaics of her ten years of research. She reread her articles. She extracted series of figures on the evolution of the M family unit, their bond groups, and their clan. She studied maps.

As she outlined and wrote, Fiona knew this was who she was. This was what she did. Her head sagged toward the keyboard, but still she wrote. And when at last she collapsed onto her cot and her eyelids dropped shut, she dreamed of elephants and wide-open plains and the African sunrise tangled in her hair.

When Rogan appeared for breakfast, Fiona began to wish in earnest for the return of that stiff wool business suit. His now-limp bush shirt hanging unbuttoned and untucked revealed the diamond of dark hair she had noticed in the night. His jaw was shadowed with unshaven beard. The hair on his head was rumpled from sleep, and she caught herself imagining what it would feel like to slide her fingers through it.

He sat in the chair at the opposite end of the table from her and stared. His eyes, framed by the tangle of dark hair, glittered like ice.

Fiona took a swallow of tea and regarded him. "Do you always dress so elegantly for breakfast, Mr. Mc—"

"Please. It's Rogan. And no, normally I shower, shave, and dress before breakfast. But then I'm usually not sleeping in a tent with growling lions outside keeping me awake half the night. And I don't usually have an African in a loincloth shaking my shoulder at dawn. And I don't often find myself in deep conversation with a khaki-and-T-shirt-clad woman at midnight."

Mama Hannah wandered out of the thatched-roof kitchen with plates full of scrambled eggs and bacon and a neat arrangement of fresh pineapple. Like a waiter in a fine restaurant, she served her steaming dishes with an elegant flourish. Her neon flip-flops pattering in the dust and the clink of silver against china were the only sounds in the clearing.

Pausing, the elderly woman regarded her guest. "Button this shirt, Mr. McCullough, please," she said. "It is good manners."

Flushing a little, Rogan quickly obeyed. Fiona could hardly contain her mirth. *Good for Mama Hannah,* she thought. If anyone could keep this rascal in line, it was she.

"God prefers that we behave in a modest way," Mama Hannah went on as she poured fresh mango juice. "It is best to wear *all* our clothes in the presence of each other. To treat one another with respect. And not to visit the tent of a young man in the middle of the night."

At this, her dark eyes slid across to Fiona, whose turn it was to feel the heat race to her cheeks.

"Mama Hannah," she said, "I just went over there to tell Mr. McCullough that —"

" 'Keep away from every kind of evil,' " Mama Hannah cut in. "The apostle Paul taught this to the Thessalonians. Do you understand, *toto?* It is not only the doing of sin we must avoid, but also we should stay away from anything that may look like sin."

"Yes, Mama Hannah," Fiona mumbled. "I'll try to remember that."

The woman's withered hand patted her arm. "For this I am happy. If only you did not bear this burden alone."

"I won't bother her," Rogan said.

"It is not you who can bear the burden of purity for my *toto*. It is God. He could help her, but she will not permit it. She must do all these things on her own."

"Mama Hannah, please, could we talk about something else?" Fiona said. "I'm sure Mr. McCullough isn't interested in my purity or in my relationship with God. Why don't you bring out a plate for yourself? We'd love to have you join us."

"No." Mama Hannah held up her hand. "I ate breakfast with Sentero. Enjoy these delicious eggs I have prepared for you."

As she walked away, Rogan chuckled. "Wow. That is some kind of mama you've got there. Cooking, cleaning, and moralizing all wrapped up in one dynamite little package."

Fiona bristled. "I'll have you know she's been wonderful — as good as any birth mother and better than most. I love her dearly."

"Relax. I didn't mean to offend. I like Mama Hannah a lot. But you're wrong about one thing you told her." He paused. "I *am* interested in you: your purity, your faith in God, your elephants — everything."

"Well, you're not going to know everything about me, so get used to it." She speared a bite of egg and decided it was time to change the subject. "This is tasty."

"I don't usually eat breakfast."

"You'll offend Mama Hannah if you don't. She takes things like that personally. And by the way, keep an eye out for the monkeys. Vervets like fruit. They'll jump on the table and steal your breakfast before you know what's happened."

Rogan glanced into the pink-lit branches of the acacias. As Fiona had predicted, the small gray-furred creatures had gathered to inspect the humans' buffet. A group of them sat on the ground a few yards from the table. As the meal progressed, they inched closer.

"If you don't eat breakfast," Fiona said, "what do you do at this hour of the morning?"

Rogan lifted an eyebrow. "At *this* hour I'm usually still asleep. But when I do get up, I read the morning paper at the table in my dining room. Next, I review my agenda for the day, check my e-mail and voice mail, and glance through the files that apply to my meetings."

"You don't eat anything at all?"

"I down a few cups of black coffee, but it's not like I have time to think about food. Two or three telephone calls usually interrupt every meal. In fact, I had a speakerphone installed in the dining room. It sits on the table."

"Right there with the salt and pepper," Fiona said, "as though it were another of the dining accouterments."

He shrugged. "I guess so."

How different his world was, she thought. Here in the middle of Africa there was no telephone jangling. No secretary buzzing. No windows being washed or vacuum cleaners whining. The sound of tires screeching, car horns blaring, sound systems pumping music was so far away as to be nonexistent.

The only sounds in the African bush

were soft ones. Sounds God had created: A stream gurgling. Doves cooing. Monkeys making quick movements. Breezes rustling the acacia leaves. The smells came softly too. Not smog and exhaust fumes and artificial pine-fragrance room deodorizers, but the scents of fresh air, eggs and bacon, woodsmoke, sun mingling with dust.

Seemingly aware of this monumental difference in their lives, Rogan jabbed at his eggs and twirled his fork slowly, watching Fiona. "You look good this morning," he said.

She smiled. "Thank you. I'm afraid you look terrible."

"Jet lag, I guess."

Actually, Fiona felt more than a little uncomfortable with the way Rogan looked. Keeping her eyes on her breakfast was simpler than facing that tan shirt and those broad shoulders. The more she thought about it, the more she realized she preferred Rogan in his suit and tie, silly as they had seemed out here in the bush. The wool suit had toned him down a little. It had contained him.

Finishing his breakfast, he stood and stretched. Muscles bunched in his arms as he stifled a yawn. "Suppose I could take a shower?" Thankful to end the intimacy of eating breakfast with him, Fiona led Rogan across the clearing to the small, canvas-enclosed shower stall. A nearby tree with branches carved into hooks held a collection of towels and white robes.

"Sentero lit the fire an hour ago, so you should still have hot water." Rogan's brows narrowed as he studied the large tank insulated with mud held in place by chicken wire. Beneath it glowed the remains of a fire. A narrow pipe ran from the tank to the showerhead.

"It's called a Tanganyika boiler," Fiona explained. "It dates back to the days when East Africa was colonized by England and Germany. And it's still very efficient. Just turn on the tap and voilà, hot water."

"What if Sentero builds the fire too hot?"

"Then steam comes out the tap, and you have to wait awhile. Or you can have a cold shower. They're very refreshing in the morning."

"Yeah, sure. Just the thing to start the day."

"Go easy on the shampoo," she instructed, slapping a heavy bottle into his palm. "We try not to alter the environment."

"Got a washing machine around here?"

He began to peel off his shirt, obviously forgetting Mama Hannah's careful instructions about good manners. "These are all the clothes I brought along."

Fiona averted her head, pretending to inventory the towels and soap. "It won't hurt you to wear those clothes for a few more hours. You can put on your suit when you get back to Nairobi this afternoon."

"I told you I'd like to stay for a few days."

"That won't be necessary. Within a couple of hours I'll have you convinced your ideas won't work. You'll see."

She turned to go, but he caught her arm. "I said I want to stay here. In this camp."

"And I've asked you to leave this afternoon." Her hazel eyes flashed as she spoke.

"Are you going to buck me every step of the way, Fiona?"

"If that's what it takes."

"Is there something you don't like about me? Because if there is, I really want to know about it."

"You're just completely different than I am. You've accused me of preferring elephants to people — and you have a point. But your relationships with people aren't the kind I'd want to have anyway."

"What do you mean by that?"

"I suspect you're used to controlling people. You've always had the power to manipulate and move people around like chess pieces. You've always gotten exactly what you wanted. You've been fawned over and showered with everything you could possibly need. Am I right?"

"As a matter of fact, you're wrong. I've worked hard to get where I am today. And the reason I worked so hard is because I *didn't* have the things I wanted or needed. I forced the world to sit up and take notice."

"Well, you won't force me into anything."

"Watch me."

He stared at her.

She stared back.

His jaw clamped shut, and his neck muscles were flickering with tension. Suddenly, he lifted his hand and flipped her hair from her shoulder. "You remind me of a Nandi flame tree — that red glow about you."

"Oh, please. And where did you learn about flame trees?"

"I like you, Fiona Thornton. I like you shy. I like you obstinate. I like you angry. And I especially like the way you feel in my arms. Warm and trembling."

"You — you —"

"Fiona," he said, lowering his voice.

"*Please* will you ask Mama Hannah to launder my shirt? In the meantime, I'd appreciate it if you could find me something else to wear."

As he finished stripping off the wrinkled shirt, it was all she could do to keep her eyes focused on his face. He folded the shirt into a neat square, lifted one of her hands, and set it in her palm.

"Please?" he repeated.

Not waiting for an answer, he stepped behind the canvas curtain and left her standing alone in the clearing.

When Rogan emerged from the shower, he saw Fiona and Sentero talking earnestly beside the Land Rover. Heads together, they were conferring at a level of intensity Rogan had come to recognize as normal for Fiona. Under one arm she carried a large packet of papers, and as she talked she jabbed at it to punctuate her sentences.

Sentero nodded, said a few words, nodded again. Fiona shook her head and pointed one long arm in the direction of the humpbacked mountain. Then she swept her hand across the horizon. But when she got to Rogan, she stopped, lowered her arm, and turned abruptly.

For some odd reason it pleased Rogan to

disconcert her. Maybe it was the fact that she was so confident about every single area of her life. He'd never met a woman like her. Oh, he'd known self-assured women, of course. As he shrugged into the clean T-shirt Fiona had draped over a bush for him, rows of self-assured, aggressive businesswomen filtered through his mind like so many automatons.

But Fiona's confidence wasn't born of clambering over others on the way up the corporate ladder. Nor was it a product of wealth and power. Fiona knew who she was. And she liked herself.

That, Rogan realized, was the true reason he enjoyed throwing her off balance. He sensed that Fiona was attracted to him, and this didn't fit her carefully plotted plan. He liked the way she had stammered when he'd stepped out of the tent last night. He liked feeling her melt a little in his arms. And he liked the way she had averted her eyes when she saw him bare-chested.

Not that he lacked female attention. But it certainly was interesting to watch someone fight it so hard.

Pushing his fingers through his wet hair, he attempted to comb it into order. A tiny mirror hung on the trunk of the acacia, and he peered into it, scrutinizing himself. The shower had done him a world of good, but he still looked like he'd been through the mill. His hair stuck out on one side. The T-shirt, obviously left behind by an assistant, was a couple sizes too small. It cut into his biceps and stretched across his shoulders like an elastic bandage. The wrinkles in his trousers would have done an elephant proud.

"Are you coming?" Fiona called across the clearing.

It was true, Rogan realized as he walked toward her. She did look like the sunrise. Her thick hair fairly glowed with an orange-red light. Her dark green shirt and matching pants were the color of the distant escarpment. Dusted with red African soil, her boots blended into the earth as if she had grown roots.

"Great shower," he commented, approaching. "That boiler idea ought to be patented."

"Why don't you go ahead? Maybe you'd make yourself another million dollars. You could invest it in Air-Tours. Then you'd be happy and leave me alone."

"I wouldn't leave you alone for a million dollars, Fiona."

Her eyes narrowed. "I hope you remember our conversation last night."

He smiled. "I remember a lot of things about last night."

Turning to Sentero, she said, "You'd better buy some aspirin while you're in Nairobi. I think I'm going to need it."

"Yes, Dr. Thornton." The African eyed Rogan. "Shall I convey a message for you, Bwana McCullough? I'm going to Nairobi now."

"You know, you speak English very well, Sentero." The American assessed the Maasai, whose plaid clothes rustled idly in the breeze. Today one beaded earlobe held a small black film canister. Bare feet with thick toenails emerged from worn sandals.

Sentero glanced at Fiona. "Thank you, bwana," he replied to Rogan. "I found it most helpful as I completed my master's degree in wildlife management from the University of Texas."

"Texas? But you're —"

"I am Maasai, bwana. I've taken the knowledge of your country, but I have chosen the ways of my people."

"Sentero is going by bus to Nairobi from the lodge at Lake Naivasha," Fiona interjected. "Do you want him to telephone your associates?"

"That's all right. I'll contact Clive on the

radio later."

Sentero accepted the packet of papers from Fiona. "Very well, Dr. Thornton. I shall return in one week."

"Give my greetings to Dr. Patel and Mr. Ngozi. And say hello to Ian for me."

"Yes, Dr. Thornton. But remember what Mama Hannah would say to you." He switched into Swahili, his face serious and his eyes devoid of sparkle. *"Kumbuka hasira hasara."* Without a further word, he set off, his long legs loping across the plains.

"What was that all about?" Rogan asked, his eyes following the Maasai.

"Just another proverb he wants me to remember."

"Well, what is it?"

"*Hasira hasara.* It means 'anger destroys.'"

She opened the Land Rover door and climbed into the driver's seat. Rogan just had time to slide in before the engine roared to life and the vehicle lurched out of camp in a cloud of red dust.

"We could have driven him to the lodge," he shouted over the deafening rattle. "It's not that far."

"He wanted to run. He says it clears out his lungs before he enters Nairobi. He dislikes the city as much as I do."

She worked the sticky gearshift as the Land Rover plunged down a ravine. Following a dry riverbed, she skirted huge gray boulders and patches of damp sand.

"Are you in a bad mood, Dr. Thornton?" Rogan asked, hoping to tease her into lightening the intense expression on her face.

"Things are frustrating enough without Sentero and his proverbs. Not only do I have to lose a morning's research, but I have to play chauffeur."

"I'm a big tipper," he shouted over the rumble. "So where are we going?"

"I'm taking you to find the M family. I need to check on a new calf."

"Why do you call them that? Does the *M* stand for something?"

"I've assigned each elephant group in the park a letter of the alphabet," she explained. She drove out of the ravine and headed across a stretch of grassland. "In each group, the elephants' names begin with that letter. It's a way of coding them."

"So they're kind of like people to you, with names and personalities?"

"No. I'm a scientist. I stay detached so I can study them objectively. If I started to feel sentimental about them, I wouldn't see them clearly."

"You're telling me they're just a herd of data? Just a bunch of carefully organized letters of the alphabet?"

She frowned. "Look, I've worked with the Rift Valley elephants for years. Even though I'm a scientist and I do keep my distance, I've gotten to know them. It was sort of inevitable. Each elephant has certain — mannerisms, you know? They have habits and temperaments. They like and dislike certain things. They tend to behave in specific, almost predictable, ways."

"Do they know you?"

"They know my scent and my presence. They show an awareness of me, and they're not afraid of me. At least, most of them aren't. Several bulls near the Suswa area are wary of any humans. They avoid me, or they threaten when I approach."

Rogan watched her drive across the plain, her slender arms shuddering with the rattle of the steering wheel. Her eyes scanned the terrain for thornbushes and antbear holes as she brushed a wisp of hair from the corner of her mouth.

"Can you walk around with the elephants?" Rogan asked. "Do they know you that well?"

"They're wild," she said. "They rule this

land, not me. I keep a respectful distance. I'm not afraid of them, though. One or two — especially the calves — like to come right up to the Land Rover to inspect it. But I stay away. I don't interfere. I let them live their lives the way they want."

She looked at him, eyes piercing, before continuing. "It's the only way to handle wild creatures. You have to leave them alone."

He understood what she was telling him. She too needed space. She needed to be left wild and free and untouched.

"Then how can you be sure you really know them?" he asked. "How can you truly understand them?"

"I don't truly understand them," she answered. "I don't think God means for us to understand everything in His world. Do you?"

They drove along without speaking for several minutes. Fiona scrutinized the golden plains for any sign of gray, ponderous pachyderms. Rogan wondered at this scientist's frequent references to God and His creation. She certainly believed in a deity, but the depth of her commitment to faith didn't seem quite the same as Mama Hannah's — a woman who had so quickly discerned Rogan's lack of inner peace. Strangely, he had been intrigued by the little African woman, her zeal for the Bible, and her devotion to strict moral values. Determination, outspokenness, and dedication attracted him. Before he left the camp, he would make time to talk to Mama Hannah about her beliefs.

The Land Rover bumped past herds of zebras, their black-and-white stripes brilliant in the early morning sun. Thomson's gazelles lifted startled heads and then bounded away. Giraffes sauntered among the tall acacias bordering the streams. Their brown-and-tan-mottled hides blended so well with the shadows that only their long necks, rising like periscopes over the treetops, gave them away.

"Margaret was feeding in this area yesterday," Fiona spoke up. "I suspect she and the other Ms slept in that clearing. And then they probably wandered toward Longonot early this morning."

She stopped the vehicle and lowered the window. A cloud of dust rolled in, settling on humans and metal alike. She flipped back the overhead hatch. In distinct gold-and-brown bars, sun streamed through the dust motes. Standing, she lifted her binoculars and ran them over the horizon.

"See anything?" Rogan emerged beside

her, his shoulders taking up more than half the space.

She wedged herself against her side of the opening. "Not the M group. Old James and Nick are over by that large baobab."

He peered in the direction she was pointing. Sure enough, a pair of gray hulks materialized out of the grass beneath a gigantic, bare-limbed tree.

"Which family do James and Nick belong to?" he asked.

"Mature bulls don't belong with any herd. Elephant families are matriarchal. They're composed entirely of females, young and old, with a few male calves mixed in."

"And the bulls?"

"They wander around doing whatever they want. Once in a while they come along and test the females to see if any are in estrus, ready for mating. Then they mate and go on their way."

"Sounds like some of my buddies. Fun with no commitment."

She lowered the binoculars. "It's an efficient way to propagate the species, which is, after all, one of the primary motivations of these animals. They want to survive, and they want to reproduce. It's an internal drive, the need to pass along their genes and biological imprints. *Fun* isn't part of the program."

"Too bad for the elephants."

She let out a breath. "You don't ever let up, do you?"

"Nope. It's part of my genes and biological imprints."

She rolled her eyes.

"So, Fiona," he went on, "why don't you start explaining all these things I don't understand about you? Like how the sunlight turns your eyes from brown to green . . . and what your hair feels like when it's wet . . . and what you think about when you're by yourself in your tent."

"I work," she said. "Assembling data."

He chuckled. "Last night, I lay awake for a long time . . . just looking at the shadows and wondering about you."

Fiona tore her gaze away and looked over his shoulder. "I'm trying not to imagine you imagining me."

"I thought about kissing you," he said.

"Must have been a biological reaction."

"Biological?"

"You know — male, female, close proximity, that sort of thing. But I think what you should know . . . ," she began, then for some reason faltered.

"What is it I should know, Fiona?"

Her shoulder was pressed against his. He felt a strange tingling sensation down his arm as the metal edge of the roof pressed into his back.

"I want you to understand," she tried again, "that I really —"

"I'm waiting."

"You see, if I step back and analyze this situation, everything is clear."

He couldn't resist taking a strand of her hair between his thumb and forefinger. "Then, why don't you go ahead and analyze things for me, Dr. Thornton? I like hearing the sound of your voice."

She clamped her mouth shut. She looked panicky, like a wounded gazelle staring into the barrel of a gun. What was she afraid of? That he actually might kiss her? Would that be so traumatic?

"Here's *my* analysis," he said. "After a great deal of scientific observation, I find that you, the intrepid researcher, have been living all alone in the middle of Africa with very little human contact. Now that's completely unnatural. The human species was made for interaction. We're social animals. We need a certain amount of communication. We rely on interplay, collaboration, fellowship."

"Oh, thank goodness!" She gave him a

118

quick smile. "I've found the elephants. Come on, let's go."

She slid down through the sunroof and landed with a plop on the seat. Rogan was still standing as the Land Rover sputtered to life and started across the plains. He loosened a strand of her red-gold hair that had gotten hooked on one of the sunroof latches. He examined it for a moment, sifting it between his fingers.

Yes, he decided, Fiona Thornton was indeed an interesting and challenging example of the human species. As he dropped the strand of her hair and watched it settle on her shoulder, he smiled.

"That's Margaret," Fiona whispered, pointing to a lumbering gray female who was eyeing the Land Rover and flapping her ears. "She's never pleased to see me at first. Poachers killed one of her daughters and two sons. She's always wary."

Through the roof hatch, Rogan watched the elephants feeding on tufts of brittle yellow grass. They all looked the same to him. Big, gray, wrinkled animals with huge ears that swayed slowly back and forth. The only differences he could discern were tusk sizes and shapes. Some of the elephants had large tusks, some had small ones, and others had none at all. The tusks were either uptilted or straight. Some had grown askew, like teeth in need of braces.

Beside him, Fiona leaned across the roof, chin resting on her knuckles. "Margaret's the matriarch, the mother of the larger females. She leads the M family. Megan and Moira are her daughters. Can you see Megan there? She's the one with the tear in her ear. Look, she's just picked up some dirt and blown it across her back."

Rogan watched the elephant and tried to memorize her characteristics: size, ear shape, tusk configuration. "Where's Moira?"

"I don't see her yet. They're all clumped together. Oh, look!" She touched his arm. "See the baby? That's Madeline's calf. He's just three days old. Watch how he nurses."

The miniature pachyderm lifted his trunk and tested his mother's skin. Then he found what he was looking for between her front legs and began to suckle. As the baby fed contentedly, his mother ran her trunk over his little body, touching and comforting him.

"Oh, you fine little boy," Fiona whispered.

"Who's that?" Rogan asked, pointing out

a large elephant some distance from the others. She was swinging her head and kicking out with one front foot.

Fiona peered through the tangle of thorny scrub that nearly concealed the elephant. "That's . . . oh, Rogan — it's Moira! I think she might be in labor."

She slid down into the seat and fumbled for her camera. Rogan joined her. "Shall we try to drive closer?"

"I don't want to disturb her. She's been having such difficulty lately."

"Here, let me do this. It'll save you time." He took the camera from her and began to load film. "Go on up. I'll have this for you in a second."

"Thanks," Fiona whispered as she climbed onto the metal roof to study the elephant.

Rogan was closing the back of the camera when she reached through the hatch and grabbed his T-shirt, half hauling him up. "She's going to give birth! I've only seen this once in all my years of study. Come on — you've got to watch."

His heart racing, Rogan climbed up through the sunroof, seated himself beside Fiona, and handed her the camera. From this vantage, they had a clear view across the scrub. The large female kept backing up and shaking her head. Just under her tail, a bulge began to appear.

"What's she doing?" he asked. "What's going on?"

"See beneath her tail? That lump? Oh, heavens, where's my notebook?"

Rogan reached into the vehicle and grabbed the small pad and pen. "You talk — I'll write."

"Nine thirty-seven A.M.," she dictated, as though he were Sentero.

As Fiona began reciting the specific indications that told her the elephant was about to give birth, Rogan realized that he had to take care to form legible words on the paper. He studied the animal. Then he watched Fiona. Her eyes shone. Her breath was shallow, and a smile lit her face.

"Nine-forty," she said, snapping a photo. "Moira is lying down. She's resting, I think. The others are ignoring her."

"She's up, Fiona! Look at that bulge now. It's moved down a foot or more. And it keeps slipping."

"She's moving. She's coming toward us. She's turning. Oh, Rogan!"

At that moment, with only the slightest push, Moira gave birth. A tiny elephant completely enclosed in a fetal sac slid to the ground.

"I don't believe what I'm seeing," Rogan

uttered, a chill skittering down his back.

"You're seeing God," Fiona whispered. "His hand. This is how I know He's real."

He nodded, unable to deny the truth of her words. "Is the baby alive?"

"I hope so."

The mother rested for less than a minute before touching the sac with her foot. Fiona and Rogan sat breathless, watching for movement. Moira bent and punctured the sac with her tusks.

The calf began to jerk its legs.

"The others are coming over," Fiona said quietly. "See how their temporal glands are streaming."

The elephant family filed toward the new mother. Long wet streams ran down their cheeks from pores on either side of their eyes. Moira had freed the baby and was attempting to lift it with her front foot.

"It's going to stand," Rogan murmured. "Uh-oh. It just fell down."

"They're wobbly at first. Can you see the baby's ears? They're pink in the back. Look, it's a female, a little girl. She's up again, Rogan. She's searching for milk. Oh no, she's fallen."

The other elephants surrounded the mother and new baby. Margaret rubbed her head against Moira's backside. Mallory rumbled, and Moira answered. Matilda picked up the fetal sac and swung it around for a few minutes. Finally she tossed it over her head.

"Look," Rogan said, nudging Fiona's arm. "Moira's got the baby on her feet again. See the two of them, right there between those other elephants? The baby's rooting around between Moira's legs."

"Has she begun to suckle yet? I can't see from this angle, Rogan."

"Yes," he said, pumping one fist in the air as if he'd just witnessed a touchdown pass. "She's up. She's nursing. We did it!"

He turned and pulled Fiona into his arms. Her camera clicked an involuntary picture as he drew her close and kissed her lips.

FIVE

Rogan and Fiona spent the rest of the day watching elephants. The M family, new addition included, inched toward the shadows of Mount Longonot. The sloping dormant volcano beckoned with the possibility of untouched vegetation and flowing streams. Overhead the sun rose to its zenith, scorching the metal roof of the Land Rover and turning the bridge of Rogan's nose a bright pink.

Neither he nor Fiona mentioned the impulsive kiss of the early morning. Instead, they fell into a routine in which she spoke her observations, and he wrote them in the little notebook. The fact of the matter was, Rogan realized over a lunch of peanut butter sandwiches and hard-boiled eggs, he'd been just as disturbed by the kiss as Fiona probably had been.

Thinking about her in his tent the night before, he had considered playing out a sort of courting dance here on the African plains. They would tease and flirt, and finally he would win her over to a romantic embrace beneath the stars of the Southern Cross.

But as the day wore on, it became clear to Rogan that Fiona hadn't been playing — not last night nor this morning in the Land Rover. As much trouble as she had breathing every time he came near, and as deeply as she responded when he held her, it was apparent that she really had no inkling of the woman's traditional role in the dating game. Which he had to admit was refreshing.

She averted her eyes from his face and wedged herself into a corner of the open hatch every time he stood to join her. When his hand brushed hers, she jerked away from the touch. Her communication consisted entirely of scientific observations about elephants.

And yet for all that, he knew she wasn't just an emotionless researcher. He had seen her eyes sparkle at the birth of the baby elephant. He'd watched her laugh aloud as the calf suckled. More important somehow, she had responded to *him*. But it wasn't the sort of response he'd expected.

She acted more like a skittish colt. Gazing into his eyes, then quickly shifting her attention to stare far into the distance. Breathless at his kiss, then turning her head. His realization that this was not a game had dawned when he'd kissed her this morning. Fiona Thornton didn't play games. Her every move was deliberate. Every response was honest. Every glance held a world of meaning.

It occurred to him that he ought to back away. He ought to steer clear of such a woman. He ought to watch his step.

It also occurred to him that he didn't want to.

The orange sun hung just over the horizon as Fiona pressed on the brake and the Land Rover ground to a halt under the spreading, yellow-trunked acacia tree. The next instant Mama Hannah hurried out of the kitchen, a butcher knife in one hand and a frying pan in the other. Her dark eyes were wide with worry as she pattered to a stop.

"Bwana, bwana! Many calls for you. All day long. The radio calls fifteen times. Maybe twenty."

Fiona stepped out of the Land Rover. "Who called, Mama Hannah?"

"The people of Bwana McCullough. A lady name *Memsahib* Ginger. 'Where is Bwana McCullough?' she asked me. I told her he is away on safari. She wanted to send a plane to find him. I said no. She said everyone from America is looking for Bwana McCullough. Everyone!"

Fiona turned to Rogan. "You must be a popular man."

"Immensely. I'll call Ginger. Mama Hannah, where's the radio?"

Rogan followed the anxious little woman into the kitchen, where the transmitter was housed. Fiona studied him as his broad shoulders pushed through the sagging door and disappeared.

It was odd how things had turned out. She had expected a day of relentless, if subtle, pressure to bring her around to his way of thinking. Instead, he'd gone straight to work as though this was some new business project he was eager to tackle. All morning he had taken down her observations — and he'd even made a few of his own. When lunchtime came and she expected to start urging him back to the camp and his airplane, she found herself avoiding the subject. He never mentioned wanting to leave. So she dropped it, deciding his assistance was worth putting up with the man for a few more hours.

Now, wandering into her tent, she rubbed the back of her neck. Her thoughts, so regulated with carefully timed observations and details, lurched into unfamiliar territory.

Who was this persistent woman named Ginger? Could she be Rogan's girlfriend? Maybe she was calling because he'd left her all alone in Nairobi. Perhaps she wanted to return to the States.

Fiona pictured this Ginger — a sandy-haired beauty with a curvy figure and a tiny waist. Unlike Fiona, Ginger wore a lovely shade of lipstick and groomed her nails with tasteful matching polish. She brushed her hair more than once a day. She knew how to flirt and tease. And her lips belonged to Rogan.

Wiping a hand across her mouth, Fiona slumped onto the cot. Sukari meowed and crawled into her lap. As Fiona rubbed the cat's ears, she decided enough was enough. She'd spent a full day struggling to concentrate on her work. The night before had been even worse. She felt robbed of the security and normalcy she coveted. This had to stop. It was time for Rogan McCullough to go.

"Hey, Fiona. You in there?" His deep voice on the other side of her tent wall made her sit up. "Just wanted to let you know I've decided to stick around a couple more days. Ginger's going to hold the fort for me."

Fiona curled her toes inside her boots.

"Fiona? Did you hear me?"

"Just a minute." She pushed back the door flap and stepped outside.

"I can stay," he repeated.

"Rogan," she said evenly, "you may not stay. You aren't needed. To be honest, you aren't welcome. There's enough daylight to fly your plane. I want you to go now."

"No," he said.

"Yes."

"No. I've decided to stay. I'll help you again tomorrow."

"Didn't I just say I don't need you?"

"You do need me. Besides, I'm just beginning to see the possibilities for this place."

"Possibilities?" She stiffened.

"Potential, Fiona. Air-Tours Safaris. I'm starting to understand the impact my company can have here. The elephants are a wonderful drawing card. The birth this morning — now that was a real coup. People will flock to things like that. The photographic opportunities out here are endless. We'll need to improve the little airstrip —"

"Stop! Just stop right now, Rogan McCullough. I've spent this entire day trying to show you that your plan *won't*

130

work. That birth was a once-in-a-lifetime thing, a rarity. Do you get it? I've only seen one other myself, and I've been out here every day for years. It just so happens that the abundant rainy season we had two years ago led most of the mature females into estrus, and they conceived. Now their babies are being born. It's not like this happens all year long. It's not like I can stage dramatic elephant births for your tourists. Besides, every elephant requires that much more record keeping from me. I barely managed with you along in the Land Rover, and then only because you were willing to take notes. Can you imagine if I had to guide a pack of tourists around every day?"

"I'll provide the guides. You can schedule and plan the tours."

"No!" She shoved his chest. "Just get out of my camp. I don't want you here. You're interfering."

He grabbed her wrists and clamped her hands in place against him. "You're being unreasonably stubborn. You won't even listen to my ideas."

"Yes, I have. And I've decided they're nothing but a bunch of bunk."

"What's bunk is that you imagine yourself completely isolated from the world and totally self-sufficient. You think you don't need anybody, Fiona. You think you can just carry on for years and years until you turn gray and shrivel up and die out here with your elephants."

"Yes, I do! That's exactly what I think, and that's exactly what I plan to do."

"Fine. I'll take my half-million dollars and my ideas for improvement and everything I have to offer you and the elephants. I'll just leave you out here to wither into a dried-up old stump of a human being who never knew what it was like to laugh and cry and love and be a part of the family of man."

"And good riddance!" she shouted behind him as he stormed across the clearing.

Dust puffed around Rogan's boots as he stalked toward the riverbed and ripped back the door of his tent. He could just see the woman years from now. Her hair would be white. She would be bent over and hobbling to her Land Rover. She would spend day after day watching her beloved elephants until one afternoon some game warden would find her, dead as a doornail with a lap full of notes.

"Good riddance to you, too, Fiona Thornton."

He stuffed his laptop and notebook into his briefcase and fumbled with the latch. Maybe he should just sell Air-Tours. It had been his father's company anyway, and it certainly had nothing to do with publishing. The only reason he'd considered messing with it was for the business challenge and the possibility of using it to coddle clients. At the least, it was something a little different. Something he could look forward to as a getaway from McCullough Enterprises.

Of course, if the deal with Megamedia came through, he would pretty much let McCullough Enterprises go. And then what would he do? He certainly wouldn't need money. He'd spent years struggling to make his organization a viable contender in the industry. Maybe it was time to relax. Time to spend a little of that money. Maybe he could buy an island somewhere. Or build a house in New Mexico. Maybe he would just sell off the businesses his father had left him and use that money to start something brand-new. Something on the cutting edge. Something risky and improbable.

He liked a challenge. He enjoyed fighting against long odds. The battles and the victories were what kept him going and made him feel alive.

"Bwana McCullough?" Mama Hannah's voice sounded outside the tent. "*Hodi,* may I come inside? I have brought your shirt."

Rogan swept back the tent flap, and the small African woman stepped in. She laid the pressed and folded safari shirt on the cot and then, like a fluttering mother, began lighting lamps and unfolding blankets.

"It will be a cool night, bwana. In Kenya, hot days can bring cold nights. Just as suffering can lead us to God's peace."

Peace again. "Mama Hannah, I won't be staying the night."

"No?" She straightened. "But I have prepared a roasted chicken with peas and potatoes."

"Sounds good, but —"

"Oh, it will be delicious. For dessert, a large spice cake with marzipan frosting."

"Well —"

"This cake is the favorite of my *toto.* This morning, when I saw that she would be upset today, I decided to bake her the spice cake. Now she will smile. You will see."

She puffed a pillow and settled it on the cot. Humming a small tune, she took Rogan's briefcase from his hand and wedged it beside the tent wall. Then she turned back the corner of the bedding, revealing a snowy white sheet beneath the blanket.

"Perhaps you will stay for this one night, bwana. Just to enjoy my spice cake and roasted chicken. Perhaps you will not shout at my *toto*. Perhaps you will sit beside the fire with her and eat. And then, perhaps, you will talk nicely. If you wish to make her smile, you will talk."

Rogan cleared his throat and scratched the rough stubble on his chin. "She's a difficult woman. Always angry."

"She is angry only with you. And this is good."

"Good?"

"I don't see her smile or shout or speak. She is always alone, thinking she needs no one. Not even God. For my *toto*, this anger is good."

It was odd to think that anger could be a positive emotion for Fiona. Especially odd, Rogan realized, because at this moment he felt strangely alive. Arguing with her had made his blood roar and his body surge with adrenaline. She certainly was a challenge. A worthy opponent. One he would savor defeating.

"Sometimes," Mama Hannah confided, "I wonder if my *toto*, the one they call

Matalai Shamsi, may one day become an elephant herself. Perhaps she will forget how to speak. She will forget to return to the camp. Her food will be the long grasses, and at night she will sleep among the elephants."

Rogan smiled. Interesting concept. He'd just been picturing Fiona as gray and wrinkled himself. "Tell me why she's called Matalai Shamsi, Mama Hannah. What does that name really mean?"

"For that story, you must ask her yourself."

"I did ask her. She gave me some nonsense about her red hair and green clothes looking like the sunrise."

"It is true. She is a woman of sunrise. But you must learn the whole legend if you wish to understand Fiona Thornton."

Mama Hannah gave the tent one last inspection before she started through the door. Rogan tapped her shoulder.

"Mama Hannah," he said, "you seem to understand a lot of things. When you first met me, you said I had no peace."

The old woman's brows lifted. "I am not wrong, am I?"

He let out a breath. "No, you're not. I just can't figure out how you knew."

"Eh-h," she grunted. "It is written in the

way you walk. In the way you speak. You do not know the peace that can never be understood."

"What peace is that, Mama Hannah?"

"When Jesus Christ lives in the heart, this peace lives there also." She tilted her head to one side. "You do not serve Him, bwana?"

"I know who you're talking about, of course, but —"

"Eh-h. Just as I know who you are." She paused a moment. "Knowing and serving are not the same. Seek Him. Serve Him. Then you will find the peace."

As she made for the door, he spoke up. "One more thing, Mama Hannah. You told me you made the spice cake because you knew Fiona would be upset when she came back to camp. How did you know this morning what she would be feeling tonight?"

For a moment the tiny African woman stared up at a corner of the tent. "A sleeping woman who lives in the pleasant land of dreams does not like to be awakened," she said. Then she turned and vanished into the twilight.

Fiona sat in her tent and listened for the cough of the airplane's engines. Surely after such an argument, after such clear instructions to leave, Rogan McCullough wouldn't consider staying another night in the camp. Surely he would figure out he wasn't welcome. Surely he would comprehend that she wasn't going to change her mind about the tourists.

She slipped on a navy blue cotton sweater and worked her hair into a loose braid. Evening shadows crept around the tent, enclosing it in a comfortable green warmth. The philodendron leaves drooped a little. The cat settled into his basket. A cricket began to chirp just outside the tent flap.

Fiona tied her small mesh window shut against a light breeze that filtered through the acacias. She turned up her propane lamp and settled at her desk. There would be time for a few minutes of study before Mama Hannah rang for dinner. Leafing through her charts, she added Moira's new baby to the M family list.

Another little female. Would this one survive the drought? Would Moira have enough milk to sustain the baby? Would the milk have enough nutritional richness for the tiny calf to develop into a strong and healthy member of the family?

Flipping open her notebook, Fiona

scanned the list of the day's observations. Bold black pen strokes recorded each moment of Moira's labor and the calf's birth. Rogan's writing. Strong downstrokes. Evenly spaced letters. Punctuation that could never be mistaken for accidental inkblots.

Fiona turned the page. Rogan had missed nothing. Every word she had spoken had been set in his dark, regular hand. He'd even added a few things she hadn't said. She scanned the writing.

11:05 A.M. Margaret moves northwest toward crest one mile past birth site. New calf struggling to keep up. Moira lagging just a little. Mallory watchful. Family stops to feed on twigs and barks of *Acacia xanthophloea* trees and dried clumps of *Sporobolus consimilis*.

Fiona frowned and reread the last sentence. She didn't remember telling Rogan the scientific names of the trees and grass that formed the primary food for the elephant population.

She skipped a few more notes she *did* remember dictating. Then her eyes fell on another notation.

Madeline searches out a patch of

Cynodon dactylon beside dried stream-bed. The grass is only a rough stubble.

Fiona stared at the page and its careful script. She tried to picture Rogan writing these words, but she saw only the man himself and not his work. A whimsical smile skittered across her lips at the image of the pair of them seated on the Land Rover roof conferring about the elephants' progress toward Mount Longonot.

Though she'd forgotten what he'd said, she remembered Rogan speaking, his mouth forming the words, then tilting at one corner in a grin that punctuated each sentence. Strands of drying hair began to lift and brush against his collar. Sun danced off the gold that spilled over his forehead. Each time he had bent his head to write, the breeze drew a random part down his scalp. She wondered if his neck had burned in the intense sunlight. His nose certainly had. She should have mentioned the name of a good healing ointment before he left.

Lifting her head, she listened again for the sound of his airplane. She heard instead the gentle melody of Mama Hannah's bamboo xylophone calling out the evening supper song.

For a moment she studied the notebook again. She slipped her fingertips across the writing, feeling the curved ridges that Rogan's heavy-handed pen strokes had embossed on the thin paper. Shutting her eyes, she held her fingers to her nose and breathed in. Then she closed the notebook and walked to dinner.

The deserted campsite, completely dark now save for the glowing campfire and a gas lantern flickering in the kitchen, beckoned. She recognized the rumbling calls of elephants from far across the plains, communication almost too low for human ears. She sat at the white-clothed table and unfolded her napkin across her lap.

"Roast chicken for madame?"

She swung toward the familiar sound of a deep male voice. Rogan emerged from the thatched-roof kitchen bearing a tray of steaming food. Mama Hannah marched behind him with an armload of plates and silverware. Still wearing the T-shirt, Rogan had topped it with one of Sentero's old school jackets. The gray corduroy sleeves hit him midarm. And the front didn't have a hope of buttoning.

He presented a fragrant roast chicken, still sizzling and popping. Opening a bottle of fresh cold water, he filled Fiona's glass.

While Rogan arranged a bowl of peas beside a basket of golden dinner rolls, Mama Hannah set the table for two.

"Mr. McCullough," Fiona began, feeling as if the world had tilted a bit on its axis, "you're certainly the most —"

"First of all, my name is Rogan. And you did make it clear that you wanted me to leave. But the fact is, it just got too late to fly out." He sat in the chair opposite her and eyed her. "I've also decided to declare a truce."

"The word *truce* implies mutual agreement, *Rogan*," Fiona said, deliberately emphasizing his name. "One person can't make that decision."

"Wrong. If one of the warring parties elects to stop fighting, you have an automatic truce."

"Or a massacre."

He laughed. "Massacre at will, Fiona. But I'm no longer in the battle."

She spooned a helping of peas and a chicken breast onto her plate. Taking a sip of water, she contemplated his words. She *could* defeat Rogan, she realized. That would be the easy way out. She could refuse to have anything to do with him. She could shout at him, run him out of the camp, send him away in his plane. Radio the authorities to arrest him if need be.

She sensed that Rogan McCullough was not a man who often called for a truce. Instead, he pressed for a surrender — on his terms. But this time, with him against the ropes, she could win. He would be caught off guard if she responded to his peace overture by banning him from the camp. He *would* go away then. And that would be the end of the strife.

"All right, you can stay," she said suddenly, not allowing herself time to weigh the consequences.

Rogan looked at her, a forkful of chicken poised at his mouth. "Truce?"

"Truce."

He chewed, mulling something over. Then he glanced up a second time, his blue eyes as bright as the stars of the Southern Cross. "Tell me the legend of Matalai Shamsi."

She stiffened. "I told you what the Africans think. It's just my red hair —"

"This isn't about you. I want to hear the legend of Matalai Shamsi. Tell me the story."

"To you, it would sound like a fairy tale."

"I'm in the mood for fairy tales. Come on, Fiona. Indulge me."

Smoothing out the folds of her napkin, she kept her eyes on her plate. How clearly she recalled Mama Hannah's patience with her skinny little *toto* who preferred fairy tales to Bible stories. "The legend of Matalai Shamsi is an old Swahili folktale," she informed him.

"Doesn't your brother study African oral storytelling? Clive Willetts told me a little about him."

"Grant collects tribal tales from all over Kenya. But it was Mama Hannah who first told me about Matalai Shamsi." Her voice drifted. She lifted her eyes to the fire, and watched the flames flicker.

"Once upon a time," she began, "a king had six sons. The youngest was named Shamsudini. The king and his sons were sitting in the garden one afternoon when a beautiful bird flew overhead. The king wanted the bird, so he told his sons to catch it for him. 'The one who loves me truly will bring me the bird,' the king told them."

"I bet the youngest son caught it."

"Would *you* like to tell the story?" She flashed him a warning look, but he just grinned. "Each of the sons was given money, a horse, and a servant. But Shamsudini's brothers were jealous of him, and they tried to kill him on the way. He chose not to fight. Instead, he gave up his possessions and set out alone to find the bird. Soon he met a gigantic spirit, who threatened to eat the prince and pick his teeth with the prince's bones. Shamsudini told the spirit that whatever God willed would happen."

"I bet the spirit didn't eat him, did he?" Rogan was leaning halfway across the table, his face animated.

"No, the spirit offered to set Shamsudini free in exchange for food. So the prince prayed, and forty pots of food appeared. After eating, the spirit offered to help the prince find the bird. They traveled to a castle, where the prince found the special bird. But the lord of this castle wouldn't set the bird free. He wanted a thunder sword in exchange."

"So the spirit took him to find the thunder sword," Rogan interrupted again.

"*Really,* Mr. McCullough!"

"Sorry, it's just that when I was a little kid —" He stopped and looked at the fire. "I like stories. Go on."

"In the castle where the thunder sword hung, Shamsudini faced another king. This king wanted the prince to bring him Matalai Shamsi in exchange for the sword.

So the spirit and the prince built a ship and sailed away in search of the Princess Sunrise. Finally they arrived at the palace where the princess's father, the sultan, lived. Shamsudini pretended to be a powerful medicine man. When the sultan asked the prince to cure his sick daughter, Matalai Shamsi, Shamsudini insisted that she be taken on board his ship for the cure to work."

"What was wrong with her?"

"I don't know. The legend isn't specific. It just says she was sick. Some people think she had a sort of sleeping sickness — she walked around in a dreamlike state from which she couldn't be awakened."

"That's how Mama Hannah described you."

"Oh no, the connection's nothing that profound. It's just my hair that reminds the Africans of the sunrise."

Rogan's eyebrows lifted. "And so the prince cured her and stole her away."

"That's right. Shamsudini had fallen in love with Princess Sunrise. But then he had to face all the other trials again. He tricked the thunder-sword king by giving him Matalai Shamsi's maid instead. He tricked the king who owned the beautiful bird by giving him a false sword that had

146

been crafted to look like the thunder sword. Finally, when the spirit and the prince parted ways, the spirit gave Shamsudini one of his feathers. The prince could summon the spirit at any time by throwing the feather into the fire."

"What about the brothers? I bet Shamsudini really let them have it."

"Actually the brothers captured the prince on his way back to the castle. They choked him until he was almost dead and threw him to the ground. Then they stole the princess, the sword, and the bird, and they went to find their father, the king. When the king asked about Shamsudini, the brothers told him that the prince had gone off on his own. The king was furious. He planned a wedding for the oldest boy and Princess Sunrise."

"Wait a minute now!" Rogan took a swig of water and thunked his glass on the table. "The prince deserves better than that. He's smart and brave. He triumphed over all the odds. He fought hard to win the princess. You can't let his brothers cheat him like that, Fiona."

"Do you want to hear the ending or not?"

"This story better end right."

"How would you end it, then?"

"If I were the prince, I'd come to. Then I'd break into the palace and challenge the brothers to a duel. I'd fight for what was rightfully mine. I'd win the sword and the bird and the princess back. Any man knows he's got to take a stand sometimes. He's got to climb to the top of the heap. He's got to win over adversity."

"All by himself?"

"Well, who's going to *help him?*"

"You're the one who's so sure people can't exist all alone, Rogan. People need each other, remember? People have to communicate, share ideas —"

"Okay, okay."

Fiona continued the tale. "What the prince did was throw the feather into the fire, and the spirit appeared. Together they went into the king's hall, where they found everyone ready for the oldest brother's wedding. Shamsudini talked with his father and told him the whole story. The prince called the princess by name. She ran to him and spoke for the first time, calling him her prince. Then the spirit's voice boomed out, 'It is true.' The king ordered the five bad brothers sewn into sacks and thrown into the ocean. Shamsudini married Princess Sunrise, and their wedding lasted many days."

"And they lived happily ever after?"

"That's not part of the original tale. In Swahili it ends with them eating rice and cakes until they could eat no more."

Rogan pondered this. "I want a happily-ever-after ending."

Intrigued that such a practical man would want a fairy-tale ending, she shrugged. "Why not? *And they lived happily ever after.*"

They sat in silence, both staring at the fire. Fiona was remembering Mama Hannah and the long evenings in the oak rocking chair when she was a child. She could almost feel the warm curve of her *ayah*'s shoulder and see her dark cradling arms. Mama Hannah had filled her *totos'* lives with love and security — both through her own devotion to them and through the Bible stories she loved to tell. But Fiona had very early come to question God's love, and instead would ask Mama Hannah for the legend of Matalai Shamsi over and over again, craving its reassurance that love could prevail and that life could be beautiful.

Mama Hannah would tell the story until her head nodded and fell against Fiona's. Then the little girl would listen to her *ayah*'s deep breathing, and she would imagine herself a beautiful princess who one day would be wakened from sleep by a handsome, brave, and wise prince. Of course she knew now that it was just a child's fantasy.

"Could we move closer to the fire, Fiona?" Rogan's face was open, beckoning as he rose and pulled her to her feet. "Sit with me, please."

They drew their camp chairs close to the fire, and then somehow his arm was around her again, warm and firm, in the silence of the night. Fiona closed her eyes and rested her cheek against Rogan's shoulder. The smells of dust and smoke mingled around him. The day's heat radiated from the skin of his neck, carrying in its warmth the essence of his male scent.

"When I was a little girl," she whispered into the corduroy, "Mama Hannah always used to tell me stories."

He held her, one hand caressing the waves of her braid. "I sat in my mother's lap for hours listening to stories," he said. She could feel the vibrations of his voice against her forehead. "But that was a long time ago."

"I don't remember my mother's stories."

"You were young when she died?"

Fiona nodded, unable to speak.

"Well, I guess everyone knows about the great McCullough scandal," Rogan said. "So that's what happened to my mom. Didn't see her much after the breakup. She never married well, you know."

His laugh held no humor.

"I don't," she said. "I don't know the story of the great McCullough scandal."

Rogan stopped breathing for a moment. He drew away from her just enough to read her face. "You don't know? You have no idea about my past — my parents, the tabloids?"

"Nothing."

"This is amazing." He pulled her close again. "Never — I've never met anyone who didn't know my past. Are you sure?"

"Positive. I'm a blank slate."

"My life has been in the news from before I was born."

"So, what's the story?" she asked.

He was silent for a long time. "Better that you stay a blank slate," he said finally. "It's not important anyway."

Fiona could feel the tension emanating from the man, the unspoken emotion that he held bridled. Barely. Though she was curious about him, she had learned to respect the ways of others, to allow for reticence, and to keep her distance.

"There is one thing about you I'd like to know," she said, meeting his eyes.

"And what might that be?"

"I'm curious about the notes you made this morning."

"What about them?"

"The grasses. The trees. Did I tell you their scientific names? I don't remember that."

"Oh." He smiled for the first time since dinner. "Crazy, huh? I know you'll find this hard to believe, but in college I majored in biology. I'd been interested in that kind of thing since I was a kid. I took a course or two in plant identification. Took pictures of wildflowers. Went on camping trips. The whole nine yards. So when I was out there with you in the Land Rover today, the plant names suddenly came back to me out of the blue."

"You spelled them right."

"Photographic memory, you know?"

He had relaxed against her, and she was beginning to decide she preferred him stiff and uncomfortable. His mouth moved close to her ear, his breath heating her hair. His hand began to slide up and down her braid again.

"I thought you mentioned publishing as a career," she said.

"Sure, publishing. That's what I do now, of course. You know," he said, "during college a buddy and I started this small on-campus student guide. Then a German pharmaceutical company asked us if we could produce a single-sponsor magazine for them. So we did. Then we bought *Manor*, the men's magazine."

"*Manor*?"

"You've never heard of *Manor*? It's a popular publication. But in those days it was floundering. My partner and I bought it and brought it back to life. Three years later we split our interests. He took *Manor*, and I took the smaller publication."

"And then what?"

Rogan paused again. When he spoke, his voice was stilted. "After the split, I started McCullough Enterprises. Right now I have a thousand employees and a fifty-million-dollar headquarters in New York. I run the thing. It's my life."

"I thought you owned Air-Tours."

"I do. My father died three months ago and left it to me, along with six other companies — most of which are in better shape. Air-Tours is just a . . . a sideline. A diversion. What I really do is publish advertising-sponsored magazines that are supplied to doctors and dentists and businesses. All kinds of professional groups. I do television, video. I have homes in New York and Florida and Monte Carlo. I own a big sailboat and three planes. I collect cars. You sure you weren't aware of any of this?"

"Of course not."

"It just seems so strange to me." His eyes studied the ground between them. "All my life, everywhere I've gone, people thought they already knew all about me. They always made assumptions. I've been pigeonholed. I've been expected to follow a certain set of prearranged rules."

He looked up and saw she was smiling. "So who are you supposed to be?" she asked softly.

"I'm this . . . this mover and shaker. This guy who rocked the publishing industry. I'm the man who climbed higher than anybody else. High enough to eclipse even my own father."

"But who are you really, Rogan?"

"I'm . . . well, I'm . . . I'm just me."

"And this is what I know about you." She took his hand from hers and settled it on the armrest of the wobbly old camp chair. "I know that you're intelligent and bold and quite stubborn. I know that once, long ago, you looked at plants and took their pictures and memorized their names. I know that this morning you understood the elephants. And that, Rogan McCullough, is quite enough for me."

SIX

Before Rogan could respond, Fiona spotted the arrival of Mama Hannah's famous spice cake. With a laugh of delight, she detached herself and hurried from the fire to the table.

During the dessert course — which Rogan declared was the best cake he'd ever tasted — Mama Hannah and Fiona went through their nightly meal-planning routine. Rogan listened, a silly grin on his face, as Fiona requested filet of Lake Turkana tilapia, a green salad, and potato soup.

"I wonder what we're really going to get," he said as the African woman padded away, arms laden with dinnerware. "Maybe spaghetti?"

"Oh, I doubt that," Fiona responded with a chuckle. "Mama Hannah has never been fond of Italian foods. There's no telling what we'll be eating. If she prepares her roast beef, you'll love it. She makes a wonderful horseradish sauce. And she has this casserole that you —" She stopped speaking and stared across the table.

"I *would* like to stay, Fiona," Rogan said.

"I think it's best that you leave tomorrow. I really have so much work to do."

"I'll take Sentero's place. I'll write the notes."

"No, Rogan. Please. I'm not going to change my mind about the tourists."

"Wait a minute now. That subject's off-limits according to the truce. I want to stay another day just to . . . to be out here. I want to see the elephants again. I'd like to go out again with you, Fiona."

She was afraid that if he said one more thing, she would give him anything he wanted. The tourists, the campsite, the elephants. The way he held her with his gaze, the way his mouth moved, the way his hair ruffled in the breeze made her completely forget to listen to what he was talking about.

"Well . . . ," she said in a blank tone. "Well, I . . ."

"The thing is, Fiona —" he reached across the table and covered her hand with his — "there's something special out here. I don't know whether it's the plains and the animals, or the dry heat, or the birth of the baby elephant. Maybe it's God, Fiona. I'm starting to believe you when you say

He's real and He's involved in this world. Maybe it's Mama Hannah and the things she tells me about God — how He can live inside a person and bring peace. . . . Or maybe it's you, Fiona. I don't know what it is. But I'm not ready to leave yet."

"But you have all kinds of messages waiting for you —"

"No. I don't want that right now. I don't want that world. I'm not ready to go back. Just give me another day here. Would you do that? No arguing. No anger. Just a quiet day watching the elephants."

"All right." The words barely sounded in her throat. "One more day. Now, if you'll excuse me —"

Before she could tumble into the pool of his blue eyes and drown there, she pushed her chair away from the table and walked across the clearing to her tent. Fighting for breath, she zipped her door flap shut and sank down on the bed. This was not good. The feelings she was having were not sane. Everything in her life was coming unraveled. Things were out of control.

On a normal night she would have sat by the campfire for another hour. She would have drunk two cups of tea with milk and sugar. She might have dozed a little. Then she would have returned to her tent and worked for several hours on her charts. Finally turning down the lamp, she would have crawled under her covers with her cat and —

"Fiona," Rogan's voice came from just outside the tent.

She clutched the edge of her cot. *Oh no.*

"Fiona, I just wanted to say good night."

"Good night," she called, hoping that would send him away. "Sleep tight."

"Fiona? Could you come out here for a second?" The zipper on the tent door started moving up slowly, metal mumbling in the night.

"Rogan," she warned. "Don't —"

He pulled back the tent door just as she was about to reach for it.

"Hey, buster!" she snapped, jumping to her feet. "You can't walk in on me like this. Mama Hannah's going to come after you with a frying pan."

"Sorry to interrupt, Fiona," he said, amusement glittering in his eyes.

She grabbed her sweater, annoyed that he knew how easily he could throw her off-kilter, and stepped out of the tent. "So what do you want?"

"About today. I want to thank you. I enjoyed myself."

"I'm glad. Well — good night, Rogan."

She backed against the tent, clutching her sweater.

"You know," he said, "I'm beginning to understand what the Africans mean about that sunrise comparison. It's the strangest thing, but in the lamplight your hair glows. And it's not just shiny hair. It's luminescent. The orange and gold inside the red light up. And then there's the way it spills down your shoulders. Did you know you have freckles, Fiona?"

He had moved to within a foot of her now, as though wanting to touch her once more tonight. Lifting a hand, he let his fingers sift through her hair.

"From my mother," she whispered. "She had freckles. Jessica, my sister, has red hair too. I think she has freckles, but Tillie and Grant —"

"They're muted. Almost invisible. But I can see them, sprinkled like fine powdered sugar."

By now his hand had slipped down her arm and then back up. With one fingertip he touched her lower lip. "Fiona, something has occurred to me."

She cast a glance at the cat inside the tent, who was having another bath, oblivious to the peril of his mistress.

"I suddenly realized," Rogan went on

when she didn't respond, "that if you don't know anything about me, then maybe there are a lot of other things you don't know. Things that are common knowledge to most people."

"I don't think that's true. Just because I never heard of you or McCullough Enterprises, I'm not ignorant. I'm not stupid."

"I'm well aware of that. It's just . . . there may be some things you're innocent about. I mean, has anyone ever told you that you have the most amazing mouth? There's something about the way your lower lip kind of pouts. And your upper lip is bowed on the top, like two smooth hills with a gentle valley between them. It's remarkable."

She brushed his hand away. "Rogan, really. I have lips just like everybody else's. Labia. The outer and inner margins of the mouth aperture, usually regarded as a source of speech."

"Speech *and* kissing." He traced the line of her upper lip. "You know, everything about the human face is fascinating. I mean, true, there's this hair of yours —"

"Cylindrical filaments composed of protein and growing out of the epidermis."

"Yes, but yours smells of flowers and lemons and sunshine."

"It's just my shampoo. Lemon is the only kind they sell at the *duka* in Naivasha."

"Feels like silk." He moved closer and lifted a mass of her hair. "Looks like fire. It's a halo. See what I mean? And I suppose you could say, sure, we all have eyes. But your eyes are unusual. They tilt up at the outer corners. And the color . . . reminds me of tortoiseshell. Strange, magic eyes. Always changing."

"Oculus," she said quickly. "Eyes are merely the organs of sight. A pair of spherical bodies contained in the orbits of the skull."

"Lovely eyes."

"Rogan," she whispered as he touched her eyebrow and then ran his finger around the tender skin, "please keep Ginger in mind."

"Ginger?" He lifted his head.

"The woman in Nairobi who keeps calling. Is she . . . well, I've thought she might be your girlfriend."

"She might be, but she isn't. Nobody is, for that matter. So, if you don't mind, I'd rather think about you."

"Well, yes, as a matter of fact, I do —"

"Fiona, I'm going to take you in my arms," he said, covering her lips with a finger. "And if you were to put just one of your arms around me, I believe you might find you liked it."

She thought her knees were going to collapse as he pulled her close and bent his head to kiss her gently on the lips. The most awful feeling welled up inside her. It was as though she were about to explode. But not in anger. Some crazy combination of fear, joy, sorrow, pain, and elation was bubbling up, threatening to froth over.

Even worse, she found she couldn't look away from Rogan's blue eyes. A flame flickered between the two of them, and she couldn't think. Couldn't reason. The small patch of skin where his finger was touching her chin seemed more alive at this moment than any other part of her body.

How odd it felt to be so moved, so affected, by another human being. She felt a little giddy with the emotion.

"Rogan," she said softly, "just look at what you've done to me. From a purely objective standpoint, the changes are . . . remarkable. My breathing and heart rate have accelerated. I feel flushed. My normal circulation has altered. Blood seems to have pooled in my knees, and I can't think straight. It's as though my brain has been deprived of oxygen."

Mirth danced in his eyes as he listened.

"Is this a scientific treatise on the effects of a kiss?"

"I am a scientist. My outlook is an integral part of me. Analysis comes naturally. I'm not the emotional, sentimental type of woman, in case you hadn't noticed."

"Hmm . . . let's put that to the test, shall we?"

He bent and brushed his lips across hers a second time. Fiona gasped. "Wait, I'm . . ." She maneuvered out of his arms. "I don't feel very . . . scientific anymore. I can't seem to keep my distance. I'm losing objectivity."

"Really?" he said with mock surprise. "Dr. Thornton, how astonishing."

"In fact, I think Mama Hannah was right. I can't do this on my own."

"Do what?"

"Staying distant. Staying pure."

He looked into her eyes. "Is that what you want, Fiona? Purity?"

She thought about it for a moment. One part of her really wanted another kiss. Lots more kisses. But she shook off the desire. "Yes," she said quickly. "That's what I want."

"Why? Because you're afraid to let a man . . . to let anyone . . . get too close to you?"

"Maybe there's some of that. I don't trust people easily. I certainly don't trust *you* or your motives." She paused, thinking. "But there's something else. Mama Hannah —"

"I was afraid she was going to come into this."

"She taught me that God requires purity until marriage. And the reason is because when humans breach that law, they're forever changed. They really do, in some strange way, become one. Spiritually."

Dismay shadowed his face. "But you said you don't bow to God's commands, Fiona. You told me you believe in Him, but you haven't given Him authority over your life."

She shivered despite the warmth of the sweater clasped so tightly around her. "Rogan, if I let anyone into my life, it will be Jesus Christ. And since you came along, I'm beginning to realize how helpless I really am."

"Helpless? Not you."

"Yes, me. And whether you want to admit it or not . . . you are too."

He gazed down at her. "This isn't how I usually do things. Not with women. Not with anything in my life. But, because it's you, Fiona, because you're . . . different somehow . . . I'm going to stop pushing for what I want. It's too late for me, but I'm going to honor what you want. Your purity."

She smiled, her heart filling with gratitude. "It's never too late for purity, Rogan. Mama Hannah says —"

"Let's let Mama Hannah rest for tonight, what do you say?" He reached out and touched Fiona's cheek. "Good night, Princess. I'll see you at sunrise."

"Toto," Mama Hannah called from outside the tent. "Fiona, wake up. Bwana McCullough is ready to go and see the elephants."

Fiona sat bolt upright in her bed. *Rogan.* The image of his face washed over her.

"Mama Hannah, what time is it? Is . . . is breakfast ready?"

"It is almost seven o'clock. Breakfast was prepared long ago. As the wise Solomon reminds us, 'A little extra sleep, a little more slumber, a little folding of the hands to rest — and poverty will pounce on you like a bandit.' "

Fiona rolled her eyes.

"Many pancakes have already been eaten by Bwana McCullough." Mama Hannah paused a moment. "And nearly all the syrup."

Fiona couldn't believe she had overslept. All night she had tossed on the camp cot while trying to sort through and analyze the flood of changes Rogan had unleashed in her. She felt silly and free . . . embarrassed and shy. She wanted to spend the rest of her life in Rogan's arms . . . and she never wanted to see another man as long as she lived. She could hardly wait to see him . . . and she wished he had never come into her life.

"*Toto?*"

"Just a moment, Mama Hannah. Please tell the bwana I'll need to shower and eat before we can go."

"He is repairing the Land Rover now. It will be ready by the time you have prepared for the day."

"The Land Rover?" Fiona stuck her head through the door flap.

Mama Hannah grinned as she jabbed a finger in the direction of the vehicle. "The bwana has told me the gears are not good. He is going to make them better for you."

"I didn't know Rogan was a mechanic."

"Oh, *toto,* that man can do many things."

"Yes," she acknowledged, "he certainly can."

"But he was not happy about the hole in

the front fender. When I told him that the big elephant, Margaret, had pushed her tusk into your Land Rover, the bwana became angry."

"He just doesn't understand Margaret." Fiona studied Rogan from a distance. He was bent over the Land Rover, one elbow jutting into the air and his head buried in the vehicle's engine compartment. "What's he wearing, Mama Hannah?"

The little woman beamed. "These are the clothes of Sentero, *toto*. Very clean, very well pressed. Even starched. These are his university clothes, bought long ago from a *duka* in Nairobi. Shorts, socks, T-shirt. Very nice?"

Fiona stared at the baggy green shorts, something an old-time English colonist might have worn. The safari shirt that had accompanied Rogan's chic tourist outfit covered a faded blue T-shirt emblazoned with the slogan Only Elephants Should Wear Ivory. The bush shirt blew open in the breeze, its tail flapping loosely at his thighs. And on his feet the new suede boots were covered with red dust.

"Very nice indeed," Fiona muttered. "He's becoming a veritable Humphrey Bogart. Next he'll be wanting to set sail on the *African Queen*. Excuse me, Mama

Hannah. I'll be ready for breakfast in a few minutes."

Humming, the African woman set off down the path toward the thatched kitchen. From the Land Rover a matching tune began. The notes intertwined, lifted through the sunlit sky, and were carried away by the breeze.

"There's James again." Fiona had spotted the lone bull as she traced her binoculars across the horizon. She and Rogan had spent the morning lurching across trackless, scorched plains in search of elephants. It was almost noon, and the old male was the first they had seen.

"He's by himself today," she went on. "I don't see any sign of Margaret or her family around here. They're probably nearly to Mount Longonot by now."

Rogan leaned across the Land Rover roof and studied the sloping mountain. "Longonot's a volcano?"

"Yes, and so is Mount Suswa, to the southwest. See it there?" She moved aside as Rogan's shoulders maneuvered the turn inside the open hatch. "Suswa has caves that are full of bats."

"Bats produce guano. It ought to be mined. The stuff could be a great moneymaker for the local population."

"Rogan, do you always think in terms of money and income potential?"

"Usually. Is there something wrong with that?"

She considered a moment. "I can see it going either way, actually. The sort of man you are . . . if you wanted to, you could be driven, aggressive, combative, intimidating. I have a feeling you might be able to manipulate people into doing anything you want."

"Whoa. Don't turn me into Hitler."

"Am I exaggerating?"

"Look, I may be a leader but I'm not evil. I just do what I need to do to stay where I am in the world."

"But you could be so much more than you are." She wondered why she was spilling the thoughts that had rolled through her head all night. It shouldn't matter to Rogan what she thought of him. And yet, she wanted him to see the vision she'd had.

"What are you talking about?" he said, a gruff note of irritation in his voice. "There can only be one person on top, and I decided a long time ago that that person was going to be me. I've worked hard to become the man I am today."

"Why? Why have you worked so hard?"

He flicked a blade of grass from the roof. "Well . . . I guess I have an inner drive to be the best."

"Why?"

"If you knew anything about my past, you'd know why. I had some things to prove. I had to show the world who I was and what I could do. A guy like me had to prove things to his father, too, you know?"

"But your father died three months ago."

"So?"

"So, now who are you proving things to?"

He stared down at the scratched green paint on the Land Rover roof. "I don't know . . . I've spent my whole life trying to show John McCullough that his son was somebody. Somebody worth noticing, worth paying attention to. But you're right. He's dead."

"Did you love him?"

"In a way. As the song goes, he was the greatest man I never knew." He paused. "What did you mean about my potential to be more than I am?"

"If you opened yourself up," she said, "softly, rather than trying to dominate, you might learn empathy. Your leadership skills could be used in positive ways. You could

171

inspire people. You could become a truly courageous man."

"I'm no coward, Fiona. I fly planes, I race cars, I'll tackle any kind of risky sport — skiing, speedboats, motocross, boxing. Mountain climbing. Caving. I love a challenge. Anything there is to conquer, I'll give it a try."

She studied him in silence for a moment. "True courage," she said, "is not the power to conquer the world, Rogan. It's the power to love it enough to save it."

"That sounds like Mama Hannah."

"Nope, that's me."

"But you're equating courage with love. Is that how you handled the charging elephant that rammed this Land Rover? Did you just sit there and love that elephant into submitting?"

"Of course I did. Margaret was very upset because I'd inadvertently driven between her and Mick, her youngest calf. It happened a few years ago, when Mick was just a new baby. The M family had been attacked by poachers not long before. They'd killed two of Margaret's sons. I understood how upset she was. So when she gored the Land Rover, I drove far enough away until she felt comfortable again. It was really my own fault. But we have an understanding now."

"You trust her not to charge you again?"

"Oh, she regularly charges. It's usually just a bluff. She's a grumpy old thing. But we're on good terms."

"I don't believe this, Fiona. You mean you'd just sit and let an elephant charge you?"

"Well, I wouldn't hold it against her. Look, here comes James. You can see he's in musth. That means he'll be a little irritable."

"Fiona, I don't think you should let these elephants get so close to you." Rogan took her arm and turned her to face him. "What if something happened? What if you got hurt — seriously wounded? One of them could easily rip you open with a tusk or crush you. I mean, they're immense!"

"Twelve thousand pounds for a full-grown male. The females are half that. But don't worry. I've never known an elephant to purposely hurt a human. In fact, they'll go out of their way to avoid it. They're gentle creatures. Very loving and kind. I've lived with them for years. I trust them, and that's that. Now, are you going to take notes or not?"

She felt oddly pleased at Rogan's concern for her safety. Not that she'd ever been particularly worried about it herself. She knew the elephants too well to be afraid of them. Rogan was flipping through the notebook, exasperation written in the downturn of his mouth.

"So what did you tell me about James?"

"He's in musth right now. That means he's ready to mate. Musth is a stage bulls periodically go through. Kind of like estrus in the females. The two conditions seem to coincide. I'm fairly sure a bull in musth can put females into estrus and vice versa."

Rogan began writing, but Fiona had a feeling his thoughts weren't on bull elephants. She hoped he was thinking about what she'd said. About how he could make a difference.

"James is smelling the air," she whispered. "He's looking for females. Notice the swollen temporal glands between the eye and the ear? They're streaming with a thick liquid. During musth, the male has a sharp, pungent odor. Can you smell him?"

Rogan lifted his head. "Hey," he said, jerking backward. "He's only ten yards from the Land Rover."

"Keep writing," Fiona said as she studied the elephant. Head high, he was testing the air with his trunk. He smelled rank. "James is showing characteristic male musth signs — head lifted, chin tucked in, ears waving. His aggression level seems higher than usual. He's constantly dribbling urine. Okay, steady. He's going to charge us."

At that moment James rumbled and flapped his ears. Shaking his head, he thundered toward the Land Rover.

"Let's get out of here!" Rogan shouted, hurling the notebook through the hatch and grabbing Fiona.

"Stop!" She squirmed free and put one hand on his arm. "Just watch. He's only bluffing."

Rogan stiffened as the enormous elephant plunged toward them. The ground shook. The air seemed to vibrate. White tusks flashed. Gray ears fanned. Fiona clenched the Land Rover roof. At the last moment the bull skidded to a halt, stared with angry eyes, and then shook his head and backed away.

"See," she said. "He's just irritable because he's in musth. Now he's wandering off again, trying to find some females."

"This is ridiculous," Rogan exploded. "That elephant is a menace! You can't stay out here and subject yourself to this, Fiona. You shouldn't be wandering around in the middle of the African bush without a gun. You shouldn't be out here, period. It's too dangerous."

"Really, Rogan. It was nothing. Just an aggressive male. You ought to understand about that."

She winked and slid through the hatch onto her seat. "Coming down, Rogan?" she called, turning the key in the ignition. "I want to check on Rosamond and the R family."

SEVEN

Sunlight, slanting low through the grass, coated the individual blades with gold. Seeds the color of platinum and the shape of arrowheads clung to each shaft. Impalas and Thomson's gazelles wore gilded saddles. Zebras' stripes glinted silver and ebony. A family of hyenas, their scraggly fur burnished with copper, crept over a rocky crest. Weaverbirds returned to gourd-shaped nests that hung shimmering from silhouetted acacia branches. A flock of vultures drifted, circling above a distant gorge like debris preparing to be sucked down a drain.

"We should look into that," Fiona said almost to herself as she drove the Land Rover across the dry, bumpy earth.

"Look into what?" Rogan had been staring out the window, his eyes fixed on a herd of shaggy, bearded wildebeests.

"The vultures. Something over there — probably a lion — has made a kill. I usually try to examine the dead animal the vultures are waiting to clean. Assuming I can find it, that is."

Rogan studied the birds as, one by one, they floated to the ground in long, lazy spirals. He'd always thought of vultures as dirty scavengers in the ecological pecking order. The low men on the totem pole. But Fiona had spoken of the birds as "waiting to clean." It was as if she saw them not as shifty-eyed beggars but as upright citizens who performed a useful job.

Once again he was struck by her view of the world. Animals were a part of the whole God-ordained life cycle, blending with plant life in supreme accord — as long as humans didn't get in the way and mess up the delicate balance. As much as Fiona loved the elephants, she admitted that they, too, had their place in the fragile web of nature. She had spoken of her worries when elephants began eating acacia shoots, of their voracious stripping of baobab tree bark, and of the horrors of human garbage in an elephant's diet. Everything had to blend in order to work. And it was man who so often threw the Creator's scales out of balance.

"I think they're landing just over that ridge," she was saying. "Mama Hannah will keep dinner waiting, so I think we'll have just enough time to check on that kill before dark."

The Land Rover bounced across a graded trail and then swerved onto the grass again. It occurred to Rogan that Fiona paid no attention whatsoever to the steady inroads civilization had made in the Rift Valley. It was as though she simply couldn't be bothered to travel on proper roads when a more direct route led across uncharted savannah. She never listened to the camp radio unless Rogan mentioned wanting to catch up on news. She paid scant attention to Mama Hannah's carefully relayed messages that came in over the radio transmitter, and from what Rogan could tell, she never returned anyone's calls. Sentero usually shopped for groceries and made her phone calls at Naivasha. Piles of unread mail lay on a table in the kitchen. Rogan had found the stack of American magazines she had mentioned. They dated back to 1988.

"Now, do you think we should go around that pile of rocks," Fiona was asking, "or cross through those trees on the left?"

"The trees look a little more manageable."

"There's a stream hidden among them, but I suspect the drought has dried it enough that we can get across. Shall we give it a try? Oh, my goodness!"

She slammed on the brakes just in time to avoid a thundering herd of elephants. They tore out of the trees, their ears flapping and the whites of their eyes showing. Tightly bunched, they kept the calves in their midst. Mothers literally pushed the babies to keep them running at the frantic pace. Fiona threw the Land Rover into gear and stepped on the gas. Dust spewed out behind the vehicle as it swerved to follow the elephants.

"It's Margaret," Fiona said, coughing on the thick red powder that billowed through the floorboard and seeped around the window glass. "Did you see her, Rogan?"

"I couldn't tell." He didn't want to admit that all the elephants still looked pretty much the same to him.

"I saw Megan. And Moira was urging her calf. But I didn't see Madeline, did you?"

"No." He wished he could have been more help. He knew that to Fiona each elephant was an individual, and each was precious.

"Oh, I wonder what's happened," she called over the rattling metal. "I think they're heading for the south ravine about four miles from here. It's where Mindy died a few years ago. I've noticed the M group seems to feel safe there."

"Maybe you shouldn't follow them. Could the Land Rover be scaring them even more?"

"They're not thinking about us. They're trying to get away from some danger. Did you hear an alarm call as we topped the ridge? I didn't hear anything. I wish Sentero were here. He would have heard it. He can hear them talking miles away."

"Talking?"

"Communicating. They rumble, bellow, grunt, groan, growl, moan, squeal — all sorts of sounds that we're only just beginning to understand." She shouted as she drove. "A lot of their communication takes place at infrasonic frequencies. It's way too low for humans to hear. We can only feel it as a sort of throbbing in the air."

"Look, they're slowing down." Rogan watched as the elephants filed through a narrow opening and disappeared into a ravine. "Is that Mallory? The big one on the right?"

"Yes." Fiona nodded, giving him a quick smile as she stepped on the brake and put the Land Rover in neutral. "She's helping Moira with her calf. And there's Madeline — and the baby."

Fiona seemed to have relaxed a little. Taking out her notebook, she began to scribble what had transpired. She lifted her head and squinted at the disappearing animals, then bent to her work again.

"Where's Matilda?" she said in a low voice. "Oh, there you are. And Mick. Yes, I see you. . . ." She wrote for several minutes, then looked up. "Rogan, would you like for me to show you something? Or do you want to go back to camp and get your plane ready?"

He focused on the dark fear that was only now fading from her eyes. "I'd like to see whatever you want to show me, Fiona."

"We'll have to leave the Land Rover and go on foot. I should warn you: it's a dangerous time of day. Lions and cheetahs hunt at dusk."

"Let's go."

Without responding, she turned off the Land Rover and swung down from the vehicle. They followed the path of rumpled grass toward the notch in the ravine wall. Slipping through a tangle of dried vines, they made their way along the sloping edge. Pebbles slipped beneath their feet. Almost nothing was visible through the dense thatch of trees and shrubbery. All at once Fiona held out her hand. Rogan took it.

"Look," she whispered, drawing him near. She pointed through an opening in the thick vegetation. "It's Margaret."

Rogan pushed aside a creeper and located the matriarch. She was walking along a dry streambed. Behind her followed the rest of her family, calm now, though their silence held an undercurrent of tension.

"She's moving toward that small outcrop; do you see?"

Margaret stepped across the streambed and began to stretch her trunk toward a collection of white objects.

"It's Mindy's skeleton," Fiona explained softly when Rogan gave her a quizzical look.

"Her sister?"

"Her daughter. Mindy was illegally speared by some Maasai warriors almost four years ago. The spear fell out, but the wound never had a chance to heal. An elephant's skin is so tough that it closes quickly and doesn't give the inner laceration time to drain. I watched Mindy fade until she wandered into this ravine. And finally she died."

She said the words with such sorrow that Rogan slipped his arm around her shoulders and drew her against his chest. The elephants had moved among the white bones and were touching them gently with their trunks. Megan lifted one. Matilda and Mick turned others over with their front feet.

"Margaret always gives a lot of attention to Mindy's head and tusks," Fiona explained in a low voice. "See how she strokes her trunk tip along the jaw? She likes to feel in all the hollows and crevices of the skull. It's as though she recognizes Mindy. I think that, in a sense, she's caressing her daughter."

Rogan watched as the elephants performed the tender ritual. Even the newborn calves fondled and touched Mindy's bones. Mick lifted a rib and, after turning it for some time, tossed it in the air.

Margaret continued to brush her trunk over Mindy's skull. Finally she hooked the heavy bone and carefully moved it a few feet. She settled it in the grass near the other bones, then gave a deep rumble. The elephants slowly moved off, shuffling through the underbrush and disappearing into the darkness of the ravine.

Rogan held Fiona for a long time. Neither spoke. Purple twilight crept through the branches. A pair of delicate dik-diks, as small and fragile as rabbits — though their tiny horns and slender legs showed them to be antelopes — picked their way across the dry riverbed and vanished into the thicket on the opposite side. Somewhere nearby a baby cried.

When Rogan stiffened, Fiona smiled. "It's a lesser galago," she whispered in his ear. "A bush baby. Can you see it in the tree there? I've been watching it for some time now."

Rogan focused on the small primate with its wide, childlike golden eyes, furry body, and curled ears. The animal stared for a moment, then cried again.

"You'd think it was human," he said, a shiver sliding down his spine. "Sounds like a tiny abandoned baby crying for its mother."

Rogan let his gaze drift over Fiona's face. The furrow in her forehead had smoothed and softened. Her mouth was relaxed, lips gentle and quiet.

"Fiona," he began, but he didn't know what he wanted to say. So he turned her in his arms, rested her head against his shoulder and stood, drinking in the twilight, the silence, the woman.

"Mama Hannah will be furious," Fiona said as she drove toward camp. "She understands if I'm a *little* late, but she hates it when the sun has set and I'm not home. She says I ruin her dinners, but really, I think she's worried about my safety. She inadvertently wound up in some amazing and frightening adventures with my sisters and brother."

"Isn't Sentero always with you on these long treks?"

"Sentero and I have been working together for only about nine months. He had trouble lining up his research grants after college in Texas. And now that he wants to begin his doctorate, he has to go to Nairobi a lot to arrange things from there. I hope he eventually decides to work with me on a permanent basis. He's great. We get along very well."

She was smiling as she drove. Rogan wondered how it could be possible for him to envy a man who had long, beaded earlobes and dressed in checkered cloths. But he did covet the smile with which Fiona favored those she treasured. He had seen it at Moira's birthing and this evening in the ravine. He had seen her special smile when Mama Hannah presented her famous spice cake. And now she wore it for Sentero.

"What's he like, anyway, this Maasai who graduated from U.T.? I'm having trouble putting him together."

"I'd trust Sentero with my life," she said immediately. "He's a wonderful man. Generous, kind, honest, intelligent. He cares about his country. He's working for the future of Kenya."

"I don't know why, Fiona, but something about him doesn't feel right to me. Maybe it's those strange eyes."

Fiona drove in silence, and Rogan wondered if she was angry with him. He knew he shouldn't have made that last statement. But he'd learned to rely on his instincts. And they told him Sentero held some deep secrets.

Maybe it was the thought of Fiona cruising around out here in the bush with hungry lions and charging elephants and nothing but a man with a spear to protect her. Or maybe he was just miffed that she reserved that special smile for someone other than him.

She looked beautiful as she drove through the pale lilac light of dusk. Her eyes shone, and her magnificent hair tumbled around her shoulders. Rogan had the discomfiting realization that if he wasn't careful, when he left Fiona and returned to Nairobi, something inside him might remain out here in the wilderness. It also occurred to him that he ought to get away. Soon.

Things were beginning to feel uncomfortable. He had the strangest sensation that he wasn't himself. Not truly. Somewhere in the deep silences and the silver moonlight and the golden elephant grass, he had begun to get tangled. Things clung to him. The dry orange dust. The smell of sunshine heating the earth. Woodsmoke. He felt he was being slowly and insidiously invaded.

And this red-haired woman . . . she was tangling him, too. The light in her camouflaged eyes told him that mysteries lay hidden in their depths. Mysteries he wanted to unlock.

"I'm going to skirt that gorge where the vultures were," she was saying, half to herself. "It might be just light enough to . . ."

Her voice trailed off. Rogan sat up as she slowed the Land Rover. Her eyes had focused on something in the distance. Brow narrowed and lips parted slightly, she stared.

"What's the matter, Fiona?" Rogan asked.

"Down there . . . in the river. Do you see it?"

He searched the dusk. "It's not light enough to see much of anything. Wait a minute . . . that little hump? Is that what you're talking about? That's not a hump,

Fiona. That's a . . . that's a baby elephant!"

He grabbed her hand as it rested on the steering wheel. She didn't move. The tiny creature stood in a couple of inches of water, its ears flapping and its head lifted piteously to the sky. As Rogan watched, he began to make out other shapes — low, slinking shapes that circled the calf and edged toward it.

"Hyenas," Fiona whispered.

"Where's the mother? That's not one of *our* babies is it? Not Madeline's or Moira's?"

"I don't recognize it. Must be a newborn. It's been abandoned."

"I didn't know an elephant mother would do that." He felt angry, filled with irrational rage at the thought of anything being abandoned by its mother. "What's going to happen?"

"The hyenas will kill it. Soon, I suspect."

"Over my dead body!" Rogan flung open the Land Rover door and jumped to the ground. Shouting and waving his arms, he ran down the slope toward the river.

Fiona drove after him, honking the horn. "Rogan!" she shouted. "Get in here! You can't do this. The hyenas will come after you."

"I'm not going to stand by and let them kill that elephant!" he yelled over his shoulder.

She slammed on the brake and the horn at the same time. "Get in! We'll try to chase them away."

He leapt into the still-moving vehicle. As she drove, he hung out the door and shouted at the predators. "Get away! Scat! Fiona — step on it. One of them's nipping at the baby's leg."

Like a woman suddenly possessed, Fiona headed straight into the group of hyenas. With a series of eerie yips and laughing barks they scattered, their hunched backs fading away in the dim light. The elephant calf screamed with alarm at the sight of the rumbling Land Rover bearing down. Smooth gray ears fanned the air as the elephant swung its trunk back and forth.

Rogan was preparing to jump out a second time when Fiona lunged across the seat and grabbed his arm. "What are you doing?" she shouted. "You can't go out there, Rogan. Those hyenas will be back within minutes. They'll tear you to shreds."

"I'm not just going to sit around and wait for them to attack that baby." He glared at her. "Are you?"

Panting for breath, he felt like a madman. Sweat dripped down his side-burns. His new safari shirt must have gotten caught on the Land Rover's metal frame, for it had ripped across the back. One pocket dangled.

"Rogan," she said softly, touching his arm with her hand, "do you remember the vultures we saw over the ravine earlier? I think this calf's mother must have been killed. Margaret and the rest of the M family may have heard her rumbles of panic from several miles away. They were fleeing when we nearly ran into them."

"How did the calf's mother die?" he demanded.

"I don't know. Poachers. A Maasai spear. The drought. It could be a number of things."

"Yeah . . . a mother elephant wouldn't just leave her baby alone, would she? The elephants I've seen today — they're not like that."

Fiona wondered at his insistence. "No," she whispered, "never. Something has happened to the mother. I'm afraid this baby doesn't stand a chance for survival."

Rogan stared at the newborn. "You're going to let the hyenas kill it, aren't you?"

"You studied biology. You know there's a

delicate balance in nature. And especially out here in the African bush. With the human population crowding in the wilderness, the drought, and the large numbers of pregnant elephants, not many of the new babies will have a chance to live. This baby is . . . it's the first casualty."

"You don't mean that. I can't believe we're just going to drive away and let it be butchered. You love these elephants, Fiona."

"I'm a scientist. There are things I'm forced to accept. There's nothing we can do —"

"You're a human being, Fiona! You love and you care. You've cried over these elephants. And you're going to help me save this baby."

"Rogan, I don't have the facilities to tend —"

"What about the courage to love something enough to save it? What about that, Fiona?"

"Oh, Rogan."

"Have you got a rope?"

She let out a harsh sigh. "I can't believe this. I can't believe I'm going to toss every shred of careful training, my ordered sense of detachment, out the Land Rover window. This is nuts." But she leaned over the seat and unlatched the metal trunk bolted to the vehicle's floor, then drew out a long coil of hemp rope.

"Take this rifle," she said, pressing a compact .22 into Rogan's hands. "Don't shoot unless you have to. If poachers killed its mother, the sound will scare the calf into a panic."

She tied the rope into a noose and continued to talk. "Keep me covered with the rifle while I walk down to the streambed. I'm going to tie one end to the Land Rover, because the baby may bolt when it feels the rope. I'll need your help if that happens."

"Fiona." He caught her arm as she pushed open the door and started to slide to the ground. "It's the right thing to do."

"It's a mistake," she said, her eyes suddenly filling with tears. "You don't understand, Rogan. It's a terrible mistake."

As she left him and made her way down the slope, she brushed away the drops that clung to her lashes. Climbing down from the Land Rover, Rogan thought about her words. Taking the helpless elephant calf away from its natural predators was interfering in the normal sequence of nature. He knew that as a scientist, she would never interfere — only observe.

But despite his concern, Rogan felt a measure of satisfaction. By saving the calf, Fiona was stepping away from the detached scientist she had always been. She was allowing herself to feel.

As Fiona approached the streambed, the baby elephant lifted its trunk to sniff the feared smell of human. Clearly a newborn, the calf wobbled and stumbled as it attempted to move away from her. In the last remnants of fading light, Rogan could discern the pink on the backs of the calf's ears — according to Fiona, a sign that it was very young.

Rogan moved slowly down the slope. He could hear the little elephant growing more and more distressed with each step Fiona took toward it, but when she set foot in the streambed and stood in silence for several minutes, the calf began to calm. Its trunk tip lifted and began to explore the front of her shirt. It moved toward her. She held up a hand and allowed the baby to touch her skin.

"I'm going to walk to the camp," she said in a low voice.

"What about the rope?" Rogan asked from behind her.

"I don't think I'll need it." She stroked the baby's fuzzy head and imitated the low rumbles of comfort Rogan had heard a mother elephant make to her newborn. Fiona caressed the baby as it continued to explore her.

"Come on, now," she whispered. "Come with me, will you?"

Turning, she began to walk up the slope of the ravine. The calf flapped its ears and shook its head.

"Come, *toto*. Come now."

The baby took two wobbly steps in her direction.

"That's it. Follow me."

Moving at a deliberate pace, she set out across the grassland. The baby stumbled after her, and in a moment its trunk settled along the back of her neck. Together they walked through the near darkness. Rogan followed just behind in the Land Rover, shining its headlights on their path.

"Toto," Mama Hannah began stoically when she saw the elephant calf, "lions will come in the night to eat this elephant. They may attack us. We trust in God's protection, but He expects us to use the wisdom He has given us as well."

"We have no choice," Fiona answered. "We're just going to have to keep watch over the calf until we can decide what to do."

"I will not watch that elephant, *toto*. I am too old. And you have missed the dinner. I prepared grilled chicken breast with a special sauce made of —"

"Excuse me, Mama Hannah," Fiona interrupted. "Rogan, I want you to radio Clive Willetts. We're going to need milk and other supplies. I need to contact the game wardens and the Wildlife Federation. We're going to have to find someone willing to take care of this calf. Maybe the Nairobi Game Park has a facility. . . ."

Rogan was smiling as he approached her. "This is great," he said. "Wonderful."

"What?" Fiona paused in her litany of concerns. The calf, though tiny for an elephant, stood almost three feet at the shoulder. It kept bumping against her and exploring her body with its long gray trunk. Barely holding her ground against the persistent nudges, Fiona had been carrying on an animated monologue — lists of requirements and analytical data that no one was listening to.

Mama Hannah, rattling out names of ingredients that had gone into the wasted dinner, kept up a nervous dance at the edge of the campfire. Every time the elephant moved toward her, she backed away.

"Rogan, did you hear what I said?"

Fiona asked. "I'm trying to explain the difficulty this situation has put me in, and you're standing there with a silly grin on your face."

"This is amazing," he said softly. "This is fantastic."

"This is going to become a catastrophe if you don't start paying attention to me. Now, you've got to contact Clive Willetts —"

"I'll fly out tonight. I'll pick up the milk in Nairobi and have it back at the camp for you by midnight."

"It's dark."

"Don't worry. Tell me what to get."

She scribbled the name of the soy-based human infant formula that was the only type of milk able to sustain elephant life. "There'll be a supply of it at the Wildlife Federation offices. It's used for several species of orphaned and wounded animals the game wardens bring in. You'll have to contact Mr. Ngozi, the director. Here's his home phone number. We can't wait. This baby is starving," she said as the calf butted her from behind and sent her stumbling into Rogan's arms.

He held her tightly for a moment. "I'll be back in a couple of hours. When you hear my plane, train the Land Rover's headlights onto the airstrip. Fiona, it's going to be all right."

And then he was fading into the darkness. In moments, the airplane's propellers could be heard beyond the streambed. They whirred to life, lifted the plane into the air, and sent it roaring across the tops of the acacia trees toward Nairobi.

As sunrise slanted over the hump of Mount Longonot and filtered through the long dry grasses of the Great Rift Valley, Fiona sat alone near the dead campfire and stared at the baby elephant, who was wandering weakly across the bare, trampled earth.

Rogan had not returned.

It occurred to her to wonder why she had ever believed he would. He wasn't from her world. In the first place, he hadn't understood why the calf should have been left to the hyenas. He'd interfered and forced himself on her in every way. He'd destroyed her serenity.

And yet, for some unknown reason, she'd come to trust him. When he held her and kissed her and told her she was beautiful, she believed him. When he insisted on saving the elephant, she had gone along — never mind that everything in her training had taught her it wouldn't work.

Exhausted from building a thornbush corral for the calf and then watching him all night, she stood and made her way toward the kitchen. Disappointment in Rogan — and in herself for being so foolish — left a palpable taste in her mouth. She would have to radio the game wardens. They would frown on her actions, of course. In the Rift Valley there was no facility and certainly no personnel to care for an orphaned elephant calf.

An animal orphanage outside the Nairobi Game Park had room for some of the smaller species. But it closely resembled a zoo, and with the large number of schoolchildren visiting, there wouldn't be room for a growing elephant on the premises. A woman had given over her estate on the slopes of Mount Kenya to the rearing of giraffes. And there were people who took in orphaned monkeys or lion cubs and nursed them to maturity. But an elephant calf?

She punched the requisite buttons on the transmitter, which began to buzz and crackle. Mama Hannah wandered in, bleary-eyed and cranky.

"The elephant has escaped from his corral," was her greeting. "He is tearing out your tent stakes."

Fiona hesitated between rescuing her home and continuing to fiddle with the transmitter. "Bwana McCullough didn't come back last night," she said. "I have to call the game wardens."

"Sukari is in your tent, *toto*. That elephant will frighten your cat."

"Mama Hannah, can't you see that I'm trying —" The flimsy kitchen walls trembled as a roar blasted over the camp. Bits of thatch drifted onto the clean pots and pans.

The African lifted her head. "Just as you wished, the bwana has returned in his airplane. Now everything will be much worse."

Half angry at the rush of elation surging through her veins, Fiona stared at the little woman. "Rogan," she whispered.

"Go to him, *toto*."

"But you said everything will be much worse. . . . What did you mean?"

Mama Hannah shrugged. "Now you will keep the baby elephant in our camp. You will forget the importance of your work for God."

"No, I won't. I'm only going to take care of the calf until I can find someone else to tend it. You'll see, Mama Hannah."

"Yes, *toto*. We will see."

In no mood for more dire predictions, Fiona stomped across the clearing to rescue her tent. In the distance, Rogan waved as he crossed the streambed.

"Fiona!" he shouted. "Everything's taken care of. I have the formula. It took a lot longer than I'd expected, but I've got three cases of the stuff. Where's the baby?"

"Tearing up my tent."

Rogan laughed. It was a deep, wonderful, rich sound. Fiona paused and stared at him. His hair rustled in the morning breeze, lifting and parting without the slightest hint of ever having been combed. A thick growth of rough whiskers shadowed his jaw. Bright blue eyes sparked with life beneath his brows.

"This is amazing," he said, chuckling. "A baby elephant. How about that? Hey, come here, kiddo —"

"The calf is a male."

"Come here, son." He deepened his voice on the final word, then winked at Fiona. "Would you look at that? He's coming! Here's a bottle for you, little buddy. Mr. Ngozi fixed it up before I flew out this morning. He wanted to show me the correct amounts."

Fiona watched as the little elephant

abandoned the uprooted tent stakes and began to nudge Rogan's chest. The man reached out and gently stroked the calf's fuzzy forehead.

"Yes," he whispered. "I've brought some milk for you. Yummy, yummy milk."

Fiona stifled a laugh as Rogan attempted to catch the waving gray trunk and hold it to the bottle's nipple. "That's his nose, silly," she said. "He can't drink through his trunk."

"Dumbo did."

"This is real life, Rogan. Hold the bottle to his mouth."

Rogan dribbled a little milk onto the calf's lower lip. The baby tasted it and lunged for the nipple. Sucking contentedly, the elephant eyed Rogan with utter adoration. His trunk slipped around the man's neck and began to fondle an earlobe. Then the trunk tested the man's ear, found it comforting and warm, and nuzzled peacefully.

Fiona had to turn away as Rogan gazed into the elephant's eyes, for there came across the man's face such an expression of bliss that for a moment her vision blurred with tears, and she was unable to swallow the lump that rose in her throat.

EIGHT

"I had decided you weren't coming back," Fiona said.

She was staring at Rogan over the breakfast table. He had cleaned his plate of three fried eggs, a half-dozen fresh biscuits, an entire bowl of sliced papaya, and three large mugs of hot tea laced with milk and sugar. Totally absorbed in the elephant calf, he sat in his torn safari shirt and dusty shorts, a smile tugging at his mouth every time he glanced at the little creature.

After downing almost two quarts of formula, the baby had hunkered down on a patch of cool grass and shut his eyes. The sound of soft snuffling snores drifted through the clearing.

"Not coming back?" Rogan asked, surprised. "I told you I'd be back. Things just take a little longer to organize out here than they do in New York. You didn't think I'd just run off, did you?"

"Commitment doesn't really seem your style."

At her words, the smile died from his

lips, and he clamped his mouth shut. He knew he couldn't argue. Oh, he was committed to certain things — McCullough Enterprises and all that went into making it a success. But Fiona had been right in one respect: he rarely bothered with other things. About the closest he ever came to charity was once a year when, for tax advantages, he signed away millions of dollars to various nonprofit organizations.

Fiona had seen beneath the impetuous Rogan of the moment to the businessman who normally existed on a detached, unemotional plane. Commitment *wasn't* his style. And lately he'd been acting completely out of character.

He thought back over the previous evening's events. Ginger's shriek of shock when he'd appeared unannounced at the hotel suite. Clive Willetts's morose head-shaking over the elephant story. And, finally, the chastisement he'd received from officials of the Wildlife Federation. Mr. Ngozi had told Rogan that the Kenyan government would be most reluctant to allow a wild elephant to be held privately in captivity and that there was no safe place the federation knew of to keep such an animal.

Now that he actually had a quiet moment to think about it, Rogan wasn't sure why he'd been so determined to save the elephant in the first place. As Fiona had argued, she knew best about the balance of nature. But the thought of leaving that baby to be torn apart by hyenas . . .

"You'll need to rebuild the corral," she was saying when he finally focused his attention on her. "And you'll have to feed the calf every three hours, day and night. He should take approximately eight quarts of milk over a twenty-four-hour period. You'll want to keep a record and watch his consumption carefully."

"Me?" Rogan clunked a glass of mango juice on the table. "Hold on a second now —"

"You'll have to make sure he stays in the shade. Baby elephants are always in their mothers' shadows. He mustn't get too hot, and he'll need plenty of playtime and exercise."

"Wait a minute, here."

"You're the one who insisted we bring the elephant to my camp. You're going to have to care for him. Day and night. You'll have to make sure he has access to fresh elephant or rhino dung to establish the right balance of flora in his stomach. When he's older — maybe nine months — you can start adding greens to his diet. When he's two years old, you can wean him. Then, assuming you can integrate him into an established herd and socialize him properly, you can get back to your publishing."

"Two years old? Fiona, you're being ridiculous. I can't stay out here. I have a backlog of nearly a hundred e-mails on my laptop right now. Clive has been complaining about my use of the airplane. Air-Tours double-booked groups of tourists, and he and the other pilot are going to need both planes. I told them I'd try to get back to Nairobi this afternoon."

"And when am I supposed to get back to *my* work? Or is your backlog of e-mail messages that much more important than my years and years of research?"

She pushed herself back from the table and stood. Rogan sprang to his feet. "Now, Fiona, let's be reasonable."

"Reasonable! I suppose you think it's *reasonable* for me to drop everything and take care of a baby elephant for two years? Never mind that I'm right in the middle of an important study of elephant family interrelationships. Never mind that Harvard just asked me to collect data on elephant communication. Never mind that *International Animal* has contracted me to write a series of articles on the effects of drought on elephant migration. Never mind that Sentero and I have begun a revolutionary study on the correlation between estrus and musth — research that Sentero hopes to use as the basis for his doctoral dissertation. Never mind that —"

"Okay, okay. Take it easy." Rogan raked a hand through his hair. "Just calm down."

"I had a well-ordered life before you invaded my privacy, Rogan McCullough. You've turned everything into havoc. My camp is a near wreck. Mama Hannah acts like she may leave here any minute. I'm sure she'd rather look after my sister Jessica's son than a baby elephant. Sentero's gone off to Nairobi, and nothing is being recorded. The Rift Valley is in the midst of a terrible drought. Babies are being born every day. And now you've saddled me with an orphan elephant to —"

The sound of a terrible roar drowned her words. The calf, eyes still shut in sleep, lay kicking and screaming with panic. Gray ears flapped, their delicate bones snapping and popping. The long trunk flailed helplessly through the air.

"What is it?" Fiona cried, grabbing Rogan. "What's the matter with him?"

He pulled her across the clearing to the

thrashing body. "It's . . . it's like a nightmare —"

"Or poison! Oh, Rogan. What if that milk was bad? What if we've poisoned him?"

Rogan bent to the little elephant and began to stroke his head. "Come on, boy. It's okay now."

Fiona knelt at the other side of the baby and rubbed his heaving sides. "There, *toto*. What's the matter now, sweet boy?"

"He's calming down. Okay now, little fella. You're all right."

At the sensation of touch, the brown eyes slid open, and the elephant struggled to his feet. Instantly he lunged into Rogan and wrapped his trunk around the man's neck. If it was possible to say that an elephant could snuggle, this one did. His two-hundred-fifty-pound body rubbed against Rogan, and his throaty rumbles subsided to almost a purr.

"He seems okay now, doesn't he?" Rogan whispered as he and Fiona petted the baby's skin.

She nodded. "I think you were right. It was a nightmare. I've heard elephants can have them. I read an article by a woman who was studying how animals adapt to zoos. She wrote about the terrible nightmares elephants experience — especially when they've witnessed something horrible in their past. Mourning can go on for months. Some elephants have been known to die of grief, no matter how much proper care and medication they're given."

"He was dreaming about his mother's death," Rogan said softly. "I think he was reliving it."

Fiona blanched, and he wondered if his statement reminded her of her own mother's death. Perhaps there had been some pain . . . some sorrow that had never quite healed.

"I need to go out to the site of the kill," she murmured. "No animal predator can successfully bring down an adult female in good health."

"You think it was poachers then?"

"Maybe."

"I wonder which elephant family the baby belongs to. Maybe there's a mother in the herd with milk to spare."

"Possibly, but I doubt it. Without an adequate supply of water and fresh vegetation, any mother's milk supply is going to be down. A lactating female will have enough trouble nourishing her own calf without taking on an orphan."

Rogan scratched the little elephant between the eyes. He had a rather thick growth of coarse black hair on his forehead and back. Together with his soft pink ears, it gave him an almost comic-book appearance. The calf explored Rogan's face with the soft, two-fingered tip of his trunk.

"He seems to like your ears," Fiona observed.

"Naturally," Rogan returned. "I have highly sensitive ears. Would you like to sample this one while the other's occupied?"

"I'll pass," she said with a smile. "It's a curious phenomenon, though. Your ears must somehow resemble his mother's teats."

"Great, Fiona. Thanks a lot."

Chuckling, she stood and stretched. "Well, have a good day, Rogan. I'm off on my rounds."

"Now, hold on." As he rose, the calf let out a rumble of dismay and began to butt Rogan's legs. "You're not going to leave me here."

"I certainly am."

"Fiona." He caught her arm. "We *both* rescued this elephant. I saw your face when you thought he'd been poisoned. You can't abandon him any more than I can. We're in this together."

"I'm not together with anyone or anything. I work alone. I live alone. I'm completely self-sufficient, remember? Just like you, Rogan. Perhaps that's why we don't get along. We're two of a kind, you and I."

"I gather you're not real big on commitment either, then."

"Perhaps not."

"All right. I guess that settles it."

"Settles what?"

"The elephant. Since neither of us has the time or energy to take care of him, and since neither of us is willing to make the long-term commitment, I guess we'll just herd him back to the streambed and let the hyenas have him. What do you say, huh? Does that sound good?"

Fiona gazed at the little shaggy-haired calf. He had wandered away a few paces and had begun exploring his trunk. For a moment he swung it back and forth in a long rubbery arc. Then he lifted his head and began to toss it up and down. Finally he sent it whirling around in a circle.

"Oh, Rogan."

"Well, Fiona? You ready to turn him over to the hyenas? Want to let the vultures pick his bones?"

By this time the elephant had tired of swinging his trunk and had popped the tip into his mouth. He stood sucking it and eyeing the pair of humans with the look of a trusting child.

"Oh my," she sighed.

"Look, Fiona . . ." He touched her arm, turning her to face him. "Why don't you go on out into the field this morning? Get some research taken care of. I'll stay here and feed the little guy. Then you come back at lunch, and we'll talk. In the meantime, I'll see if I can think of something. After all, solving problems and coming up with grand schemes is sort of my specialty."

"All right," she whispered, gazing up at him with her big camouflage eyes.

If there had ever been a moment when he wanted to abandon a promise, this was it. He felt a huge, unbidden urge to throw his arms around Fiona's neck, kiss her passionately, and then act like a complete idiot. Gush about the elephants, caper around the campfire, insist that the fairy tale never end. Demand that this stubborn woman and the baby elephant and everything wonderful they had brought into his life stay just as they were forever.

Instead, he swallowed the knot in his throat and watched her walk away.

Fiona returned to the camp just as Clive

Willetts's airplane bounced onto the landing strip. She pulled the Land Rover under the shade of an acacia tree and sat for a moment, watching the scene in the clearing.

Rogan was crouched in the dust, one arm around the little elephant and the other holding the large milk bottle. The calf, trunk nestled along Rogan's neck and toying with his ear, gazed adoringly at the man. Soft gray ears fanned the air, lifting and scattering Rogan's hair. In the background Mama Hannah trudged back and forth, her arms full of dishes. She was humming — always a good sign. Occasionally she said something to Rogan, who responded. And they both laughed.

Fiona rested her forehead on the sun-warmed steering wheel. Though she had firmly refused to allow God into her heart since her mother's death so many years ago, she suddenly found words of surrender forming on her lips.

"Dear God, how has this happened?" she murmured. "What can I do? I need Your help. I need You, God. I really need You."

Once there had been a man in a stiff wool suit who demanded that she allow tourists into her camp. Now, as she lifted her head again, she saw a man who fit in, whose skin had been darkened by the sun, whose clothing matched the soft taupe grasses, and whose boots were red with African dust. She saw a man who whispered into an elephant's ear. A man who stroked his fingers through a baby's dark hair. A man who belonged.

"Lord, I ought to send him away, shouldn't I?" she whispered. "What should I do? Why won't You talk to me the way You talk to Mama Hannah? Would You do that if I let You in? If I gave You my heart?" She shuddered. "I don't even know where to begin. I don't know *how* to let You in. To let anyone in. But you're both coming in, aren't You, Jesus? You're both storming the walls."

If Rogan had changed in the past few days, Fiona knew she had been transformed. For the first time since . . . well, she couldn't even remember . . . she craved a human touch. She ached for the sight of this man's smile and his deep laughter. Worse, she longed to hear his voice, arguing, teasing, discussing — it hardly mattered. She wanted to talk. Human words. Human expressions. Human feelings. She needed them all. And she was scared to death by that need.

Trembling, she slid out of the Land

Rover. She ought to send him away. She had to make Rogan leave if she was ever to get her old life back. And the most terrifying thought of all was the realization that she wasn't sure she wanted her old life back.

"Fiona!" Rogan lifted a hand as she approached. "Two quarts since you've been gone! How about that? He's getting really frisky, so watch out."

When the elephant calf caught Fiona's scent, he pulled away from the bottle and headed toward her. Wobbly legs flying, he greeted her with a loud rumble. Head raised, ears spread and flapping, he tucked in his chin. His trunk looped around her arm, then unlooped. Then he backed away, spun in three complete circles, and bumped into her legs with his bottom.

Trying not to laugh and frighten him, Fiona responded in kind. She caught the elastic trunk and wrapped it around her arm. She lifted her head up and down. Then she turned circles and backed into the baby.

"What is she doing there, Mr. McCullough?" Clive's voice broke in among the human and elephantine rumblings.

"It's the greeting ceremony," Fiona explained. "All the elephants in a family do it when they've been apart. It's usually very intense and emotional."

"Good heavens. I'd no idea." The lanky pilot scratched his sparse mustache. "Well, at any rate, here's your man, Mr. McCullough. He's a Kikuyu from up in the highlands. He tells me he worked on a big coffee farm, and he thinks if he can take care of horses, he can take care of elephants."

Rogan and Fiona both stared at the compact African. Cleanly dressed in a neat pair of gray trousers, a navy sweater, and a striped shirt, he looked as if he had just stepped out of an office in Nairobi.

"My name is Moses," he said, holding out a hand. "I will work for standard wages and one weekend off per month. You must provide my bus ticket home. I will sleep in the camp, and I will require my food. Now, this is the elephant?"

Obviously this *was* the elephant. Moses took the bottle from Rogan's hand, and within a few minutes he had the calf sucking contentedly. As he moved the baby into the shade, he called back over his shoulder, "You may return to Nairobi now, Bwana McCullough. All will be well."

Rogan looked at Fiona. "I, uh . . ." He cleared his throat. "I took the liberty of radioing Clive and setting things up."

"But I have no way to pay this man."

"It's okay. I'll take care of that. It's the least I can do."

"Yes," she said. "Well . . ."

"Well, everyone," Clive filled in the silence between them, "I guess it's time to leave. Do you two have things worked out now?"

Neither spoke for a moment. Fiona tried to moisten her lips, but her mouth was dry. So this was it. Rogan and his money had solved everything in one neat package. The elephant would be taken care of. Rogan would fly to Nairobi and then to New York. She would return to her research. And that was that.

"Yes," she said softly, "everything's been worked out."

"Will Air-Tours be flying in here, Mr. McCullough?" Clive asked.

"No," Rogan said. "That's not going to be possible."

The pilot nodded, as if to say he'd known all along the plans wouldn't work. "So, Dr. Thornton, where are the elephants these days? I have two groups in this week. I thought I'd fly over the park and let them have a look at your friendly pachyderms."

217

He had pulled a map from his hip pocket and was spreading it wide. Fiona stared at the familiar lozenge shape of the Rift Valley Game Park nestled between the two volcanic mountains, Longonot and Suswa. With her help, Clive had partitioned the map into the same grid she used for tracking elephants.

"The M family is in D-2 heading north toward Longonot," she said, pointing out the position. "The Js are in A-3. They're looking for water. You'll find the Os in D-7. They're near the Suswa bulls — Jesse James and his gang. You've been seeing the Cs a lot lately. They're in E-4 right now, but I wouldn't advise flying over them. They're very jumpy. Poachers killed Calliope yesterday."

"You don't say. That's too bad. Did they get her tusks?"

Fiona nodded, trying to block the memory of the bullet-riddled elephant whose face and trunk had been hacked away. "She was the calf's mother."

"Well, it's a good thing you saved the little chap and I found Moses to watch him. Now he'll have a chance to grow into a big tusker like his mum."

"If he's lucky," Fiona said.

"Thanks for the tips, Dr. Thornton. If

you're ready, sir, we'll start back. Your secretary's nearly frantic with messages for you."

"Yes, okay . . ." Rogan murmured as the pilot set off toward the plane. "Fiona, I'll set up an account for you to use for Moses' salary. And . . . I'll write to find out about the elephant."

"Of course."

"Is there anything you need from Nairobi? Anything I can do for you?"

"No."

"Well, then . . ."

"Good-bye, Mr. McCullough." She held out her hand.

"I've enjoyed my visit." He took her hand and held it. His thumb stroked her palm. "Fiona, I —"

"Rogan, you'd better go."

"Yes." His lips brushed her cheek, and then he was pulling away, crossing the streambed and climbing into the nearer of the two Air-Tours planes.

"Mama Hannah," Fiona said as she passed the cook, "there will only be me for lunch. And you should know that Moses has joined our camp crew to look after the elephant."

"Yes, *toto.*" Mama Hannah looked forlornly at her table, all set for a great company. "I prepared a wonderful egg salad."

"I'm sorry, Mama Hannah."

"Will the bwana return one day?"

"No. He's not coming back."

Mama Hannah lifted her head as the planes flew over the camp. "Perhaps you are wrong, *toto*. God's ways are not our ways. Perhaps he will return."

"No."

"But he has forgotten to tell me *kwaheri*. And he failed to say good-bye to his elephant."

"Well, at any rate, he told *me* good-bye."

"No, *toto*. If you will remember, it was *you* who told *him* good-bye."

With that, Mama Hannah turned her back and began removing plates and silverware from the table.

As Rogan's plane flew over the camp, he tried for one last look at Fiona. He couldn't find her. It felt to him as though she had already reintegrated with her world. Her red hair had melded with the rich soil, her glowing skin with the shadows of the trees, her clothing with the shades of the grasses. She had rid herself of the alien invader and instantly adjusted to life without him.

Things weren't going to be so easy for

Rogan. Remembering his father's comments to Clive about Africa, Rogan felt the first touch of affinity with his late parent. In Africa, John McCullough had been able to relax, to rest. In Africa, he'd felt like himself. Now Rogan knew what that meant. He began to glimpse an understanding of the mysterious, powerful father he'd hated and loved with an intensity that had driven him for more than thirty years. Maybe his father was not so different from himself.

Rogan flew low over a thicket of thorn trees lining a river, then lifted the plane so as not to frighten a herd of zebras grazing nearby. Sun beat on the top of the aircraft and seemed to melt through the metal roof onto his head. Clive's plane flew not far to one side, its silver wings as bright as mirrors.

A group of long-necked giraffes, their shadows tucked neatly beneath them, wandered in the direction of Mount Suswa. Rogan wondered where the Ms were today. Was Margaret searching for water? Was Mallory hovering close to Madeline's new baby, keeping watch? And what about Mick? Was he tossing dust over his back or running with ears flapping toward a patch of not-so-dry grass?

Rogan flipped on the radio and contacted Clive. "See any elephants down there?" he asked.

"Not a chance. They're almost invisible from the air. That's why I ask Dr. Thornton to tell me where she's been tracking them."

"What's that? The shiny patch just to the southeast?"

"A little water hole. The Maasai use it for cattle. It's just outside the park boundary. The King family built that old stone house down there. That and the water hole. The Kings were colonists, you know. But the house is empty now. Falling apart."

"Too bad . . . hey, is that an elephant? At two o'clock?"

"You have sharp eyes, sir. Those are the Suswa bulls. Mean old devils. Swing down and take a look at the tusks on those chaps."

Rogan banked the plane and zoomed over the three bulls. They shook their heads and trumpeted at the sound of the engines. Their huge bodies looked small from this height, vulnerable somehow. There were so few of them. And their hold on this golden kingdom seemed so tenuous.

As soon as he got to Nairobi, Rogan decided, he would radio the camp. He would
find out how the little calf was managing in
the hands of Moses. He would ask Mama
Hannah what she was planning for dinner.
Was there any spice cake left? Maybe
Mama Hannah would copy the recipe for
Rogan's own cooks back in the States. And
what about the rest of the camp? Were the
vervet monkeys behaving themselves? Any
sign of rain? Was Fiona planning tomorrow's outing?

Fiona.

An ache that tightened the muscles in
his chest gripped him as he thought of her.
She was still so close. And so far, out of
reach, intangible. He could almost smell
the lemon-flower scent of her hair. The
memory of its red-gold waves tumbling
down her back seemed so real. He felt he
could almost touch her smooth skin. He
could see her camouflaged eyes, mystical
and enigmatic.

It was a good thing he was getting away.
He couldn't allow himself this intensity of
feeling. He didn't want the burden of responsibility that came with caring. Fiona
was too much for him. She was too strong,
too honest, too real. He preferred a surface
sort of woman. One who didn't have too

much to give but didn't take too much either. The sort of woman his father . . .

His father. John McCullough. A man who craved power and wealth. A man who couldn't commit, not even to his own wife and child. A man who skimmed the top, who refused to deal with anything strong, honest, and real.

How Rogan had hated his father. He'd hated the man, not because he was his father but because he wasn't. He'd despised the man, he'd fought him, he'd struggled to prove himself to him . . . and, in the end, he'd become just like him.

Rogan let three days go by. He forced himself to concentrate on his work. Ginger reported that a man who owned a hotel on the coast wanted to work a deal with Air-Tours. The CEO of Rogan's huge oil-refinery operation had wired, asking for a meeting the minute Rogan could get back to the States. Megamedia had been calling every day, trying to finalize the buyout of McCullough Enterprises. Rogan's personal manager had phoned to find out whether to open the Florida home for the traditional end-of-winter bash, or whether Rogan planned a ski trip to New Mexico. There were calls from several stores in New York with messages that Rogan's new spring suit and casual-wear selections were ready, calls from dealers with new airplanes or cars on the market, calls from his accountant, calls from six foundations inviting him to patrons' dinners.

Rogan sifted through the pile of messages. His leather-bound appointment book perched on Ginger's stocking-clad knees as she filled line after line with crisp black-ink notations. He met with the Mombasa hotel owner. It wasn't a particularly good deal — not the sort of thing he would normally accept. More like a losing proposition, if the truth were told. But it would give Air-Tours some business. And business would keep it alive.

"Now, about the museum benefit on the fifteenth," Ginger asked on his fourth morning back in Nairobi. "Shall I call and tell them you'll attend? It's in Washington — and you've already set up a meeting in New York for that morning. But if you flew down —"

"That's fine. Fine."

"And I've been on the phone with the airline. Shall I go ahead and make reservations for us to fly out tomorrow morning? You could talk to that fellow in Amsterdam who's interested in a partnership —"

"Tomorrow morning?" Rogan looked up. "Leave Nairobi tomorrow?"

"You do have a meeting with Mega-media in New York on Friday. It would give you a little time —"

"Ginger, where's the nearest radio?"

"There's a CD player over there, sir. I'm sure a radio comes with it."

"Not that sort of radio. A transmitter. The kind of thing you can call places with."

"Clive Willetts has one at the airport. That's where I called you from when you were out at that camp in the middle of —"

"Get my coat, Ginger."

"But, sir, I have all these messages to go over with you. And there's the —"

"My coat, Ginger."

"With all respect, Mr. McCullough, I don't think it would be wise for you to go out in public right now. You haven't shaved since the meeting with the hotel owner two days ago. And your clothes —"

"Where is that blasted coat?" He stalked across the room and rummaged through the closet. Jerking the mended bush jacket from its hanger, he tossed it over one shoulder. "Call down to the limo, Ginger. I want to go to the airport."

"Yes, sir. What about your conference call with Megamedia? It's scheduled in ten minutes."

"Tell them to call back later."

"*Later?* It'll be the middle of the night in New York, Mr. McCullough. Sir —"

The door closed before she could finish her sentence.

Striding into the empty Air-Tours hangar, Rogan noted that both planes had flown out with tour groups. Clive's plane would spend a week crossing three game parks, he remembered. The other, piloted by Oliver Kariuki, would fly around Mount Kilimanjaro and Mount Kenya.

After unlocking Clive's small office, Rogan spotted the large black radio transmitter. He sat at the desk and fiddled with the buttons and switches. Unable to produce more than a spatter of static, he jerked at the desk drawers to look for a set of instructions. Locked. All of them.

That irked him. It was one thing to keep private, confidential materials locked up. But Air-Tours was just a simple charter company. Securing the company files was probably Clive's idea of maintaining an image as a businessman.

Returning to the radio, Rogan eventually

managed to find the frequency used by the elephant camp. And at last he heard Mama Hannah's voice through the buzzing transmitter.

"This is Rogan McCullough, Mama Hannah," Rogan shouted. "How are things at the camp?"

"Bwana McCullough, is that you?"

"Yes, Mama Hannah, it's me. How is everything?"

"I am preparing steak with black pepper. It will be delicious, bwana."

"Sounds good. How's the elephant?"

"Moses does not like our camp."

"I'm sorry to hear that. What about the elephant? Is the baby elephant still there, Mama Hannah?"

"*Two* elephants now, bwana."

"Two elephants? Calves?"

"Sentero found another one in a ravine. Last night they knocked down your tent."

"How's . . . how's Fiona? Dr. Thornton . . . how is she?"

"Quiet."

"Quiet, did you say?"

"Not talking."

Rogan stared at the Air-Tours logo embossed on a stack of writing paper. He could see Fiona's silence. He could feel it. Her mouth closed. Her eyes hidden. Her face half in shadow.

"Have you found it?" Mama Hanna's voice interrupted his thoughts.

"Found what?"

"The peace that you were looking for."

While Rogan was trying to come up with an answer, she went on. "You would like this steak, bwana. Lots of fresh black pepper . . . and mango chutney. I make it myself."

"How about spice cake?"

"Today I have baked my very special coconut pie. It's good. Perhaps you should taste it, bwana."

"Perhaps I should."

"I will select for you a very thick steak and a very delicious slice of my coconut pie. Good-bye, Bwana McCullough."

As the radio crackled, Rogan shouted through the empty hangar to the limousine driver, who was polishing a windshield. "Hey, out there! Hey, Duncan Gitau! Find out how I can rent an airplane, would you?"

"An airplane, Mr. McCullough?"

Rogan grinned. "I've got a dinner engagement."

NINE

Fiona drove the Land Rover along the track toward her camp. Evening sun silhouetted the acacias and baobabs. Dust, pink-lit and fine as talcum, sifted through the cracks beneath the doors and settled on her boots. A stack of papers slid back and forth in the back. A pen rolled and bounced around the floor.

"Shall we search for the J family tomorrow, Dr. Thornton?" Sentero asked. "We haven't recorded anything about them in a week. They were near Longonot last time. We could check on the Ms too."

Fiona nodded but said nothing. Sentero flipped through a few sheets of paper attached to a clipboard. His long earlobes dangled against his neck as he searched the file.

"In the J family, you recorded four females in estrus two years ago," he said. "Janice, Jennifer, Jill, and Jody. It would be a good idea to find out if there have been any births."

"Yes."

"What about the poaching? They've killed Calliope and Cindy. And we haven't seen the old bull, Custer, lately. Do you think the kill is stepping up? Should we alert the wardens?"

"They need to know."

"Dr. Thornton, I've been thinking about what we discussed earlier — about the new age-group being initiated. Perhaps I should speak to the Maasai elders."

Fiona sighed. "If you would, Sentero."

She didn't feel like talking. The day had been long and discouraging. That morning they had found Cindy's carcass not far from Calliope's. She, too, had been shot and butchered for her tusks. The C family was jittery and hiding nearby in a thicket of trees. At the sound of the Land Rover, they bolted. In the same moment, Fiona realized that Charlie, the young bull, had been wounded. Blood dripped from his mouth and trunk as he struggled to keep up with the others. His tusks were tiny. He wasn't even old enough to have marketable ivory, but the poachers had shot him anyway.

And then Sentero had mentioned the initiation of a new group of young Maasai males. Fiona knew from experience that every few years the Maasai clans circumcised all teenage boys within a certain age-group. When they recovered from their ordeal, these young men would be called *Ilmoran*. Warriors. To prove their bravery, they would spend months searching for wild animals to kill — even though hunting was against the law in Kenya. Lions were the favorite, but elephants often fell prey to the spears of young Maasai warriors.

With the poachers, the drought, the age-group initiation, and the calves being born, the Rift Valley elephants could not hope to fare well. Fiona felt the ominous certainty that every few days she would begin to find dead elephants. Matriarchs and old bulls slaughtered by poachers. Young females pierced by spears. Calves collapsed from starvation.

And there was nothing she could do. Oh, Sentero could talk to the elders. But they would never agree to call a halt on their warriors — even though they knew the *Ilmoran* could be prosecuted as poachers or shot on sight by game wardens.

She could speak to the wardens themselves. But how much could a few ill-equipped men do against efficient poachers armed with automatic rifles? Especially when the killers were motivated by the black-market fortune to be made from a world hungry for ivory trinkets, earrings, and tiny carved boxes.

And, of course, the drought. Only God knew when that would be over. Why? She questioned the Almighty for the hundredth time. Why couldn't it rain? At least the babies would be spared. A new generation.

Fiona was under no illusions. She knew wobbly elephant babies could never take the place of the stately old matriarchs who carried with them the collective memory of generations, who knew where to dig for water during the dry seasons and where the best patches of grass could be found. But, given a chance, the babies would grow and learn and one day fulfill their own destinies on the golden plains.

"Airplane," Sentero said.

Startled, Fiona lifted her head and scanned the camp. She could see a small plane on the distant airstrip — it was something modern and red. Certainly not one of Air-Tours' big Catalinas. Her heart sank.

Chastising herself for allowing the thought of Rogan McCullough to enter her mind again, she tried to focus on other matters. Who might have flown to the camp? Another researcher? Somebody from one of her supporting wildlife societies or universities? When should she drive to the park headquarters to speak to the wardens? What would Mama Hannah have prepared for dinner?

But, as the past three days had proven, nothing — not even drought and poachers — could erase Rogan from her thoughts. Again and again she had imagined him climbing the stairs to a huge jetliner, settling into his first-class seat, and winging away to Europe and America. She knew it wouldn't be long before he forgot all about his brief interlude in Africa.

Fiona had been a mere annoyance to him, that was all. An irritation. He would sell Air-Tours, since it wasn't making enough money to suit him. And before long he would be settled back into his world — negotiating deals, flying planes, racing cars, buying houses, whatever multi-millionaires did.

She, on the other hand, had been left in a silent world filled with his memory. When she rose in the morning, she thought of their breakfasts together by the campfire. When she settled into her Land Rover, she found herself wishing it was Rogan's heavily muscled body in the next seat — and not the thin-framed Sentero. Even when she was studying the elephants, she seemed to hear his deep voice, low and murmuring, as he spoke his observations. His handwriting filled pages of her notebook. The T-shirt he'd worn hung on the line.

And alone in her tent at night, she faced long, quiet hours when thoughts of Rogan McCullough would sift through her mind. Snatches of conversation replayed. Memories of his smile. His laugh. His blue eyes gazing into hers. She would close her eyes and curl into a tight ball and try to will him away. But in the end, she would hear his voice again.

"Bwana McCullough," Sentero said. "He has returned, Dr. Thornton."

"What?" Fiona shifted her focus from the dusty road to the camp, now bathed in shadow. A jolt ran down her spine as she recognized, standing beneath an acacia, the dark figure with broad shoulders and shaggy hair. "It *is* him," she breathed. "What's he doing here?"

"No doubt he wants to check on the elephant calf."

"Oh, that must be it."

"Perhaps he has developed a new plan for bringing his tourists to the Rift Valley."

"Yes, maybe so."

"Of course, at this moment you will notice he is waiting for *you*."

"Well, I don't think . . ." Fiona unconsciously smoothed her hair as she pulled the Land Rover to a stop beneath the tree. She wished she'd worn something other than this faded yellow T-shirt and olive-drab trousers. And if she had just worn a hat, she wouldn't have such pink cheeks.

"Oh, well," she muttered.

"Hello to you too," Rogan lifted a hand as he approached the Land Rover.

"What are you doing here, Rogan?"

"Mama Hannah invited me for dinner," he explained. "She says there's a new baby. Besides, I wanted to see you again, Fiona."

"Have a pleasant evening, Dr. Thornton," Sentero interrupted, speaking in Swahili. His face a mask, the Maasai strode into the fading dusk. As he rounded the kitchen, the tip of his spear glinted in the last rays of sunlight.

"That guy gives me the heebie-jeebies," Rogan said. "What did he say just now, anyway?"

"It's nothing. He was just wishing me a good evening."

"I don't see why he can't speak English and say what he has to say outright. If he went to college in Texas —"

"Rogan, please." She faced him. "Why did you come back? I thought you were going to the States . . . to your work. I thought we had settled everything."

He studied her eyes. "Nothing's settled, Fiona. You know that."

"But the elephant calf is fine. We have a strong enclosure now, and Moses is looking after him. The other one we brought in seems to be responding too."

"Fiona."

"Sentero's back, and he's going to talk to the Maasai elders about the initiation problem. You don't know about that, but it's a difficult situation. We've contacted the authorities about the drought. And we're going to tell the wardens about the increase in poaching."

"Fiona . . . ," he said again.

"Rogan, I explained to you, I won't allow tourists in the camp. I'm only just now getting back to my research."

"I missed you, Fiona."

She looked away and bit her lower lip. "Oh, I see."

"It's just that . . . well, I've never known a woman quite like you. For some reason I can't get you off my mind. Sounds corny, huh?" He paused. "Did you miss me, Fiona?"

She glanced at him as much as she dared. "I've been very busy, of course. There's the research and the poachers . . . and the drought . . . and two calves . . ."

"While I was gone, did you think about the afternoon we spent sitting on the Land Rover's roof watching elephants, Fiona?" He stroked her hair, cupping a mass of it in his big hand. "Did you remember the way we talked under the stars? Did you miss the feel of my arms around you, holding you close and warm?"

"Oh, Rogan," she mumbled. What else could she say? The touch of his fingers in her hair felt like heaven. The warmth of his breath on her neck brought a sigh of contentment. She slipped her arms around him and allowed his jaw to graze her cheek. His mouth touched her ear. She shivered.

"Oh, Rogan," she said again, because it was all she could manage. She wove her fingers through his thick hair and leaned her head against his chest.

Fiona had never needed anyone's strength before, not since she had grown up and learned to live on her own. But now, oh now, she drank in this man's presence like a sponge absorbing water. His firm muscles moved under her fingers. His

238

beard grazed her skin like fine sandpaper.

"Fiona," he breathed into her ear, "I want to take you to Nairobi. Just to be together and relax."

Her eyes lifted and traced his face. "Nairobi? But I can't leave. My research —"

"Sentero can do it for a few days. You managed without him while he was in Nairobi. Now it's your turn to get away. Please, Fiona."

"But the elephants. We have two of them now, and they're so rowdy."

"Moses can watch them."

"Moses isn't working out very well, I'm afraid. He keeps forgetting the feedings. And he's afraid out here in the bush. He won't admit it to me, but Mama Hannah says he's terrified at night."

Rogan studied her face. "What am I going to do about you, Fiona Thornton? I don't want to leave you out here again. There's something between us. I can sense it in you. I can feel it in myself. It intrigues me, Fiona, and I want to find out what it means."

"You can't force me to go with you, Rogan. I'm tied to this place and these animals much more strongly than I could be to any visitor."

"A visitor? Is that how you see me?"

"Dinner's served," she said softly. "Will you stay, Rogan?"

Awaiting his answer, she listened to the muted melody of the bamboo xylophone as it drifted across the evening. A pair of doves added their own sweet five-note call to the refrain. Crickets began their shrill high-pitched chirps. Somewhere in the streambed a frog launched into his nightly croak.

"I'll stay for dinner," Rogan replied. "But, Fiona, I want you to think about what I've asked. You've turned me down on everything else. Come with me to Nairobi for a few days. You need a rest. And I'd like the chance to be with you a little longer, to get to know you better."

"The only place you can really know me is here, Rogan. In the bush. This is where I belong."

"Just think about it, will you?"

She nodded. He tucked her under his arm, and she rested her head against his shoulder as they walked toward the campfire. *You don't know, Rogan,* she was thinking. *You have no idea how easy it seems just to drop everything and do what you ask. For the pleasure of looking into your blue eyes and the tingle of your hands on my skin, I could walk away from it all.*

But — she realized even as she was thinking those thoughts — *this is merely a physical attraction. It's only temporary. You have your life, Rogan. And I have mine. Blue eyes and warm arms can't change that.*

After dinner they settled beside the campfire. The elephant calves were visiting Sentero. He had agreed to take over the night feedings in place of Moses, who was too much trouble to awaken anyway. Mama Hannah had placed a pot of steaming tea, two china cups, milk, sugar cubes, and a plate of buttery cookies on a small table between the two rickety chairs. After the ritual of planning tomorrow's meals with Fiona, she had retired for the night.

"Fiona, have you thought about —"

"Shall we just drink our tea?" she cut in. "Please."

"Would you let me tell you the reasons why I'd like to take you to Nairobi?"

"I can't go to Nairobi, Rogan. I don't like the city, and there's so much to do here that I —"

"Fiona." He caught her hand and pulled her around so that she was forced to meet his eyes. "Just give me half a chance, would you?"

"All right."

"I'm supposed to be heading back to the States. I really ought to leave tomorrow. I've got meetings and all kinds of appointments set up with various people and organizations. But the only thing I can't let slide is the company that wants to buy me out."

"Someone is buying McCullough Enterprises? But what will happen to you?"

"The point here, Fiona, is that I have to meet with the Megamedia people. But they have a small office in Nairobi and a bigger branch in London. I can handle most of this with conference calls."

"And? What does that have to do with me?"

"Afterward, I'd be free to stay a few more days in Kenya."

She thought about the idea for a moment. He was offering to make her little fantasy come to life — they would be together. But what good was that? If she spent any more time with Rogan, it wasn't going to be easy to stay casual. And surely she didn't want any deeper involvement. Did she? No, of course not.

"Rogan, the thing is, I just don't see the logic behind this." She tried to choose her words carefully. "Practically speaking —"

"Forget practical, Fiona. Put away your

scientist's brain for a moment, and let yourself feel a woman's emotions. I saw your face this evening when you realized I'd come back. I felt the way you hugged me."

"I'm a woman, but I don't intend to spend the rest of my life flitting around with my emotions on my sleeve. I am a scientist. I've worked hard to control my feelings and keep myself detached. That's the way I choose to live, Rogan. Please try to understand."

"I hear your words, and I know you mean them. But look at you! All I can see at this moment is Fiona the woman — your smile, your glowing eyes, your long neck, your hair drifting around your shoulders."

"But you can't have just the woman and not the scientist. They go together."

"Okay," he said. "Here's why you should come to Nairobi tomorrow morning. Logically speaking."

She leaned forward, almost willing him to come up with something.

Rogan took a deep breath. "I've lined up a meeting with the national museum in Nairobi. I'm going to propose a partnership with the executive board, to promote both the museum and Air-Tours in one package. You come to the meeting. I'll give you fifteen minutes to talk to them about your elephants."

"Fifteen —"

"Half an hour. No interruptions, I promise. And —" he paused, as if scanning his brain — "and there's this embassy thing I was invited to. A party. We'll go together. It's a chance to meet diplomats from everywhere."

"Burundi? Zimbabwe?"

"What about them?"

"They're two of the countries in Africa that haven't signed an agreement to allow Switzerland to monitor the trade in registered tusks. Most of the illegal ivory poached in Kenya goes through Burundi or Zimbabwe, Rogan."

"Yes, we'll talk to their ambassadors. Sure thing. Why not?"

"And?" she asked. "Are there any more reasons I should go to Nairobi?"

He smiled and shook his head, letting out a breath. "Well, let's see. If you can't count dining in the finest restaurants, shopping for new clothes, going to the theater, walking hand in hand, and —"

"No. I can't, Rogan."

"How about if I got you a spot on Cable Television News? I know their correspondent in Nairobi. He worked for McCullough Enterprises years ago when he was starting out. He could interview you for CTN, Fiona. That's big time. Worldwide exposure."

Was this man the devil himself? she wondered. When would he get to the part where he asked for her mortal soul in return? She looked down at their entwined fingers. "I've never been on television."

"Just talk about the elephants. Talk about Margaret and the others. Talk about the babies."

"Satan," she said, "you drive a hard bargain."

He grinned. "I'm not that bad, am I?"

"Just as sly."

"Then you'll go?"

"I'll think about it." She stood, feeling frightened by her own vulnerability. "Good night. I'll see you in the morning."

"Fiona." He rose and caught her hand again. "There's something else I've been thinking about."

"Yes?"

He hesitated, as if there were a hundred things he wanted to tell her. "I bought a notebook," he said finally.

She studied his blue eyes and felt their intensity. "A notebook."

"With blank pages."

She nodded. "Oh . . . blank pages." What other kinds of notebooks were there? Why was he telling her this? And why did his fingers feel so strong? Each one pressed separately into her skin and sent messages that she couldn't read.

"I've been writing in the notebook. Collecting things." He turned his head and shuffled a foot, as though unsure of how to proceed. "Well, anyway . . ."

"What kinds of things?" she asked.

"Oh . . . stuff. Never mind."

"Rogan, what are you collecting? I'd like to know."

"Well . . ." He studied the moon. "Uh . . . flora."

"Flora? You mean flowers? Leaves, plants, specimens — that sort of thing?"

He nodded. "I started with bougainvillea. Did you know they don't really have petals? At least, not flowers of any consequence. The colored parts are bracts. So I broke some off and pressed them in the *Current Financial Strategy* book I bought in the airport the other day. And then I got to looking at the Cape honeysuckle growing up the wall outside my hotel suite. And I found some frangipani trees, but when I tried to save the specimens, they turned brown. That's when I bought the notebook

246

and started writing down my observations. I began to notice all these different varieties of hibiscus. I wandered into someone's yard, and an old lady with hair like cotton came out of the house and took me all around her garden, showing me things. And, I don't know . . . pretty silly, huh?"

"Will you come with me, Rogan?" Fiona said. She pulled him along. "I want to show you something."

She told him to wait outside her tent while she went in and turned up the lamp that hung from a hook overhead. After shooing the cat off her cot, she removed a big philodendron from the top of a black metal trunk and set it aside; then she opened the lid. She rooted around, placing things on the floor — a small photo album; a child's diary with a tiny brass key on a ribbon; a thick, hand-knitted wool sweater; two teacups with red roses and green leaves on a pink background. And, finally, a large book.

"Here," she said, stepping back outside, "my father gave me this years ago. You're welcome to borrow it, Rogan."

He took the book and gazed at the slick cover imprinted with brilliant red blossoms and bearing the black-lettered title *Plants of Kenya*.

"I used to read it all the time," she went on, stepping to his side to peer at the book. "See, I saved actual specimens of each of the species I found. It was sort of a dream of mine to collect every one."

With tanned fingers he turned the pages one by one. His shoulder leaned into hers. She reached across him and stroked the paper-thin petals of dried flowers.

"Floss-silk tree," she murmured. "Flame tree, red-hot poker tree, jacaranda, desert rose. Africans use the desert-rose sap as an arrow poison, did you know? It's toxic. Here are some yesterday-today-and-to-morrow blossoms. Look — purple, cream, white. All from the same shrub. Candle bush, angel's trumpet, snow on the mountain, poinsettia, hibiscus, crown of thorns."

"Looks like you got them all."

"Not the baobab." She smiled. "You know those thick trees with bark the elephants love to eat?"

"Adansonia digitata."

She laughed in surprised delight at his instant recall of the scientific name. "Baobabs hardly ever have leaves. And you almost never see them in flower. I tried and tried, but I couldn't get a specimen. And I've lived in Kenya all my life. Nearly, anyway."

"Nearly?"

"My sisters and brother and I were sent to boarding school in England once, right after our mother died. That experiment didn't last long. And then, of course, I did some of my university work in the States."

"Why didn't your boarding-school experience last long?"

"Oh, England . . . well, you know."

"No."

She lifted her head. What did he expect her to do — blurt out all the pain she had worked so hard to bury? Just come right out with everything as though it didn't matter? As though she could just casually shrug off her past and the things that had hurt so much?

"I suppose my experience was something like yours," she said finally. "All the things you don't like to talk about, you know. About your parents and the memories."

"I don't see much similarity between your life and mine, Fiona. Did your parents get divorced, and did your father take you on ski trips with his mistresses? Did your mother marry five different men in a row and hate each of them within a month of the wedding?"

"My mother died."

"How?"

"Well, they killed her."

"Who killed her?"

She gestured vaguely in the air. "They. Somebody. People."

"Somebody *murdered* your mom?"

"Rogan, really, I think you'd better go now." She brushed her hand across her forehead. "I have to compile some data from this morning. And I have a full day planned for tomorrow. If you don't mind . . ."

"Fiona." He took her shoulders. "You can talk to me — talk about anything. I want to hear it. You can say the words that seem so hard. You can cry if you want to; I won't mind. You can be angry. I'll take your anger and hold it for you."

"When have you ever shared *your* tears or anger, Rogan?" she asked. "When have you ever spoken of those things that were so painful?"

He looked away. "We're alike, aren't we? Both buried in work so we won't have to feel, both stuffing memories that hurt too much, both sidestepping anything that requires emotional commitment."

She swallowed. "I guess we are alike. In some ways."

"Fiona, thank you for the book," he said, holding it between them like a barrier. "I'll read it tonight."

"You can take it with you if you want.

Just send it back to me when you're finished."

"Okay. Thanks."

"Well . . ." She stood there, not wanting him to go but not knowing how to make him stay.

"Breakfast tomorrow then? And you'll let me know about Nairobi."

"All right."

He walked across the triangular patch of lamplight that fell across the grass. "Fiona —"

"Rogan."

He turned and retraced the steps he had just taken. She came into his arms, her own sliding around his back. Her face tilted to his, and their lips met.

"Fiona," he whispered.

"I'm glad you came back."

"I thought about you all the time."

"I thought about you too."

"Please come to Nairobi with me," he whispered. "I'm not ready to walk away from you again."

She drank down a deep breath. "All right."

"You will?"

"For the museum and the embassy party and maybe CTN. For the elephants."

He nodded, backing away from her tent.

He looked dazed, like a teenager dizzy with emotion. "Okay. Okay, that's fine. For the elephants."

She watched him leave, his face bright with a smile she'd never seen before.

TEN

When Rogan emerged from his tent by the streambed, Fiona was deep in conversation with her small staff. The two baby elephants trotted around the dead campfire, running with floppy ears. Due to the elephants' orphan status, Fiona had given them names that would not tie them to any particular family. She hoped they would form their own bond group — a goal that now seemed feasible. When Johnny tripped on a tree root and fell, Fiona stopped speaking and moved to help. But instantly the older orphan — a female she'd christened Olivia — rushed to Johnny's aid. She nudged his gray backside, pushing with her trunk and front foot until the little calf was standing again.

Smiling, Fiona lifted her focus and watched Rogan make his way across the clearing. He wandered toward the shower, his head high, his attention on the branches of the acacias and the monkeys cavorting there. He wore a soft expression, completely readable. He looked nothing like the man who had first come to her camp in a wool business suit, with carefully parted hair. He looked happy.

Before stepping into the shower, he raised one hand toward her. She waved back. Then, feeling the dark eyes of her staff on her flushed cheeks, she returned to the conversation.

Her leaving, she realized, was not something anyone had anticipated. Mama Hannah would be going with her and Rogan — in the hope that she might catch Fiona's brother, Grant, in Nairobi. The small woman wanted to know what to do with all the fresh fruit she'd just bought in Naivasha. And should she take the coconut pie with them on the airplane? Moses complained, pointing out for the third time that morning that he'd been hired to watch only one elephant and asking whether she intended to employ another man to look after Olivia. Sentero studied Fiona in silence, his dark eyes shifting from the woman to the shower to the woman again.

"I'll be away two or three days at the most," she assured them. "Just to speak to some people in Nairobi about the elephants."

Moses shook his head, dark eyes forlorn as he gazed at the pair of baby elephants now resting in the shade. Sentero stared at her, his impassive face revealing nothing.

In time, breakfast was eaten and all the arrangements made. Rogan, clean shaven and dressed in tan trousers and a blue shirt with a button-down collar, insisted on carrying Fiona's half-empty canvas knapsack and Mama Hannah's small cotton bag to the plane. Fiona had on her least faded pair of khaki slacks and a white blouse sent as a Christmas present from her father years ago. She had never worn it.

Now, feeling silly in long puffed sleeves and a stand-up collar buttoned to her throat, she paused at the airplane door and called last-minute instructions to the men.

"Be sure the babies don't get too hot," she shouted to Moses over the drum of the propellers. "And keep an eye on the M family for me, Sentero. Check Rosamond's wound again, will you? I'm afraid it's festering. And Charlie, too. He can't last much longer. If you see anyone suspicious around the camp at night, radio the game wardens. And —"

Rogan's hand closed over hers. She turned to find him smiling patiently. "Everything will be all right, Fiona."

She nodded, her heart beating too fast. "And, Sentero, please keep an eye on Sukari for me."

"Yes, Dr. Thornton."

"I don't want him to feel neglected. And check that he has fresh water."

"Fiona." Rogan drew her gently inside the plane and reached past her to shut the door. "Relax now. They'll manage."

Relax? How could she possibly relax? She grabbed Mama Hannah's hand as Rogan taxied the small plane down the airstrip. What if something happened to one of the elephant calves? What if Moses quit while she was away? What if Sukari panicked and ran off? And then there was the matter of this tiny plane — she'd always hated flying. It seemed so uncertain. And Rogan. What about him? How could she possibly be doing something so impulsive as abandoning her staff, her research, the elephants, to go off to Nairobi with this man she hardly knew!

She sucked in her stomach as the plane lifted into the air. Oh, she'd thought about Rogan. Thought about him nearly all night. Thought about the wonder of him. And the magic. Of course, that was all he was. Illusory magic. These amazing feelings wouldn't last. They couldn't. Yet here she was in her puffed blouse zooming over her camp, bound for the city.

"I don't like Nairobi," she said to Mama

Hannah in a low voice.

"Such a big place." The little woman nodded, her head wrapped in a bright green scarf. "So many people."

"Dangerous things happen in cities. You can't simply walk down the street anymore."

"You are thinking of your mother, *toto*. You have not allowed God to heal your heart. If you would let Jesus Christ live in you, you would know that He is the same in the city or in the grasslands where your elephants walk."

Fiona glanced away. "The thing is, Rogan will expect me to do things . . . to be normal. To follow him to his embassy party and talk to the museum directors about the elephants. He'll expect me to blend into his world."

"And what else will he expect?"

Fiona looked at the man in the pilot's seat. His strong profile was lit by the early morning sun, outlined in gold. Though she couldn't see his eyes from where she was seated, she could easily picture the way the light would dance through them, skipping on the white flecks and darkening the navy circle around each iris. He was smiling that little smile from the night before. One corner of his mouth turned just enough to make a crease in his cheek. His skin glowed from the razor, and his hair, still damp, clung to his neck.

Fiona thought about the conclusions she had come to in the night. She had forced her mind away from the mystery of Rogan's kiss. She had made herself think about practical things. About her work. About the elephants. And finally her thoughts had come full circle, back to Rogan.

"I'm old enough to handle this, Mama Hannah." Fiona leaned toward the older woman to make herself heard. "You don't have to hover so much."

"You are not an elephant, you know. An animal. God has created you for purity. I like the bwana very much, but I fear he does not understand this. He has tried to go into your tent. In the city he will want to be alone with you. It is not pleasing to God for a man and woman to come together this way before marriage."

"Shh, Mama Hannah!" Fiona squeezed the old woman's hand. "Be quiet, for heaven's sake!"

"I will be at your brother's house. You will be alone, and you will need to call upon Jesus Christ."

Fiona glanced at Rogan again. He was

studying the clouds just overhead. His hands, strong and tanned, skillfully guided the small plane. He read gauges and set switches. And every now and then he leaned over and looked out the window.

"There's the edge of the park," he said in a strong voice that carried over the engine noise. "Ever seen it from the air?"

"No," she called back, wishing her stomach wasn't lurching and her palms weren't so sweaty. It was just the plane ride, she told herself. It had nothing to do with Mama Hannah's prediction.

"Look down," Rogan urged, glancing over his shoulder at the two women. "See that empty stone house and the water hole? Clive tells me they're located right on the park's borderline. And can you make out Mount Suswa just to your right? It's kind of far away."

"Oh yes, I see it."

"Won't be long before we fly over the escarpment and into the highlands. Did you bring a sweater? Nairobi can be chilly at night."

"Yes. A sweater. I brought one."

"Great. Okay, Nairobi, here we come."

A long white limousine met them at the airport. Fiona climbed onto the lushly padded leather seat and wedged herself into a corner beside Mama Hannah. Rogan stretched out, his long legs angled across the floor as they drove through the city. Fiona shut her eyes, willing away the honks and growls of traffic, the sway of the car as it swung around corners, the *ding-ding* of bicycle bells.

In no time the limousine pulled into the shadow of a high marble arch. The door opened, and Fiona stepped out onto hard pavement, followed by Mama Hannah and then Rogan. Rogan cupped Fiona's waist, his fingers trailing along her arm as he informed the driver when they would need the car again.

And then they were climbing the hotel's cool marble steps. Walking through a door held wide by a smiling, red-coated African. Standing in a carpeted elevator that swished up and up with stomach-sinking swiftness.

"Here we are," Rogan said, a note of pride in his voice. "Great location. Lots of space."

She tried to smile as he fitted a key in the brass lock. The doors were huge and antique, carved and studded with brass. Brought up from the coast, she imagined, where they had once graced an Arab house. Rogan gave her a small nudge to move her into the suite.

Instantly a tall, thin woman leapt to her feet and hurried around a huge carved desk. Fiona observed that her hair stuck straight up from her head in little blonde spikes.

"Mr. McCullough — you're back! Oh, thank goodness." Seeing Fiona and Mama Hannah, she stopped suddenly, her ankles nearly giving way atop her high heels. "You're . . . you've brought someone."

"Ginger Smeade, this is Dr. Fiona Thornton," Rogan said. "And this is Mama Hannah."

"Of course, the elephant researcher. So pleased to meet you, Dr. Thornton. And, ah, Mrs. Hannah."

Fiona shook the proffered hand, amazed at the length of the fuchsia nails extending from the secretary's fingers. How did she ever type?

After shaking Mama Hannah's hand, Ginger turned to her boss. "Mr. McCullough, I have a stack of messages for you, sir. Megamedia has been on the phone for hours with me, and I just don't know what to tell them. They've been sending e-mails too. Mr. Barnett called from New York. He's very concerned, sir. And the man in Frankfurt —"

"Ginger, would you be so good as to show my guests across the hall to the suite I radioed you about? And see if you can scare up something for us to drink. I'm parched."

"Yes, sir. But about the messages —"

"Go ahead, Ginger. Show Dr. Thornton and Mama Hannah around. I'll take care of things."

As she walked back through the carved doors, Fiona looked behind her at the man who now stood at the desk. A telephone receiver was wedged in the crook of his shoulder and neck, his fingers riffling through a stack of papers, his eyes scanning an opened laptop computer.

"Yes," he was saying, the softness gone from his voice. "I need New York, please. . . . Yes, get me New York."

Fiona followed the secretary's swaying hips across the carpeted hall and into another suite. She was standing in a massive living room. They continued through the door at the far end into an immense bedroom, one side lined with closets and the other containing a smaller boudoir area with a love seat and plants. There was a luxurious bathroom with rows of lights over the double sink, a big pink-marble tub, fluffy white towels.

"When your suitcases are brought up," Ginger was saying as she opened one of the closet doors, "you can hang your clothes in here."

"Oh, this is all I've brought." Fiona lifted the knapsack that hung from her index finger by a frayed loop. "I'm not staying long. I'm only here to . . . to talk to a few people about the elephants."

"Of course." Ginger smiled, fuchsia lips spreading over pearl white teeth. "Is there anything I can get for you, Dr. Thornton?"

Yes, Fiona wanted to say. *I need fresh air and green trees and dust on my feet. I need my elephants, and I need Sentero's dark eyes watching the landscape, and I need my white cat curling onto my lap.*

"No, thank you," she managed. "I'll just use the phone and try to reach my brother. Everything's fine."

"Well, then. I'll go get those drinks and see what else Mr. McCullough might need." The secretary appraised Fiona from head to toe. Then she smoothed the skirt of her purple linen suit and hurried from the room.

"Oh, Mama Hannah! What have I done?" Fiona sat on the end of the bed. She stared at her safari boots, worn and creased and reddened with dirt. She stared at her hands, knotted around the wrinkled knapsack. Then she stared at the immense room, the gold-and-crystal chandelier, the mauve silk bedspread, the heavy curtains that muffled the sounds from the street below. Blinking back a tear, she fiddled with a string on the hem of her blouse and tried to figure out what to do with herself.

"Ready to go?" Rogan burst through the half-open door to find Fiona slumped on the edge of the bed, staring at her feet. "Fiona? What's wrong?"

She raised her eyes. "I shouldn't have come. I need to get back, Rogan."

"Hey, now." He strode to the bed and eased her to her feet. "I had a few things to take care of. I'm free for the rest of the afternoon. Let's go out. I'll buy you something to wear to that embassy thing tonight. What do you say? Mama Hannah, you come along too."

"I am going to take a taxi to the house of my *toto* Grant," the older woman told him, her dark eyes serious. "I am going to leave this *toto* here . . . with you."

"That's great. Wonderful. I'll take care of Fiona, and you have fun with Grant." He was grinning. "We'll walk you down to the lobby, Mama Hannah. Make sure you get your taxi. Then Fiona and I will go shopping."

Fiona met Rogan's eyes. She wondered if the man who pressed hibiscus flowers was still in there somewhere. "I can't accept charity, Rogan. Besides, these clothes are fine, and I don't want a dress. I'd never wear it again."

"So what if you never wear it again? We'll wave my magic credit card. Anything wrong with that, Fiona?"

She pondered the question. "I'll admit I've thought about buying myself some new clothes. I just haven't gotten around to it. But I don't need your money —"

"Fiona, you haven't allowed me to contribute to your project in any way so far. Let this be my donation to the cause. Look on it as an investment with potential for good returns at the embassy party tonight."

"Well . . . as a donation . . . still, I don't feel comfortable in cities, Rogan."

"I'll be with you every minute. Come with me now. We'll shop till we drop."

She walked between Rogan and Mama Hannah into the living room. He stopped before a full-length, gilt-framed mirror. Then he turned Fiona around, letting her take a long look at herself — at the red-gold hair, the girlish white blouse tucked into worn trousers, the dusty boots.

"Remember this," he whispered in her ear. Then he led her across the hall and poked his head into the front room of his suite, where Ginger was sorting through a file.

The secretary looked up. "Going now, Mr. McCullough?"

"We'll be back by six." He started to leave, then stopped and pulled Fiona into the open doorway. "Ginger, what colors would look good on Dr. Thornton?"

"Colors?" Ginger stood and cocked her head. "Colors, oh, let's see. Red, maybe? Orange. And pink. Any shade of pink."

"And fabrics?"

She stuck the end of a fuchsia spike into her mouth and thought. "Velvet. Brocade. And knits."

"Thanks, Ginger." Rogan winked. "Catch you later."

He wheeled the two women down the hall toward the elevator. Chuckling, he slipped his arm around Fiona's waist. She stepped through the steel doors feeling more queasy than she had before.

"Red?" she said as the elevator sucked them down.

"Pink?" Mama Hannah added.

"And, Rogan, brocade and velvet? Please, I —"

"Oh, think of this like when you and Mama Hannah plan your meals. Whatever Ginger suggested, we'll do just the opposite. Personally, I'm picturing you in green silk."

Rogan and Fiona packed Mama Hannah off in a yellow taxi and began their stroll down the streets of Nairobi. They lunched at The Thorn Tree, a sidewalk café under the spreading branches of a three-stories-tall acacia that had been planted in the city's center. They wandered in and out of galleries and boutiques, examining necklaces of amber, malachite, amethyst, and tigereye . . . admiring dyed batik dresses in shades of purple and yellow . . . touching fine olivewood carvings . . . studying oils and watercolors of Africa and her animals.

At first Fiona clung to Rogan's arm. Unable to stop herself, she kept glancing behind her. She jumped when a car backfired. But as the afternoon wore on, she began to relax. The press of people held mostly friendly faces. When someone bumped her arm, there came an instant apology. Rogan focused her attention on the wonders of the shops, the aromas of curry and cinnamon and freshly baked bread in the little stalls, the array of bananas, papayas, mangoes, and tomatoes being hawked by street vendors.

"This is it," he announced as Fiona emerged from the fitting room of a dress-filled boutique. "This is the one."

She pivoted in front of a three-sided mirror, staring at herself with flushed cheeks. The gown, a rich blue-green silk, fit closely, its narrow skirt skimming down her hips. Pale silk stockings, at Rogan's insistence, were added to a stack of lacy lingerie. Matching blue-green pumps covered in sequins went into a sack, along with a cashmere shawl in a complementary shade of midnight blue.

Later in the afternoon another boutique provided a simple matching jacket and skirt in pale yellow linen. The short skirt was accented with a pair of pretty black heels. As she left the store, Fiona clutched the bags against her chest, unable to believe she was the owner of such up-to-date, expensive, well-matched, and fitted clothing.

"Now your hair," he said, turning her into a beauty salon.

"Rogan, I like my hair just the way —"

But in moments she was seated in a reclining chair, enjoying the feel of practiced hands massaging her scalp with thick lather. Her hair was treated to the luxury of rich conditioner, fluffed with a modern electric blow-dryer, and finally curled and styled. When the stylist turned the chair so Fiona faced the mirror, Fiona gasped so loudly that everyone in the salon turned to look.

Her hair, swept and piled on her head, gleamed with copper lights. Tendrils almost too wispy to see softened her face at the ears and nape. The lifted hair revealed things about her that Fiona had never known. She had high cheekbones that gave her eyes an exotic almond shape. And her neck. How long it was! Long, thin, meeting her shoulders with swanlike grace. She turned, admiring her own ears for the first time in her life. She smiled and realized she had a lovely mouth. She blinked and saw long dark lashes flutter.

Next she was handed over to a woman who showed her how to apply makeup. A soft foundation and translucent powder made her skin glow. A gentle liner, eye shadow, and mascara brought her sparkling eyes to life. Contours blushed her cheeks. A stray brow hair was plucked here and there. And finally a glossy lipstick showed how pretty her lips really were.

When Rogan walked into the salon after her three-hour ritual, Fiona stood, turned, and walked to him, feeling like the loveliest woman alive.

And his eyes agreed.

"Fiona," Rogan said in a low voice as they stood together at the embassy party, "it's almost midnight. Are you ready to leave, princess?"

"Will my dress turn into a T-shirt and jeans at the stroke of twelve?"

"No, but I might change into an ogre if I'm forced to make small talk any longer."

She laughed and took a last sip of punch. Ladies in gorgeous gowns tittered with men strutting in black-tie tuxedos. Faces from Asia, Africa, Europe, and South America mingled. Languages, accents, laughter, and music floated through the high-ceilinged ballroom. Scents of rich perfumes blended with the aromas of exotic food — curries, tropical fruits, spices.

Rogan had introduced Fiona to a diplomat from Zimbabwe. The man had listened to her animated words about the plight of the elephants. Then he had smiled, commented, "How very interesting," and sidled off to find himself another drink. But Rogan had blotted out her disappointment by whirling her off to the buffet before introducing her to yet another diplomat. And each time they found themselves alone in the crowd, his arms came around her, his eyes memorized her face, and she drifted away in twin pools of deep blue.

Oh, this day had toppled her off balance, Fiona realized — from the morning's plane ride away from her camp to the afternoon of shopping to the utter physical transformation of Dr. Fiona Thornton. She felt frightened and light and so, so vulnerable. She had let herself laugh and meet people. She had graced Rogan's arm, chatting inanities that she imagined were proper and polite.

And all the while she tried to keep in mind that this was normal. Completely, utterly normal. Fluff and brilliance and perfume decorated the prancing peacocks of the world of people. Rogan was her suitor, trying to win her approval with touches and compliments, with his handsome suit and his gifts — just like a weaverbird won a mate by building the perfect nest or a bull elephant triumphed by dominating the other males.

And Rogan dominated. How he dominated! His smile sent the women into flutters. His handshake held a power that transfixed men. He stood tall and handsome, the white shirt matching his smile, the black bow tie accenting his bronzed skin.

"All right, I'm ready," she said at last. He escorted her through the ballroom and into the limousine. He drew her close in the darkness of the leather padding.

"Fiona," he said in a low voice, "you're beautiful."

"Yes," she concurred, "beautiful." She allowed her eyes to drift shut, savoring the nearness of this man. *Yes,* she thought. *I am beautiful. I'm a beautiful, beautiful woman. And this is my chosen male. The male who selected me. This is simple and natural,* she told herself, *perfectly normal.*

Fiona awoke with a gasp and sat straight up in bed. Where was she? A mauve spread lay rumpled over an expanse of bed bigger than her entire tent. Sunlight spilled between pleated curtains. Hot tea, plates covered by silver warmers, and a single red rose in a fluted vase crowded a bamboo tray beside her bed. The aroma of eggs and bacon drifted through the room.

Grabbing her throat, she glanced down at herself. White nightgown. Her old one from home. Buttoned to her neck. The blue-green silk dress draped over the love seat in the boudoir. Sparkly pumps perched together on the Persian carpet.

"Oh, dear Lord." Once again she caught herself in prayer.

Flopping back on the bed, she flung an arm over her eyes. Oh, what had she done? What hadn't she done? Why had she done it? Where were Sukari and her philodendron and the chime of Mama Hannah's xylophone?

"Good morning, *toto.*"

She bolted upright again as Mama Hannah walked into the room and sat beside her. "Do you wish to eat any of this, or are you going to sleep all day?"

"Oh, Mama Hannah." She threw her arms around the old woman. "You're here. I'm so glad. Last night, I —"

"You went to sleep in the car. Bwana McCullough carried you inside and placed you beside me on this big bed."

At those words, a vague memory drifted back into Fiona's mind. Half asleep, she had stumbled out of the limo and been lifted into Rogan's arms. She didn't remember the elevator, but she recalled the door to her suite, Mama Hannah's warm voice, the soft coolness of the sheets.

"But what are you doing here?" she asked. "I thought you were going to stay with Grant."

"That *toto* keeps as busy as you. We talked through the day, but he and his wife had made a plan to go to their research camp in the bush. In the afternoon, after tea, they went away."

"And left you alone?"

"No, they put me into a taxi, just as you did. Now, I am here with you in this room."

Fiona let out her breath. "I can't believe I fell asleep in the limo. I guess I was worn out from all the shopping and beauty-parlor business."

"You were out very late, *toto*. Your usual bedtime is eight-thirty."

"In the camp, Mama Hannah. This is the city. People stay up late here. It's the normal thing to do."

"Eh-h, normal," Mama Hannah gave a snort. " 'It is useless for you to work so hard from early morning until late at night, anxiously working for food to eat; for God gives rest to His loved ones.' The bwana waits for you."

"Where is he?" She glanced toward the

living room of her suite. "Out there?"

Mama Hannah nodded.

Mortified, Fiona crawled out of bed and padded to the door. Opening it a crack, she poked her head through. "Hi."

"Morning, beautiful."

"Um, sorry about last night."

"No problem." He was smiling as he walked toward her. "Our museum meeting is at ten. After that I'll take you to lunch at the Norfolk Hotel. And then we'll meet Fred from CTN at two."

"All right."

"Wear the yellow suit."

"Rogan . . ."

"You're beautiful, Fiona. Beautiful in the morning. Beautiful at night. Even beautiful when you're snoring."

"I snore?"

"You snore," Mama Hannah confirmed, behind her.

"Very daintily," Rogan clarified. "See you in an hour."

Fiona couldn't imagine taking an hour to shower and get dressed. She shut the door and headed for the tray of breakfast foods. After a croissant and a cup of tea, she hurried into the bathroom. The water was steamy, the soap filled with cream and lather and sweet perfume. Thirsty towels drank beads of water from her skin. She rubbed lotion over her legs and arms. She practiced with the makeup and blow-dryer. And she brushed out her hair so that it tumbled in thick burnished waves.

Finally, with only minutes to spare, she dressed in the yellow suit. Mama Hannah elected to stay behind, saying she would venture out later to shop. Giving the elderly woman a quick kiss, Fiona hurried across the hall and stepped into the living room of Rogan's suite. Ginger glanced up, and her mouth fell open, revealing her set of pearly teeth and a wad of chewing gum. Rogan stopped dictating.

"Fiona."

Color crept up her neck and settled in hot points on her cheeks. A vague memory slipped forward — a little girl in a lacy pink Easter dress standing on a porch. White-gloved hands clasped a shiny white purse, and tiny white shoes rocked her shyly back and forth.

"Why, Fiona . . . how adorable!" a young voice said. "Look, John, isn't she beautiful?"

And then another, deeper voice. "I should say so. Takes after you, Beryl, darling. My, my, my."

The memory faded, and with its leaving came the sharp sting of tears. Fiona tried to remember her mother's face . . . the red-gold hair . . . the smiling eyes . . . but she, too, had faded.

"Fiona?" Rogan was at her side.

She swallowed and forced a smile to her lips. "Shall we go? I'd hate to keep the curators waiting."

Ginger swept up a file from the desk. "Here, Mr. McCullough. The file for your meeting with Megamedia." She placed it in his hands, but her eyes were on Fiona. "You look great, Dr. Thornton," the secretary said. "I mean, it's a regular miracle."

"Thank you, Miss Smeade. It's a temporary miracle. I'll be leaving tomorrow morning. Would you please find out whether Clive Willetts will be free to fly Mama Hannah and me to my camp? I'd like to leave as early as possible."

"Sure. Of course, Dr. Thornton."

And then Fiona and Rogan were on their way. The museum meeting rushed by. Fiona's presentation drew a rumble of approval from the board. Board members asked pertinent questions and offered their pledge of support. There was talk of setting up a budget allocation for the Rift Valley Elephant Project.

At lunch Fiona imagined herself completely in control — the museum meeting had gone better than she'd expected. Now she was fully prepared to face the cameras of CTN. She felt confident, efficient.

But then Rogan nudged her hand.

"Would you like a roll, Fiona?"

As she reached for the basket, she suddenly heard the whispered voices again: *"Bread, Fiona, dearest? Mummy baked it just for you. And marmalade? Oh, sweetheart, do have a bit of butter."*

And the deeper voice: "You bake the best bread in eleventy-seven counties, Beryl. I swear it. I'd bet money on it."

"Darling!" And then a high, tinkling laugh that tumbled down into Fiona's heart.

"Fiona?" Rogan touched her cheek. "Fiona, what's the matter? Is something on your mind?"

She focused on his eyes. "Oh . . . oh, it's nothing. I was just remembering something. Something I'd forgotten."

He watched her, a look of concern on his face.

But she was stunning before the cameras. The interview went beautifully. Fiona communicated her passion for the elephants with clarity and sincerity. Fred asked if CTN might come to her camp and film a segment on the elephants of the Rift Valley. She said she would think about it and let him know.

And then Rogan slipped his arm around her, and they walked together to the limousine. In the car he held her hand, toying with her fingertips. He said nothing, and she couldn't bring herself to speak.

They rode the elevator to the penthouse, and Rogan gave Ginger the rest of the day off. "Relax here, Fiona," he said, opening her suite door. "I'll be at my meeting with Megamedia until around six. Then we'll have dinner together."

She nodded.

"And Fiona, if you want to stay another day, I'd like that." He touched her arm. "I'm not crazy about the idea of sending you off tomorrow."

As he shut the door behind her, she sank onto the bed. The voices slipped over her again: *"John, darling, I just can't send the children away. They're too small. Let them stay here another year."*

The deeper voice: "What about school? We must see to their education, Beryl."

"Better unschooled than lonely. Look at dearest Fiona. She's obviously intelligent — that will work in her favor. But she's so shy, so small and fragile. She's just a child, John. I'm afraid she would be easily hurt."

"All right, Beryl. Keep the children with

you. Fill them with all that extra love you seem to think they need. And when the time comes, we'll figure out a way to educate them."

Fiona squeezed her eyes shut, seeing the faces. Oh, her mother. Her father. How long ago it had been. And how very warm and secure.

With the heel of her palm she smeared tears into her cheek and shook her head. Why now? Why was she suddenly swamped with memories of what she had lost so long ago? Why did she feel like that little girl again, wanting warmth, wanting comfort, wanting security . . . wanting . . . no, aching . . . for love?

ELEVEN

When Rogan returned from his meeting in downtown Nairobi, he found Fiona seated alone in his living room, staring out the window, one fingertip trailing down the mounted ivory tusks that sat on the table. Bare feet emerged from the ragged hems of her jeans. A navy T-shirt clung to the curve of her back.

"Fiona?" Rogan walked toward her, uncertainty in every step. Though her physical appearance had returned to the norm, emotionally she seemed drained, evaporated, and so silent.

She turned and gazed up at him, her eyes deep. "How was your meeting?"

"Looks like I can have the deal wrapped up in a few weeks. If I decide to make the final move."

Her mouth curved into a faint smile; then she returned to tracing invisible lines down the tusks.

"So, what have you been up to while I was gone?" Rogan asked, setting his briefcase on the floor and loosening his tie.

"I answered the telephone for a while. But then I gave up and let it ring. I didn't know what to tell people. They all wanted you."

"Don't worry about the phone. It's the bane of my existence. I leave it off the hook half the time anyway. . . . So, what else have you been doing?"

"Trying to pray. Not succeeding. Are these yours?" She tapped the tusks.

"The suite was furnished. They were in here with all the other stuff."

She returned to tracing.

"Where's Mama Hannah?"

"She went to have dinner with some of her nieces and nephews."

"Where would you like to eat, Fiona? Chinese, maybe? Or Indian?"

"I had cheese and crackers at sunset."

"Man cannot live by cheese and crackers, Fiona. I'm famished." Getting no reaction, he studied the back of her head, copper hair tumbling over her shoulders. She was despondent, obviously homesick for her camp and the elephants.

Rogan wandered into his bedroom, unbuttoning his shirtsleeves and rolling them to his elbows. Fiona might have performed superbly for two days in his sphere, but he had to recognize her behavior as just that — a performance.

What had he expected, anyway? Had he hoped to show her life in the fast lane, the pleasures money could buy, the importance of knowing all the right people? Had he hoped to impress her with things he was beginning to doubt himself? Did he really expect her to respond to a man who had reached the pinnacle of power, when that man was starting to question the point of striving?

He had tried to force her out of her world into his. And look what it had done to her.

"Is it those tusks?" he asked, stepping out of the bedroom in his bare feet. "Is that what's bothering you, Fiona?"

She turned, her eyes revealing a trace of surprise at his tone. "They bother me, of course. I keep thinking about the elephant they belonged to once. Maybe she was a matriarch, with lots of sons and daughters and a mind full of wisdom about where to find the best patches of grass and how to search out water during the dry season, and . . ."

She fell silent.

Rogan reached around her to grab the heavy tusks. "Here. I'll just put these things where they belong." He strode across the living room and hurled the curved tusks into the huge stone fireplace. Their weight shattered a half-burned log. "I'll set them on fire. Isn't that what the Kenyan government said to do with ivory? Just burn the stuff? Will that make it go away, Fiona? Will that erase some of the pain?"

"Rogan —"

"Fiona — what would make a difference? I'm just one man. I can't round up all the poachers and stand them in front of a firing squad. Believe me, if I could, I would. It's not going to be solved that easily. Look, I'm sorry if you're down in the dumps. I thought you might have fun in the city. You know — shopping, eating out, things that would relax you and take your mind off your worries. And I wanted to be with you. But I guess it was a mistake. You're miserable, and I'm —"

"Rogan, will you please stop talking?"

He clamped his mouth shut and watched her walk across the room, her bare feet silent on the thick Persian carpet. She looked like the sunrise coming toward him, her hair glowing, her slim body covered in shades of indigo. He wanted to hold her and take away everything that hurt her. It angered him to realize that for all his money and connections, he didn't have the

284

power to make her smile. He couldn't heal her.

"Rogan," she said, crossing her arms and staring into the fireplace at the sooty tusks, "there are other things."

"What things?"

"When you haven't spoken your deepest thoughts in twenty years," she murmured, as if to herself, "how do you just start all at once? Words don't form on your lips so easily anymore. Feelings don't want to be dredged out of hiding."

"Talk to me, Fiona. Please."

"Memories have been flooding through me for the past few hours," she went on. "Things I haven't thought of for years. It's as though you . . . your human touch . . . your kind words . . . have somehow opened me inside. Doors have swung wide, and windows have lifted. I'm tasting my own feelings again. I'm reliving things I didn't even know I remembered."

His heart hammered in response, and he knew he felt the same. "I'd like to hear everything. Whatever you want to tell me."

"I realize that after this night, I'll never see you again," she said softly as she lowered herself to the stone edge of the raised hearth. "That ought to make me feel safe enough to talk. Since I met you, I've been remembering things. Things about my life. I guess I'd shut them away a long time ago. But the way you've talked to me and . . . and treated me in the past few days, I've slipped back in touch with those other sides of myself. It's been a little strange for me. Difficult."

He settled beside her on the hearth. Elbows resting on his thighs, he linked his fingers loosely and kept his eyes from her face.

"A long time ago," she began, her voice just above a whisper, "when I was young . . . five years old . . . we all went to the States to visit my father's family for Christmas. Boston."

When she stopped speaking, he tensed. He wanted more than anything to reach over and take her hand. Or cradle her in his arms. But he was afraid she would slip away from him.

"Boston," he said. "Big city."

"Yes." She sat in silence. He heard her swallow twice. "My brother and sisters stayed home with Grandma one evening, while I went Christmas shopping with my mom and dad. Snow was falling. I remember walking through mounds of it, white on my black boots. They were shiny boots."

"New ones, probably."

She nodded. "And we were walking around a corner. I had a big white package under my arm. A new pen for my father. A very special paintbrush my mother had been wanting . . . it had some sort of bristles that made it absorb the paint better. She was an artist, you know. And I was holding her hand, our gloved fingers all tangled up. Daddy was . . . my father was walking just in front of us with my grandfather. They were laughing about things they remembered. My mother was singing me a silly song she'd made up about snow . . . 'sweetheart, watch it blow . . . and which way will it go . . . it settles on my nose and seeps between my toes . . . it sparkles, oh so white, like sugar in the night' . . . and then I heard a . . . sound . . . very loud. . . ."

She let out another breath and it came in trembles. Rogan took her hand and wove their fingers together.

"It was a car. Boys laughing and hanging out the windows. Shouting. Waving bottles. And a loud sound . . . a boom . . . or a bang . . . and a bright light. My mother fell into the snow, and I tumbled on top of her because she had my hand. I heard screaming and shouting. Sirens. My father

287

was running down the street and then running back to my mother. Someone picked me up. I wiggled and cried, because I wanted to be with my mother — her hand had felt so warm on mine. But then I saw . . . spreading across the snow around her head . . . a stain . . . like a red halo. And I don't remember anything after that."

Rogan stared at their hands. He couldn't make himself breathe deeply enough to fill his lungs. "Your mother . . ."

"She died. The police never found out who the boys in the car were. A random shooting, they told us. They killed my mother . . . just for kicks."

She rubbed the end of her nose. "I felt so empty after that. Things died inside me when my mother was murdered. We went back to Africa, and my father kept teaching anthropology at the University of Nairobi. Mama Hannah came to take care of us kids. I loved her big brown eyes and skin like ebony and her soft smile. She sang made-up songs the way my mother had. She told us God loved us and had a good plan for our lives. And she always rocked me while she told us stories."

"Like the one about Matalai Shamsi."

"And lots of others. My father seemed to sort of go away. He didn't talk or laugh anymore. He never took us to church. He put my mother's paintings in a room and locked the door. He worked all the time, and he got angry if anyone bothered him. He shouted if I touched the tagged yellow bones on his desk. He wouldn't let people come to our house. He had no friends. Then . . . when I was a little older, he decided all us kids should go to England to boarding school."

She gave a laugh that sounded more like a sigh and shook her head. "That was awful. They had to practically pry me from Mama Hannah. I screamed and cried and dug my fingers into her skin. She kept saying, 'Okay, *toto* . . . okay, *toto.*' But it wasn't okay. I didn't last very long in England before they expelled me."

"Expelled you? What for? You were just a little kid — what harm could you have done?"

"I ran away from school. We all did, actually — Grant, Tillie, Jessica, and me. Six times in the first two months. They couldn't find us for days at a time. We hid in scary places. Beneath a bridge. In somebody's barn. And finally they just gave up and sent us all back to Africa. My father hired a tutor. And that was that. I grew up. I met a woman studying lions, and she helped me plan my graduate work and get research grants. And from then on, I've lived with the elephants."

"Did Mama Hannah stay with you when you were sent back to Kenya?"

"Yes, but by then it was really too late, you know. I had decided I didn't like people any more than my father did. I kept Mama Hannah at arm's length — wouldn't sing with her, blocked out her Bible stories, refused to listen to the Scriptures she was always quoting. She said I had hardened my heart, and she was right."

Rogan listened, feeling grim inside. How different he and Fiona had once seemed — yet now, how alike.

"I was young," Fiona went on, "but I wasn't stupid. I figured out that people had killed my mother for no reason. For fun. How could I trust anyone after that? People had beaten me with a cane for running away from school. People had laughed at me when I cried and hid under my bed. I didn't need anybody or want anybody. Even my brother and sisters learned to keep their distance from me. They knew I was happiest alone."

"And you still are."

She lifted her head. "That's the strange part. Yes, I'm happy enough, and I'm content with my work and my life. But for some reason lately, things have begun feeling very . . . odd. I've started remembering my mother. My father and mother. Our family. I can remember laughing and singing songs. I can remember all us kids hugging and tumbling down a grassy green hill. For the first time in ages I've started wanting . . ." She stood suddenly and walked across the room. "Oh, I don't know . . ."

"Tell me, Fiona. What is it you've been wanting?"

She stood still, her back to him and her arms tightly crossed, hugging herself. "It's like I went to sleep years and years ago. And now I feel as though I'm awake. I've found myself longing for what Mama Hannah has. I want to be open enough to let God in, to forgive Him for taking my mother, to surrender to Christ. And people . . . somehow I want them too. I want . . . I want to be . . . touched."

He knew those words had taken great courage. He knew she could give nothing more. Slowly he went to her. His hands slipped down her bare arms, and his fingers wove through hers.

"Fiona," he whispered, "I'm . . . I'm sorry. I'm sorry you've been hurt so badly.

Not everyone is going to hurt you." He turned her around in his arms.

"People lie," she said. "You might be lying."

"I'm not lying. It's true that no one is perfectly good. And it's true that there are people — a lot of them — who don't care about anyone but themselves. But it's also true that there are people who care. People who try to do the right things. People who heal and save others, and people who fight for justice."

"And which kind of person are you, Rogan?"

He studied her camouflaged eyes, and he knew the answer. "I'm one of those who's been walking around in the middle. I don't murder or steal or poach elephants. But I've spent a lot of years focused on one thing — Rogan McCullough. I haven't really cared who I stepped on to get where I wanted to be. And I've had to do a lot of thinking about what you told me the other day."

"What was that?"

"You said I could use my assets to improve the world instead of trying to dominate it."

She studied his face. "And?"

"And I haven't figured out how to do that, Fiona."

"Well, I don't know how to let people into my life. I don't know how to let them touch me."

He cupped the side of her face and tilted her head. "Fiona, letting someone touch you is the easiest thing in the world."

"I don't know . . . it makes me feel very vulnerable when you start . . ."

"When I kiss you?" He touched his lips to hers. Her mouth felt dry, as though she'd used everything up in telling him her past.

"Yes, that."

"Vulnerability is good sometimes, Fiona. It's okay to trust."

"Even to trust God?"

He thought about that, about how God had become so much more real to him since he'd met this woman. About how he had always controlled his own life — and had never found the inner peace he was seeking. And he thought about his own yearning to give up, to admit he couldn't do it all, to ask God to take over.

"I've been thinking Mama Hannah may be right," he said. "Maybe it is best to let God be in control. I know it can work that way with people — to let go of the reins you hold on to so tightly, to just relax with someone you trust."

"Can I trust you?"

"Always."

"Now is all I care about, Rogan. Can I trust you for now?"

"Now. Tomorrow. Forever."

He gathered her hair in his hands, wanting her to know she was cherished. Not for anything in the world would he hurt her — or allow anyone else to hurt her. She'd endured enough pain for one lifetime.

"Fiona, there are things about you that make a man wonder what he's been doing all his life. You have such honesty, such immediacy. There's no pretense in you. Your inner spirit seems to radiate outward . . . through your shining hair and your smile. Did you know you have a certain smile that you save just for the things you love?"

"I do?"

"For the elephants. For Mama Hannah's spice cake."

"Spice cake!" She laughed. Then she grew solemn, as if afraid he might see that special smile when she looked at him. Lifting a hand, she smoothed the hair above his ears, then let her fingers drift down his short sideburns and onto his cheek. He knew his skin, shaved that morning, now wore a fine dark shadow of beard. She let her fingers trace his jawline.

"I suppose you've been told hundreds of times how handsome you are," she said.

"Not by you."

"I think you're very . . . very beautiful."

"Beautiful?"

"Yes. Blue eyes. Strong features. And you have such a wonderful mouth. When I first saw you, I thought I could dismiss you from my mind. But I couldn't stop thinking about your mouth. Your lips."

Watching her mouth form the words, he felt his breath grow short. "Fiona." Struggling with his thoughts, he knew his hands were too hard on her shoulders. "Fiona, I want your trust," he said. "I want that more than anything. I want you to know that I'd never do anything to make you lose faith in me. Do you understand that?"

"Yes."

"The thing is, Fiona, I've never had much practice at being particularly noble and restrained. And when I hold you and kiss you . . . and when you look at me with those unbelievable eyes . . . I start to feel like those bull elephants."

She bowed her head. "I understand that. I'm having a hard time myself."

"I don't want to hurt you, Fiona. I don't want to be someone who passes through your life and uses you and then just goes on." He let out a hot breath. "But purity. You said it was never too late. What did you mean?"

"Have you noticed how God is always starting over with His creation, Rogan? In America, the seasons are a part of that. The trees lose their leaves and seem to die. But in the spring, new leaves burst out, filled with life and health — completely pure once again. Here in Kenya, the animals always remind me that life doesn't stop with death. Babies are born all the time. The rains come, and the barren ground becomes green and lush. Mama Hannah used to say, 'There's a time to be born and a time to die.' "

"I thought you didn't listen to Mama Hannah's Scripture quoting."

She smiled. "Maybe I was listening more than I knew. Anyway, she always said that birth was the start of life, but death wasn't the end of it. She said my mother was living still, because she had given her heart to Jesus Christ before . . . before she was murdered."

Pausing, she moistened her lips. "But Mama Hannah also used to say that in our time here on earth, there can be deaths and new lives. She said we can die to our old ways. We can be reborn as new people, with new values and purposes . . . new character. And that's what I was thinking of when I said it was never too late for purity."

"You mean I can somehow cut away that part of me? My past?"

"Well, God can." Fiona sighed. "I wish Mama Hannah were here. She could explain it a lot better."

At Fiona's words, Rogan felt a surge of overwhelming desire — not for her but for this thing she had described, this newness. "Did she tell you how to do it? Did Mama Hannah say how to become a new person?"

"You have to admit you were wrong." She paused, frowning as she searched for the answers. "Confess. Repent. Surrender. I think that's it."

"Confess what? That I wasn't pure in the past? That I did everything my own way, and it still left me empty? I don't have any problem with that. I know who I've been, Fiona. I've created myself in my father's image — and I've become just like the man I never wanted to be."

"The Father's image. That's it. Mama Hannah said we can surrender ourselves and become reborn into the image of God."

"How?" He squeezed her shoulders. "How, Fiona?"

"I don't know. I've never done it."

"Well, what did Mama Hannah tell you?"

"She said I have to open my heart and let God in. I have to admit that Jesus Christ is the Son of God — that He is God. I have to believe that He came to earth and died on the cross and rose again, all to take away my sins."

"Sins of the past? But I've already admitted that was wrong."

"And then repent. It means turning your back on the old ways and walking the opposite direction."

"I can do that. I want to do it."

"Do you believe what I said about Jesus?"

He nodded. "I do. I need to know more, though. I need to know what He taught. I need to know . . . to know *Him*."

"Well, you'll have to read the Bible. Mama Hannah says it's the only way to know God."

"I can do that too."

Her eyes searched his. "Well, then. I guess you've done it. You confessed your sins. You repented. You acknowledged Jesus and what He did for you. And . . .

and now you just have to surrender." She looked away. "I have to surrender," she whispered.

"By surrender, do you mean stop trying to control everything myself?"

"Open up," she agreed, as if speaking to herself. "Let go. Let Jesus come inside. Ask Him what He wants you to do . . . and do it. Obey. Yield. Let Him . . . let Him touch you."

Suddenly her eyes flooded with tears. Rogan pulled her close. "Fiona, what's wrong?"

"I have to go. I need to be alone."

"But it's so right — don't you see?" He held her and closed his eyes as the flood-gates broke open inside him. "I can do it. I have done it! I've let Him in, Fiona!"

She broke away from him. "I can't, Rogan. I can't be here right now. Excuse me."

Breathless, dazed, he watched her run across the room and into the hall, slamming the door behind her. He dropped down onto the hearth and covered his face as tears overflowed his hands.

TWELVE

Fiona curled on the couch, her face pressed against a pillow as she tried not to cry. How had she been reduced to this? She was strong, independent, intelligent. Yet she felt like that small, lonely child she'd been so many years before. What had she needed then? What did she need now? Where was she going to get it?

Love. That was it. The missing thing inside her.

Mama Hannah would tell her she needed God's love. Rogan would tell her she needed human love. Maybe she needed both, but she wasn't sure how to find them or get them or keep them. Most of all, she was afraid. Love meant risk. If she loved someone, she would be vulnerable. And then what? So easily . . . in the blink of an eye . . . the loved one could be snatched away.

Not God, Mama Hannah would tell her. *God won't ever leave you or forsake you.* Was that right? Fiona groaned into the pillow, wishing she could cry and trying so hard not to.

A knock on the door brought her out of her cocoon. She knew who it was. Rogan. He would want to talk, want to touch her. Oh, how could she keep holding back? It was too hard! And she was too lonely.

"Fiona?" His face appeared as she opened the door.

Loving the sound of her name spoken in his deep voice, she drew back the door and let him inside. He took her in his arms and held her tightly.

"Fiona, what is it? Why did you leave?"

She brushed her hair from her cheek and slipped out of his embrace. He followed her to the couch, so she took a chair instead. "All these years," she said, tucking her legs up under her, "I've worked so hard to suppress myself. After my mother died, lots of feelings shut down of their own accord. And I struggled to hide away the rest. When I was sent to boarding school, I didn't want to feel the pain of letting Mama Hannah go. And I didn't want to be hurt over my father's withdrawal. Eventually — out in the bush — I just wanted to be as much like the Africans as I could. Like Sentero, you know?"

"Sentero?"

"Sentero is enigmatic. I like that about him. I never know what he's thinking or feeling. He's always right on track with our research. Nothing gets in the way of his observations. He's so emotionally level that his other senses have had the opportunity to heighten. He smells and sees and hears much better than I do. I wanted so badly to be like that. But now . . . since I met you . . . all my hard work is . . . useless."

"What do you mean, useless?"

"Everything — all the feelings I'd locked away or buried — suddenly it's breaking loose inside me. I feel so out of control."

"Is that a bad thing?"

She shrugged. "I don't know yet. I feel emotional. It's like all the dams inside me burst and everything is rushing out. I'm sort of in shock."

"You aren't the only one."

Lifting her head, she read the solemnity in his expression. "Tell me what you mean, Rogan."

"It's fairly simple. When I met you, I was one kind of man. And now I'm completely different." He shook his head. "So simple — and so unbelievably complicated. Back there in the room a few minutes ago . . . that's when it happened. That's when the change became permanent. I could feel it coming on, feel that there was something opening inside me and that I was beginning to want to change. But it didn't happen until you taught me what to do."

"I taught you?" She blinked. "Rogan, I don't even know how myself."

"Yes, you do. You took me through the steps I needed to give myself to God. And now . . . well, it's done. I'm never going back."

"What does it mean? How will your life be different, Rogan?"

"I'm not sure." He took her hand. "I've been accused of being indifferent to people — even using them. I've been the guy women wanted but never loved. And I know why they haven't loved me. Because I couldn't commit to that kind of nonsense. I cultivated my image so that everyone knew where I stood — women and men alike. I wanted them to know they couldn't expect a lifetime of devotion out of Rogan McCullough. That's why I have no real friends. I didn't have it to give."

"And now?"

"Now, that's all I want. The important stuff. First of all, I want to know everything I can about God. I'm hungry for Him. I'm starving." He paused for a moment. "And you. Here you are, Fiona, this woman who's so beautiful inside and out. This woman who has trusted me to be the first one in years to touch her. Who has let me breach the walls that have been her fortress nearly all her life."

Fiona listened, fighting the truth in his words. "Rogan, I'll be going in the morning. I need to get back to my work. Maybe the walls are down, but I have so much to —"

"Fiona, wait." He came to her, kneeling at her feet. "Fiona . . . if only you could understand what you've done for me. What you do to me. I need to tell you —"

"*Toto*, I —" Mama Hannah stopped in the open doorway. Her mouth fell open. "Excuse me, please. I did not know you were here, Bwana McCullough."

Fiona stood quickly and stepped over Rogan's bent knee. "You're back, Mama Hannah! How was dinner?"

The little woman stepped into the room. "Delicious. And I learned much news. But perhaps I shall go away again. It seems you have a guest, *toto*."

"It's all right," Rogan said. "I hadn't realized it was so late. Fiona, I'll see you at breakfast."

Pausing beside Mama Hannah, he bent down and kissed her cheek. "God bless you," he said, folding her into a bear hug. "And thank you."

As the door shut behind him, Mama Hannah's dark eyebrows lifted. "This is a change," she said.

Fiona let out a sigh. "That's the understatement of the evening."

"By this, what do you mean?"

"I mean," she said, "Rogan became a Christian tonight. Somehow . . . and I haven't figured this part out . . . somehow I led him to it. Can you believe that?"

"Of course. You have known the path since your childhood."

Fiona shook her head. "I have no idea what to do about this."

"Perhaps you should join him on the path."

"Or perhaps," she said, "I should just go to bed."

Leaving Mama Hannah, Fiona headed for the bedroom . . . certain she couldn't get away fast enough.

Fiona woke Mama Hannah at the crack of dawn. They ordered room service, bathed, packed, and ate without speaking more than a sentence or two. Filled with a panic she couldn't explain, Fiona knew only that she needed to get out of this place — away from the city, away from her fears and emotions, and most of all, away from Rogan McCullough.

She scribbled a brief note, thanking him for the opportunities to promote her cause. Setting it on the dining table, she called down to the lobby for a taxi. In moments, she gathered up Mama Hannah's bag and her own; then she bundled the little woman out the door into the hall.

The sight of the tall man leaning against the opposite wall took Fiona's breath away. "Rogan," she said.

"I was hoping you hadn't forgotten breakfast."

She cleared her throat. "Breakfast? Oh, well —"

"We have eaten already," Mama Hannah filled in. "It was not good. Only toast and jam with a little tea. The tea was not hot, and I am sorry to tell you they forgot the milk altogether."

Rogan straightened. "You ate?"

"Yes, we are going away," Mama Hannah continued, "so that we will not see you again. This is the plan of my *toto*."

Fiona grew hot. "I wanted to make sure we didn't miss the flight. Clive said —"

"You don't need to worry about Clive," Rogan said. "In fact, you don't even have to leave today. I'll tell Clive to spend the day tinkering with his airplanes. Fiona, I'd like to talk with you about some things."

"Rogan." Now Fiona felt a chill wash over her. "I need to get back to my camp. Sentero and Moses will be wondering what's happened to me. And the elephant calves . . . and the research . . . I should go."

She started down the hall, but he stepped out and called her name. "Fiona, don't go. Not like this."

"I had a lovely time in Nairobi, Rogan. Thank you so much. For the clothes. And dinner. And everything."

He took her shoulders. "Listen to me here, Fiona. I've asked you to stay one more day. I think it would be a good idea, considering last night and the things we haven't talked about."

"I said much more than I should have, Rogan. I ought to go."

"I am the one who will go," Mama Hannah said, taking her bag from Fiona's hand. "I will tell the taxi driver to wait."

Before Fiona could stop her, Mama Hannah headed for the elevator. "Fiona, I know we've had some disagreements in the past," Rogan said, turning her to face him, "but last night we . . . well, we shared something."

"Rogan, please." She bit her lip for a

moment, hearing herself preparing to express carefully formulated thoughts that had begun to sound like lies. "Last night, I talked about myself. And you opened up too. But that was all we shared. Neither of us is prepared to make anything more of it. We agreed we're not people who are good at committing. And we both know how different our lives are. We don't fit together. We don't belong —"

"That's wrong, Fiona! It's baloney, and you know it. You told me things — things I already knew about, in a way, because I'd felt them myself. And then you helped me find something I've been searching for without even realizing I needed it. We connected, Fiona. Is that something you're just going to shrug off so you can get back to your elephants?"

"What am I supposed to do? Do you want to turn this into something difficult? What happened was a conversation. I hope it was healthy for both of us. But it was simply a discussion."

"Was it?"

She stared at him, hands clenched. *No,* she ached to say. *No, it was wonderful and miraculous. You're a new man, and I feel opened and vulnerable for the first time in my life. I feel alive. Truly alive. And it's all be-*

cause of you, Rogan. You and only you. No one else.

She swallowed and studied a beam of light filtering across the carpet in the long corridor. She couldn't speak.

"I want to marry you, Fiona," he said suddenly.

She caught her breath at the bluntness of his pronouncement. Tears flooded her eyes. *Let me go, Rogan,* she pleaded silently. *Let it be the way I'd planned it. Let it be simple and uncomplicated and nothing more. Please, Rogan.*

"I want you to be my wife, Fiona. I want to hold you and cherish you and love you forever."

"Rogan, please."

"What's your answer, Fiona? Tell me. Say it, Fiona — yes or no."

She squeezed her eyes shut, fighting the tears. "Marriage is not part of my plan. I'm just a . . . I'm not like other women. You know, elephants don't marry. It's be- cause —"

"Elephants! Is that how you think of yourself, Fiona? That you're an elephant matriarch? Marching through life without human emotion, human need, human love?"

"I have to go, Rogan."

309

She turned away, but his hand tightened on hers. "Fiona, stay. Give us a day to sort this out. Will you do that?"

She held her breath, knowing that everything inside her was weeping. How she loved this man's blue eyes. How she longed for his voice. How she wanted his wisdom, his strength, his warm arms. How she needed —

No, she didn't need him. She didn't need anyone. Not Rogan. Not Mama Hannah or her family. Not God. And if she stayed, she would only want more than she could allow herself to have. It would only be that much harder to leave.

"Rogan," she said, trying to swallow the lump in her throat and failing. "Rogan, good-bye."

On the airplane to Frankfurt, Germany, Rogan switched on the overhead light and stared in the semidarkness at an airline magazine — one his own company published. Ginger sprawled beside him, sound asleep. A thin wool airline blanket covered her legs and bare feet. Her high heels stuck out of the seat pocket in front of her. Her blonde spiky hair was mashed down flat on one side of her head.

Rogan smiled for the first time in twelve

hours. Ginger was the sort of woman a man needed to have around. She was reliable. She did her job. She didn't complain or talk about herself or expect anything out of him.

As opposed to a woman like Fiona. Obviously her type was trouble from the word *go.* She was stubborn, independent to a fault, and self-centered. She couldn't focus on a thing except those elephants.

Rogan tugged at his collar and flipped a page of the magazine. His eyes scanned something about Dutch cheeses. Windmills. Tulips. Delftware. Maybe he would go to Holland. Spend a couple of weeks there just for fun.

Fun. Rogan flipped another page. He tried to think of things that would be light and enjoyable. Bike racing, maybe. Holland was so flat there wouldn't be much challenge in it. Maybe he should go to Switzerland. Climb a mountain. Or Monaco. Have one of his cars shipped over and race it.

He flipped another page. Oh, great reading material here. An article on grief. Just what a guy needed to be thinking about thirty-five thousand feet in the air. He'd have to speak to the editor in charge of the publication. Death, dying, grief —

wonderful. He scanned the sidebar that listed the stages of mourning people went through: denial, anger, bargaining, acceptance.

It was obvious he'd never felt an iota of grief about his father's death. He wasn't in denial. He wasn't angry. He wasn't bargaining to get the old man back. No. The only thing Rogan was angry about was Fiona Thornton.

He skipped a couple of pages of in-flight entertainment listings and found the map at the end of the magazine. Red arcs zipped from city to city around the world, showing where the airline flew. His eyes traced the line he was on from Nairobi to Frankfurt.

It was a good thing he was getting out of Africa. The place had never held much attraction for him in the first place. He would sell Air-Tours and be done with the whole mess. As for Fiona, she would soon be forgotten — another woman, in and out of his life. No big deal.

His gaze traveled to the tiny spot on the map where the Rift Valley Game Park nestled beside the highlands. What would she be doing now? Probably settling onto her cot, turning out her lamp, petting her cat. Her hair would spill out over the pillowcase. She would tuck her feet inside her nightgown. She would shut those camouflage eyes.

He deserved a little more from her than just a quick good-bye and fare-thee-well. He'd offered her half a million dollars for her elephants. He'd flown her to Nairobi and gotten her in to talk to some bigwigs. He'd even bought her a bunch of new clothes. Not that she owed him anything for all that, of course. But the least she could have done was . . .

Was what? What had he wanted from Fiona — marriage? What was he thinking when he'd blurted that out? Had he really expected her to say yes?

Why wouldn't God answer his questions for him? He closed his eyes, trying to think how to pray. Was there a right way to pray? Was it okay to ask God about every little thing? But Fiona wasn't a little thing — she was everything. He didn't know the rules, but he was beginning to know God. And he trusted that God would listen. So he began to talk to Him.

"Father," he whispered, realizing that word now held new and potent meaning for him. It meant that he could be a child. "Help me, Father. Help me to know what to do about Fiona. And help me know what to do about myself."

He didn't hear an answer, but he had laid the prayer in the lap of God. He knew it was safe there and would be answered in God's time.

Looking down, Rogan flipped the slick pages of the magazine back until he found the grief article again. He studied the first two stages: denial, anger. Was it true Fiona had meant nothing to him? Was it true he was only angry with her because she wouldn't bend to his will? Or was he actually mourning the loss of her red-gold hair and soft voice and gentle ways?

Leaning his head against the seat, he stared up at the tiny lightbulb. The last thing on the list of stages was acceptance. Acceptance. He couldn't imagine a time when he would ever accept the fact that Fiona was gone. That he'd lost her.

All right, he would give himself two weeks. Two weeks of vacation. Fun. He would send Ginger back to New York. He would stall Megamedia and cancel all his appointments. He would just have fun zipping around Europe doing things he enjoyed. In two weeks, with God's help, maybe he would be over this little romance. If you could call it that. It was awfully one-sided.

Rogan set aside the Bible he had bought, now underlined in a hundred places. Beneath the Bible lay the tattered airline magazine. He picked it up and leafed through it as he sat on the edge of his bed in a Swiss chalet. Après-ski boots barely warmed his icy cold feet. He savored the thought of plunging them into the Jacuzzi.

Rogan lifted a gold pen from the hotel letter set and began marking through the list of mourning stages. All right, he was over his *denial.* Two weeks without Fiona had taken care of that. He couldn't negate the fact that she had come into his life. She had touched him in a way no one else ever had. He couldn't pretend not to care about her. He wanted her — more than just physically. He wanted to know her and to be a part of her life. And he'd lost her. She had chosen to go off into the bush without him. He couldn't deny that either.

Anger. Well, he wasn't mad anymore. After all, she was right. They really had nothing in common. She wouldn't last a week in New York — not with all the hustle and bustle, with the traffic and people and parties and meetings that made up his world. And no way could he exist in her isolated world. No, he wasn't angry.

His pen tapped at the edge of the third word — *bargaining.* What was that supposed to mean? Bargaining with whom — God? Rogan had already tried that and gotten nowhere. With Fiona? He had no intention of trying to get her back by bargaining her into it. There was nothing to bargain with. The facts were all too clear. They'd met. Spent time together. Talked. Briefly touched each other's life. And gone their separate ways.

He stared down at his boots. He had always enjoyed late-winter skiing. The slopes weren't as crowded. The snow was good. But a week of sliding down mountains hadn't held its usual allure. He was bored. He tossed the magazine into the wastebasket.

Bowing his head, he prayed again for God to grant him the ability to forget this woman whose face still haunted his dreams. The week before, Rogan had found a little church in the alpine village and had talked to the minister there, asking when his prayers might be answered. But the elderly man shook his head and told Rogan that God hears prayers, but He doesn't always give the answers man desires.

"*Gott* knows best," the minister said in

316

broken English. *"Gott knows best, ja!"*

If God knew best, Rogan wondered, why wouldn't He take away this torment? He studied the laces on his boots. What would Fiona be doing right now? Certainly not sitting around in ski boots. It was late evening in Kenya. She would probably be sitting by the fire with a cup of tea. Mama Hannah would be going over the menu with her. Maybe Sentero would be slithering around in the background, looking things over with his small dark eyes. And the elephant calves? They were probably taking their night feeding. Or settling into a patch of grass, their soft ears flapping with contentment.

He kicked off a boot. It had been two weeks since he'd seen Fiona. Maybe he should try to reach her. She never had given him an answer, had she? It wasn't every day a woman got a proposal of marriage. And he had never — ever — wanted to take that step. Certainly he'd never stuck his neck out and asked anyone to be his wife. At the very least, Fiona could give him the dignity of an answer. He reached for the telephone.

"I'd like to send a telegram, please," he told the operator. He waited a moment while she connected him. "Yes, I want this to go to Kenya, East Africa. Send it to Dr. Fiona Thornton, director of the Rift Valley Elephant Project. Cable it to the safari lodge at Lake Naivasha. They'll get it to her."

"What will the message be, sir?"

Rogan studied his feet again. There were a thousand things he would like to say. Things he wanted and needed to tell her. But Fiona had been brief with him. He would respond in kind.

"This is from Rogan McCullough," he said finally, adding the address of the hotel chalet.

"And what will the message be, sir?" she asked again.

"Just . . . uh . . . just put down three words. *Yes or no*. And a question mark."

"Yes or no?"

"That's right. Just *Yes or no?* Send it like that."

As he hung up, Rogan opened his Bible once again.

Fiona was unloading a shipment of soy-based milk formula from Clive Willetts's plane when Sentero drove the Land Rover into camp. Her hair, tied in a loose braid, whipped around in the wind that had sprung up suddenly from the west. She rubbed a hand over her fore-head, brushing at the sweat that trickled down her temple.

"Is that it, Clive?" she called over the rush of wind.

His head emerged from the cargo com-partment. "That's all they sent. Will you be needing more soon?"

"Of course. This is barely going to last us a fortnight." She tapped a toe against one of the blue-and-white cartons stacked beside the plane. "Look, Clive, I want you to get a message to the Wildlife Federa-tion. Tell Mr. Ngozi I'm going to need an-tibiotics as well as regular large shipments of formula. And I'll need for him to send a vet out here the next time you come."

"Dr. Thornton, I can't fly into your camp on a weekly basis. Or even every other week. I have my regular work. And we've had rumors of a shutdown."

"A shutdown of Air-Tours?"

"I got a wire from Switzerland a few days ago. Mr. McCullough wants a de-tailed inventory of the assets. He said he's thinking of selling off. That means I've got to haul tourists about, write up this blasted inventory, *and* plan for my own future. I've been bringing these formula shipments as a favor."

"A favor to whom?"

"To you." He stared at her, pale hair whipping around his head. "Well, I'll admit, Mr. McCullough did instruct me to keep you in supplies. But that was before he started talking about selling Air-Tours."

"You still work for Rogan McCullough, Clive. And you're still bound by his wishes. Until you're told otherwise, I expect you to fly the formula to my camp."

"Yes, Dr. Thornton." A bitter line, unconcealed by the wispy mustache, formed around his mouth. "But I'd think you might consider the welfare of others once in a while."

Fiona grabbed a box of formula and wedged it against her stomach. "Stack another on this one, please, Clive."

"Get Sentero to do it," he snapped. "I've a group of tourists waiting at the lodge for the plane."

He slammed the cargo door. Fiona felt fire flush her cheeks and heat her blood. She marched toward the pilot.

"For your information, Mr. Willetts," she fairly shouted, "I spend ninety-nine percent of my time considering the welfare of others. I have three elephant calves to care for now. Three! Babies are being born and orphaned in the park almost every day, and I could take in twenty if I had the room. But I have three here — and three is almost more than I can manage. Moses, the man you found to tend them, fled a week ago. My research has gone straight down the drain. The camp is in chaos. There's almost nothing in the park for the adult elephants to eat, and they're starving. Maasai warriors speared James to death two days ago. Rosamond has a septic wound, and I'm out of antibiotics. I've been so busy considering the welfare of others, Clive, that I've let my own camp run out of food. Thank goodness Sentero had the presence of mind to drive to the lodge this morning and buy a few supplies on his own initiative, or we'd be starving as well."

"Dr. Thornton —"

"I'm not finished, Clive. You can tell your employer the next time you talk to him that he left me in one fine mess out here. He ought to just come and see what a wreck everything is — except that the minute I saw him, I'd want to stake him to an anthill for the jackals and vultures."

"Dr. Thornton —"

"What is it, Clive?"

"Sentero has something for you."

Fiona turned as the thin African stepped

forward bearing a slip of yellow paper. "A telegram," he said. "It was waiting at the lodge when I went this morning. It's from Bwana McCullough."

She snatched the envelope from his fingers. Squelching the mixture of anticipation, fear, desire, and joy that flooded through her, she tore open the paper. Three words stared back at her.

Yes or no?

"Well," she said finally, setting the message back into Sentero's palm. "It seems he's still interested in bringing his tourists out here."

She pulled a slim notebook from her back pocket and a pen from behind her ear and scrawled out her one-word response to Rogan's query. Then she folded the paper and handed it to Clive. "Clive, send this telegram to your employer the minute you get to Nairobi." Pushing the aching memories of Rogan out of her mind and into the wind, she firmed her shoulders and bent to the cartons.

"Come on, Sentero," she growled. "Load me up. We've got things to do."

Rogan was sitting on the balcony of the chalet, sipping a steaming mug of mocha and trying to pay attention to the Frenchwoman he'd met on the slopes that afternoon. A petite brunette with pale eyes and a wide smile, she had been chattering on about things that didn't interest him in the least.

"So what brings you to the slopes, Rogan?" she asked, rolling the R in his name.

"Uh . . . elephants." He realized belatedly that he'd said the first thing that came to his mind. And it was the wrong thing.

"Elephants?"

He sat up and took a deep breath of crisp evening air in hopes it would waken him. "Elephants. Yes, you see, I was in Africa looking into one of my smaller business interests. I met a woman there who was studying elephants."

"Oh, you're recovering from a broken heart!"

"No, I'm . . . I'm just —"

"But you have no idea how thrilled I am! I am the queen of curing broken hearts."

"Really, Babette, I —"

"Oh, Rogan." She rolled the R again. "Don't deny me this pleasure. I've found there's nothing so interesting as a wounded man."

Weary, Rogan gazed at her, wondering how he was going to detach himself from this vixen with a fetish for broken hearts. He turned back to the snowy slopes, transfixed by the red-gold glow of sunset. Fiona's hair was that color. And nearly as shiny. He could almost touch it. Almost smell it.

"Rogan?" Babette tapped his wrist. "Someone is speaking to you."

He lifted his focus to find a portly bellman, a flat silver tray balanced on one palm. "A telegram for you, sir. From Nairobi."

"Nairobi?" Rogan tipped the man and began unfolding the pink slip of paper. For some reason he was suddenly wide awake.

As the bellman left, Babette and the opulent chalet and the last vestige of exhaustion faded away. Rogan uncreased the telegram and read the one-word response.

Yes.

For a moment he could do nothing but stare transfixed at the brilliant hues on the horizon. Then his head shot up, his mouth dropped open, and his voice emerged like that of a frog coming out of hibernation.

"Yes," he said, lifting his eyes to the mountains. "She said yes! Thank You, Lord! I'm going to marry Fiona."

THIRTEEN

Fiona bent over her desk, Sentero at her side, a detailed grid map of the Rift Valley Game Park spread before them. As he read aloud the list of sites where elephants had been poached, she marked them with dots of red ink. In the past two weeks, the park had lost eleven elephants to poachers. Eight males. Three females, one of them a nursing calf who had taken a bullet meant for her mother.

"There's a pattern here, Sentero," Fiona announced as she placed the final red dot along the eastern escarpment. "I have no doubt about it. It's almost like the poachers know each elephant family intimately. It's like they can predict and track the family's every move."

The African studied the diagram but said nothing.

"Can't you see what I mean?" she insisted. "Look, here are the Js heading south toward Mount Suswa. James is shot on a Wednesday, just over the road to Narok. Two days later Jack is killed at the foot of Suswa. But on that same Friday, the Ps are hiding in the bush near Nairagie Engare and someone shoots Paul. Now, how could the poachers have known where the P family was if they were busy tracking the Js?"

"Perhaps there are two groups of poachers."

Fiona slapped a hand on the map in frustration. "Maybe so, Sentero, but you know poachers never work this efficiently. They're never this fast. They never accomplish so much in such a short time."

He shrugged. "Perhaps they are learning better skills. And the drought is certainly slowing the elephants."

He was right, of course. The elephants were so hungry they were risking exposure in order to search out the last remaining grass. And with continued exposure, more and more of them became victims.

"Still . . . look up here in the north," she argued, aware that her emotions were running high. "See how the pattern of poacher kills follows the pattern of elephant movements? I could understand if it were just one family being tracked, or even two. But members of five families are being slaughtered at the same time in different places. It's uncanny."

When Sentero said nothing, Fiona thought she was going to explode. She jumped up from her chair, toppling it backward onto the canvas tent floor. Storming to the door opening, she gripped the central pole as she struggled for control.

Ever since Rogan McCullough had invaded her life, nothing had been the same. Her emotions had come raging up like molten lava. She cried at the drop of a hat. She shouted at the occasional warthog who happened to run in front of the Land Rover. She mourned the loss of each slain elephant with such intensity that it almost consumed her.

This couldn't go on much longer, she thought. She was a wreck. Her carefully regimented world was tumbling down around her — and she was crumbling right in the middle of it.

Oh, how she missed Rogan! Every single day that passed seemed to cut into her, carving one more notch in her heart. His smile haunted her. The blue of his eyes followed her in the huge cloudless sky. Even the dry grass seemed to mirror the soft golden lights of his brown hair.

"Dear God," she whispered. Prayer had become a regular habit as she begged for release from pain during the long weeks since he had flown away from her forever. Often she found herself with her head bowed and eyelids shut tight to the slow deaths of the elephants, to the barrenness of the landscape, to the unbearable ache inside her.

She had never needed anyone in order to be a complete person. That still held true. For the first time in her life, however, she had come awake to her deep need for communion. She wanted someone to talk to. Someone to laugh with. Someone to love and to be loved by.

It seemed odd to her that in the midst of death and destruction — a perfect opportunity to rail against forces beyond her control — she had discovered that missing sense of communion within her own dormant spirit. She began to connect. Her prayers seemed to travel toward a divine ear. And though she received no quick answers, she knew she was heard. Somehow, in the silence, in a moment she couldn't quite pinpoint, she had let God in.

There was no blinding light, no miraculous healing, no majestic transformation. The drought didn't end. The poachers didn't stop their killing. But in her life, Fiona sensed God's caring presence. She felt His sacred Spirit in the breath of wind that brushed her face each night. She saw the Father's hands mirrored in Mama Hannah's. She heard the power of God's almighty Son in the roar of lions on the savannah. As certainly as Fiona felt the soft nudgings of the baby elephants' trunks, she knew at last the presence of Jesus Christ in her life.

"Dr. Thornton?" Sentero's voice rippled through her thoughts. His brown hand tapped her shoulder. "Dr. Thornton, Clive Willetts's plane has returned. Perhaps this time he has brought the vet."

She nodded, unable to speak.

"Dr. Thornton," he said again.

"What is it, Sentero?"

"You know the vet cannot heal all the wounded elephants."

"I know."

"You know also that God has given Africa one great gift."

She glanced up, trying to read the message in his small dark eyes. "No, Sentero. I'm not sure about the gift God has given Africa."

"This gift we Maasai call *im-booti*, the seasons. Now we're in the midst of *alamei*, the dry season, when the sun scorches, the grass withers, and the earth cracks. This is

329

the time when cattle trails are dusty and hills are bare. The people and the animals face despair, destruction, death. But one day God will spin the cycle and we will have *alari,* the rainy season. Then a green blanket will cover the earth, streams will overflow their banks, crickets and frogs will sing, nights will be cold, and the Maasai huts will begin to leak. During *alari,* we'll feast and sing and rebuild as we prepare for the return of *alamei. Alamei* will come and go, Dr. Thornton, just as surely as *alari* will come and go. *Im-booti* are God's great gift — and also His great curse."

Fiona studied the somber face, knowing from a lifetime in Africa that Sentero's words were true. Yet she was also aware that Kenya's rains had been known to fail for several years in a row — until there was such severe drought that other nations had to send financial aid, doctors, nurses, and shipments of food for famine relief.

And this was the worst drought Fiona could ever remember. Not only were the people growing hungry, the animals were starving. With quick and easy money to be made, poachers were slaughtering elephants at a faster rate than the creatures could ever hope to overcome through their normal reproductive cycles. Orphaned

330

baby elephants — weak and hungry and dying — seemed to dot the landscape.

And with the parched bleakness of Fiona's world, she too felt dry and dead.

"Sentero, if the vet has come, please go and talk to him," she said softly from her place beside the tent pole. "Show him the three calves and ask him to examine them. In the morning we'll drive out and try to find the wounded elephants. Maybe there's something he can do."

Without answering, Sentero took up his spear and brushed past her through the tent opening. Fiona sagged onto the end of her cot and covered her face with her hands. She didn't want to flee, to run away. She wanted to fight — and win. But how? The odds against her seemed over-whelming. Even though she had finally given in and agreed to let Rogan bring his tourists out, she had little hope that the extra revenue would really do much good.

Sukari crawled into her lap and began to groom himself, first with one damp paw and then with the other. Fiona rubbed the warm spot between his ears and heard him begin to purr. A smile crept over her lips as she stroked the cat's silky white fur. His tail wrapped around her arm, much the way the baby elephants' trunks twined around her in greeting.

Pondering the three calves with their floppy ears and rubbery trunks, her heart warmed. The rest of Africa might be dying, but at least three elephants would survive. God willing.

But if the babies were to survive, they would need her care. Standing, determined not to give up, she pushed back the tent flap to reveal a tall figure blocking the late-afternoon light.

"Fiona. Hello."

The voice rocketed into the marrow of her bones. She drew back, rigid with disbelief. Yet there he was. Rogan. Broad shoulders, khaki jacket and shorts, tan socks, dusty suede safari boots. It was as if he had never gone away but had only faded for a moment. His blue eyes traveled over her face. His mouth was slightly parted, as if he wanted to speak but wasn't quite sure what he should say.

"Rogan." It was all she could manage. "You're here."

"Of course."

She brushed a hand over her eyes. "Why?"

Life infused him suddenly. "Why? Your message. Fiona, you said you'd marry me. I dropped everything and came back."

"Marry you?"

"I took the first flight out. It was all I could think about the whole way." He took her shoulders and gripped them as he spoke. "I want you to tell me everything. When did you realize you loved me as much as I love you? Have you thought about how we can manage it? And a home. Have you considered where we should live?"

She stared at him. "Rogan? What are you talking about?"

He frowned, his eyes red-rimmed and tired from the long flight. "Your message. I asked for your final decision, and you said yes."

"What?" A gasp of disbelief burst from her lungs. "I wasn't answering a marriage proposal."

"You weren't?"

"I thought your telegram was asking if I had reconsidered your offer of assistance. For the elephants. You left me in such a desperate situation that I didn't have any choice. So of course I said yes."

Silence fell over them.

"Assistance." Rogan said the word in a monotone. "I wasn't asking about that. I was asking if you were ready to give me an answer . . . if you were willing to marry me."

"You were?" A sick feeling welled up inside Fiona. She fought to squelch it.

"Yes. I was."

They looked at each other.

"You thought I was saying yes . . . I'd be your wife?"

"Are you telling me you won't?"

She looked away. "I need your help, Rogan. Right now that's all I can think about."

He cleared his throat and crossed his arms. "So, what can I do for you?"

Fiona bit her lower lip and stared over his shoulder. Images of Rogan flying all the way from Switzerland assaulted her. "You traveled here just to . . . just to . . ."

"Just to find you," he confirmed. "I came back to take care of you. I came to be with you, Fiona."

"Oh, Rogan." Unable to help herself, she slipped her arms around him. "I've missed you so much."

The warm scent of his skin flooded through her like an awakening. She shut her eyes and rested her head against his cheek. His strong arms gripped her tightly, as if they would never be willing to release her.

"Fiona, I can't just walk away again," he said. "And I can't let you walk away from me, either."

Her fingers squeezed the fabric of his jacket. She ached to believe those words. Ached to know Rogan could fill her and she could fill him — and they could make it all work.

"I don't see how," she began. But his mouth covered hers with a kiss that burned away the pain of the past lonely weeks.

"Fiona," he breathed.

She clenched her teeth, fighting tears, battling away the overpowering surge of emotion that rolled over her. He was back. He was holding her again. His words held sweet promises.

"Since you left, everything's fallen apart," she whispered.

"Tell me." His eyes searched hers.

"The drought . . . three calves . . . Moses ran away . . . and the poachers . . . and . . . and, oh, Rogan, I can't believe how much I've missed you."

Rogan gazed down at her, watching the tears stream down Fiona's cheeks. "No one ever cried over me before," he mused. "No one ever cared enough."

At his confession, something inside Fiona's heart broke loose. Rogan crushed her more tightly against him, and she realized she coveted his need of her. She wanted her own pain too — the pain she had felt for him.

"For once in my life," he said, "I know what it's like to be needed. Missed."

"Longed for," she whispered.

"My money —"

"No, not that. Not your business or your money or your influence, Rogan. You. I missed you."

"Fiona, I'll do anything to keep you feeling this way. I'll protect and nurture you with my life."

He didn't brush the tears from her cheeks. Nor did he kiss them away. Instead, he watched them, as if hungrily memorizing their shine on her skin.

"Fiona, tell me everything that's going on," he said. "I want to know about the elephants. Tell me about the drought and the poachers and how you ended up with three calves. Tell me everything."

She sniffled. How many years had it been since she'd let loose with such a flood of weeping? She thought she should feel foolish. But the tenderness written in Rogan's eyes erased everything but warmth.

"Let's go sit by the fire," she said softly. "Mama Hannah will be ringing for supper soon."

Mama Hannah's smile had never been

so broad as that night when she served a specially prepared dinner of roast chicken basted in garlic butter, fluffy brown rice with groundnuts, and spinach salad.

"I almost feel guilty, feasting like this when I know people and animals are starving out there," Rogan commented as he toyed with a spinach leaf.

"Don't feel guilty," Fiona said in a quiet voice. "Eat what God has blessed you with, and be thankful for it. And then do what you can to help others."

"Save the world, you mean? There's only one Savior, Fiona."

"I know," she said. "I understand now . . . now that I've let Him inside." She looked up, welcoming the pleased surprise she read in his expression. "But you can do your part, Rogan. I still believe it. God has gifted you with so much."

He shook his head. "If I have a gift, it's for railroading people and amassing money."

"That's a worthy gift. Not many people can do it."

"It doesn't save the world, Fiona."

"It might help."

She cut a bite of chicken and savored it slowly. Then she spoke again, telling him about the situation in the Rift Valley. He listened, asking occasional questions as she explained the severity of the drought, the Maasai ritual spearings, the uncannily patterned paths of the poachers, and the numerous births of baby elephants.

Fiona followed his gaze as it wandered to the three little pachyderms cuddled together in the soft grass beneath an acacia tree. The smallest lay on his side, one gray ear flapping. The other two had hunkered down face-to-face. Johnny explored Olivia's face, touching her long sparse eyelashes and damp temporal glands with the tip of his trunk. Their rumbles of contentment slipped through the clearing to mingle with the calls of night birds, the laugh of a hyena on the plains, and the cry of a bush baby.

"I'll stay up and feed the calves tonight," Rogan said when Fiona paused in her discourse on the Wildlife Federation and the need for a consistent supply of formula.

"It's all right," she protested. "I've been feeding them every three hours day and night for almost two weeks. I'm used to it."

"But I want to do it."

She pondered the idea of letting Rogan back into her world. Feeding the elephant calves would allow him to touch what she had been touching, feel what she had been feeling. It would bring them close once again. She wasn't sure she could handle it — because she knew that eventually Rogan would want an answer to his question. And this time she would have to give him one.

"Rogan," she began, "it might be a good idea for us to talk tonight. I feel strange about all of this. I mean, you came back to the camp expecting to find me ready to marry you. I don't know exactly where you've been, but Clive Willetts told me you've been away from your work for almost three weeks. Things haven't been . . . normal . . . for either of us. My research is in a shambles. I just think we should talk over this situation."

His blue eyes traced the features of her face. Finally he spoke. "We both know what's going on between us, Fiona. We just don't know what to do about it."

She swallowed and turned to watch the elephants. His hand, large and warm, covered hers. She shut her eyes, soaking in the human touch.

"Fiona, I want to take care of the babies tonight," he said, his voice deep. "I want you to get some sleep. We'll talk tomorrow."

"How long can you stay?" She blurted

the question before she had given herself time to think. Feeling foolish, she stood. "No, don't answer that. . . . Good night, Rogan."

She walked quickly to her tent. But he was behind her, taking her shoulders before she could step through the door flap. "Fiona, I'm here now. That's all that matters to me. I've lived three miserable weeks thinking about you and missing you and wondering how I had been so stupid to let you get away from me. I tried everything possible to make myself get on with things. I decided I'd plunge back into my work, so I canceled the sale of McCullough Enterprises to Megamedia. I put Air-Tours on the market. A fellow in Bonn made me an offer. I spent time in Europe trying to have fun and make myself forget. I wanted it all to be over between us, so I could just get back to my old life."

"It sounds like you succeeded."

"Hardly." He stared into her eyes. "I wanted to be with you so badly I could taste it."

Lifting her face, she met his lips with all the pent-up emotion of their weeks apart. Night birds and crickets went unheard. All she knew was the warmth of his arms around her.

"It's not going to be easy to leave you tonight," he murmured. "But I've got a few little things to take care of. Three, to be exact."

He touched her chin and lightly kissed her cheek. Then she watched him walk away, his broad back silvered by moonlight and his brown hair ruffling in the night breeze.

In the morning Rogan was gone. His plane had flown long before sunup. Mama Hannah was dismayed, of course, having prepared a huge breakfast of pancakes, sausages, omelets, and fruit salad. Fiona stared at the empty airstrip, her mind and heart a blank, but it was only a moment before Mama Hannah hurried out of the kitchen with a note printed in large block letters.

"For you, *toto*," she announced. "I believe Bwana McCullough wrote it."

Fiona took the note. "Did some thinking last night," it read. "Back by sunset. Gone to do my part. Rogan."

"Is it from the bwana?" Mama Hannah asked, straining over her shoulder.

"He says he'll be coming back tonight."

The African nodded as she walked away. "Oh, yes. Of course he will return. Perhaps I shall bake a spice cake."

★ ★ ★

Rogan's plane flew into camp just as the sun's last light flickered out over the horizon.

Sentero had arrived in the Land Rover only minutes before. Standing beside her, he watched the plane taxi across the bumpy ground and creak to a halt. "A good pilot," he commented.

She smiled, watching Rogan climb out of the plane, long legs descending first, followed by his chest and head. "A good man," she stated.

Sentero said nothing but watched with her while Rogan sauntered over the dry streambed and across the clearing beneath the acacias. He lifted a hand, a grin brightening his face in the gathering dusk.

"Well, I took care of a few things," he announced, clapping Sentero on the back. "Got us a place to keep the three elephant calves. And more, if we find them."

"A place?" Fiona tilted her head. "Where?"

He jabbed a thumb toward Mount Suswa, at this time of day just a purple hump in the distance. "The old King house over by the edge of the park. The house itself is crumbling, but there's a water hole, plenty of trees, some stone cattle corrals, and lots of acreage."

Fiona stared at him. His blue eyes looked downright merry as he gestured back and forth, describing his day. "Flew into Nairobi," he was saying as she tried to concentrate and at the same time figure out how to tell him that his dream was an utter impossibility. "Took this fellow, Masika, out to the site around noon. House could use some work, but I'm a fair hand with a hammer and paintbrush . . . back into Nairobi . . . put up the cash. The bank was very helpful . . . deal should close within two weeks . . . got the papers right here . . . planning to work it all out with the wardens tomorrow —"

"Rogan!" Fiona finally interrupted him. "Rogan, please. Listen to me. It may sound like a good plan to you, but —"

"It's a great plan. We'll borrow a truck and haul the little fellows over there. We'll straighten things up —"

"Rogan, stop. You can't be serious about this. I couldn't possibly find the time or the money to keep something like that going. Besides, this camp has been my home for almost thirteen years. I just can't see this."

"That's because I'm the one with the vision." Smiling, he flung an arm around her shoulders. "Come on, Sentero. Let's go sit by the fire. You two hardheads hear me out, and then we'll make a decision."

"But you've already bought the house," Fiona protested as he urged her across the clearing.

"Paid more than it's probably worth, too. But I figure it's a great long-term investment. Once I get the orphanage set up."

"Orphanage?" A slightly hysterical shriek emanated from somewhere in her throat.

"Sit down, Dr. Thornton. Now just listen."

Fiona watched him settle into a sagging camp chair. She formed a mental image of him seated behind a huge, polished mahogany conference table in New York as he prepared to propose some outlandish plan to his board of directors. He positively beamed.

"What I've got in mind here is an elephant orphanage," he said, hardly able to keep his smile under control. "A place for baby elephants — orphaned by poachers or the drought or anything else — to find a haven. You or the game wardens can bring them in when you find them. We'll staff the place and keep it supplied with everything the little tykes need. Then, when they're old enough, we'll head them back into the bush and find their family group — or another one that will accept them. It shouldn't be too hard if they're not still nursing."

Fiona shook her head. "Oh, Rogan, I can't . . ."

"Now just listen, okay? We'll fund this thing by letting tourists visit and see the operation. They'll love it. Baby elephants. It's perfect, Fiona. People will go out to the orphanage in tourist buses. They'll pay a fee to get in. We'll sell T-shirts and hand out packets of information on the need to save the elephants, and then we'll take any donations they happen to want to give. We'll plow everything back into elephant work. I can just see it — better equipment and more vehicles for the wardens to use in stopping poaching, plenty of formula for the calves, vaccines, maybe a full-time vet, even funding for your research. Can you envision what I'm talking about here?"

Fiona glanced at Sentero. His face, as usual, was unreadable. She cleared her throat. "It's interesting."

"It'll work, Fiona. I'm telling you. I know how it can be done."

"So, you just went and bought the house?"

"Sure. I didn't want to wait around on

this thing. No telling how many of the little fellows are standing around right this minute with hyenas nipping at their feet."

"Well . . ." She looked at Sentero again. "Well, the idea might have merit. But I don't have time to manage such an operation, Rogan. And who's going to work there? These elephant calves have to be fed and tended constantly. You know that."

"Like I said, I'm planning to talk to the wardens tomorrow. It can only be to their benefit to go along with me. The park will make money, the poachers will be deterred more effectively, and the elephants will have a greater chance of survival. As for workers, we can't judge everyone by that bum Moses. These will be steady jobs."

"So, this is how you've decided to save the world?"

"Yes, ma'am. This is it."

Fiona looked at Sentero. He studied her in silence. After a long moment he placed his *rungu* stick on the ground in the Maasai sign that he had made up his mind to speak.

"Bwana McCullough," he began, "in Kenya we have a saying: 'a holed calabash cannot be filled.' It means that the will of God cannot be changed. This has always been our belief. When something is set in motion, it cannot be stopped. The seasons run in endless cycles. Birth, life, and death must come to all men. And I fear that you are proposing to fight a battle that cannot be won — even with money from tourists. Tomorrow go out and see the elephants. Then you will understand. Good evening."

Taking up his *rungu* and spear, Sentero walked away from the fire without another word. Rogan studied the tiny orange flames that licked brown logs atop a pile of white ashes. A dry breeze lifted a strand of hair and sifted it across his forehead. In his jaw a tiny muscle flickered. "Well, I guess we know what he thinks," he said finally.

"Sentero's discouraged, Rogan. The situation is so terrible." She struggled to keep images of dying elephants from her mind. "But he has forgotten that the Africans have another saying. One they believe in with equal conviction."

"What's that?"

" '*Dawa ya moto ni moto,*' " she said. " 'The remedy for fire is fire' — or as they say in America, 'fight fire with fire.' "

"And?"

"And I'm ready to fight, Rogan. I'm ready to fight with you to save the elephants."

FOURTEEN

When the sun peeked above the escarpment of the Great Rift Valley and sent a golden light streaming among the silver grasses, Rogan and Fiona set out across the plain. The Land Rover jumped over rutted tracks and ground up hills, its riders bouncing with each bruising jolt. Fiona looked back from the passenger seat at the old wicker hamper Mama Hannah had packed for them. Despite the rough ride, its cargo of water bottles, hard-boiled eggs, potato chips, mangoes, and other goodies appeared secure.

"Where shall we go?" Rogan asked, glad to feel the wheel beneath his palms. It pleased him that Fiona had trusted him with the Land Rover, showing her faith in his driving ability on the rugged plains and acknowledging his growing familiarity with the park.

"Let's find the M family," she said. "I haven't seen them for almost a week. Sentero recorded them in D-4 three days ago. They were heading west."

"D-4. Let's see . . ." But before Fiona could cue him in, he pictured the grid map in his mind and located the spot. Just north of the road to Narok.

He noted the smile that crept onto her lips as she leaned back on the gray vinyl seat. She shut her eyes, and he enjoyed the play of sunlight across her eyelids and on her arm resting on the open window. The scent of dried herbal grasses being crushed beneath the tires mingled with the ever-present red dust drifting through seams in the floorboard.

"You know," she said, "contrary to what I might have expected — your return has brought peace back into my life. I slept well for the first time in ages, knowing you were watching the elephant babies all night. And breakfast was more pleasant than any I can remember in years."

Rogan nodded. Mama Hannah's grin had been radiant as he wolfed down seven pancakes, a matched pair of poached eggs, and three slabs of ham. The aroma of hot coffee and woodsmoke, the sounds of doves cooing, the antics of elephants frolicking with joy over their milk — all had combined to imbue the camp with a blessed aura of wholeness.

"Strange, isn't it?" she asked, speaking

almost to herself in the familiar way she did when recording her observations.

He glanced at her but said nothing.

"You were so annoying in the beginning," she went on. "I thought I'd never met anyone as bullheaded and politely obnoxious in my life."

"Politely obnoxious?"

"You were a gentleman about everything. But your ideas . . . concrete water holes, a camp full of tourists, noisy generators . . . they were impossible."

She laughed a little and closed her eyes. He reached across the stick shift and took her hand. Her eyes opened as he twined his fingers through hers.

"They may have seemed impossible to you," he said, "but we're making them happen. Just not at your camp."

He thought of the old stone house at the park border. With its huge green acacias bordering a stream and a water hole, the place held great potential. But the once-manicured croquet lawn was now a tangle of weeds. The rock garden was barely evident, and the house itself was in disrepair. Nevertheless, its facade of past glory gave it a faint charm . . . a sense of peace.

"I think you're crazy to take on that old

house," she said. "It was probably a show-place at one time. I can almost imagine lace curtains in the windows, a white wicker table, and chairs on the lawn. . . ."

"I'm going to paint the gables a deep green," he announced. "And the flowers are already fantastic. Bougainvillea, bird-of-paradise . . . liberally mixed with weeds, of course, but even so, it's stunning. But it could use a woman's touch. Why don't we drive over there this afternoon?"

Fiona ran a finger over the chrome door handle, absently dusting it. "I doubt there's much hope for that house, Rogan. It must be nearly a hundred years old. Every time I drive by it, I expect it to have fallen down. You'll want to put your tourists in tents, I'm sure. For safety."

"Tourists aren't going to hang around there except to watch the baby elephants. The house will be a residence."

Her eyes darted to his.

"You should see the floors," he continued. "Old wood parquet. Beautiful stuff. It's been allowed to dry out, and some of the pieces have started to come up. But it's nothing that some gluing, sanding, and waxing won't take care of. Apparently the roof leaks. I've hired out that job. Should be done in a week or so."

"Don't forget, Rogan, you're not in the States. Here, a week might turn into a month — or a year."

He shrugged. "The rooms will need new paint too."

"White," she said quickly.

He looked at her and smiled. "White, eh?"

"It's . . . it's a good color in Africa," she finished. "It brightens things."

"Sort of stark, though."

"Not with pictures on the walls and furniture upholstered in deep shades. Houses in Africa tend to be invaded by the landscape. You open a window and it comes drifting in — scents, dust, sunlight."

"Even a monkey or two."

She laughed. "It's possible. White walls keep everything blended and pristine . . . even with the occasional invasion of a vervet or a stream of safari ants . . . or geckos, who love to hide behind the pictures."

"Okay, white walls. I can go for that. But what about the furniture? You mentioned something about upholstery."

"A chintz, I would think, covered with huge cabbage roses in maroons and emerald greens. Wicker pieces in the garden. Those should be white. And a white tablecloth in the dining room. Deep curtains

. . . something to block the sunlight. It creeps in so persistently. And bookshelves in the library. Does the house have a library?"

"Sure does."

"I thought so. All the old colonial homes had them. You can put potted plants in there, and ficus grows well indoors."

"What about the philodendron in your tent?"

She looked at him. "You can't have my philodendron, Rogan."

He glanced her way, pleased to have teased her into a reaction. Interesting how she had run on and on about the house, as though it were somehow partly hers.

"It's not my house," she said. "I live in a ragged green tent, and I'm quite happy there, thank you very —"

"Hey, is that Margaret?" Rogan interrupted as he stepped on the brake.

Fiona sat up and scanned the horizon. "It *is* Margaret," she confirmed. Lumbering over a ridge as if they had all the time in the world came ten red-gray elephants. In the lead, Margaret lifted her trunk to test the air. Her tattered ears flapped, and she shook her head. "She's annoyed that we've found them."

"They don't look too good, do they?"

"They're starving."

She said it so matter-of-factly that he turned to her, concern knifing through his chest. "Well, what's going to happen here? Are they just going to drop dead with no one even trying to prevent it?"

"What can we do, Rogan? We can't make it rain. It's almost April, and there's not a cloud in the sky."

"What about taking food to them?"

"In my recent issue of *Zoology*, Dr. Hodges — he's an acquaintance of mine — reported the yearly diet of one zoo elephant at one hundred thousand pounds of hay, twelve thousand pounds of dried alfalfa, fifteen hundred gallons of grain, two thousand potatoes, sixteen hundred loaves of bread —"

"Okay, okay. I get the picture."

He sat slumped against the Land Rover's door, watching the elephants file down the hill to graze among a spindly stand of acacias. Megan and Moira tore at the young tree shoots, eating tender leaves and new buds. Margaret set to work on a giant gray baobab. Piercing the bark with her tusks, she tore sheets of it away to reach the spongy central core.

"That can't be good for the tree," Rogan said.

"It will kill it eventually. But Margaret's not thinking about the future. She's thinking about now. She knows she has to stay alive because she's the only one in the family who can get them through this drought. She's lived through other dry seasons, and she can lead the others to hidden patches of grass and acacia stands. She even knows where water can be found beneath dried riverbeds. When there's no more water in the ponds or streams, she'll take Megan, Moira, Matilda, and the others and teach them how to dig for water with their tusks."

Rogan absorbed her words as he studied the old matriarch stripping away the baobab bark. Beside her, Madeline's calf knelt to nibble at fallen scraps of the core, its wobbly gray trunk unable to perform such a delicate maneuver as picking them up. Mick, who had always been Rogan's favorite in the family, stood alone, his antics vanished and his head lowered.

"Mick looks depressed," Rogan said, fighting the emotion that welled up inside him.

This time it was Fiona who reached across the open space and took his hand.

"You know," he said finally, "when I was a kid, I used to feel powerless. I hated it."

He paused for almost a minute, struggling with words that didn't want to come. "I feel powerless now."

Fiona held his hand tightly. "You're not powerless, Rogan. You've done something. You saved the calves, and you bought the house for them."

"That's nothing. Three babies — that's not enough. It doesn't help this situation."

"Yes, it does."

His growl of frustration negated her words of support, but he couldn't stop it. He detached his hand from hers and crossed his arms over the top of the steering wheel. Staring at the floorboard between his legs, he fought the urge to curse.

"I hate this," he repeated. "When I was a kid, there wasn't one thing I could do about my situation. And I promised myself I'd never let that happen to me again. But here I am, angry and not able to do one blasted thing —"

"Rogan, you're not that little boy any-more."

"But I was." He sighed, lifting his head. "I was that helpless kid. My father — John McCullough, real-estate mogul, patron of the arts — decided to have an affair with a showgirl from Las Vegas. Someone from the tabloids took a picture of them together, and the scandal hounds were loosed. My mother screamed and cried and threatened him. He stalked around the house in stony silence. And there wasn't one thing I could do to fix it."

"You were only a child."

"I wanted to save her . . . protect her."

"Your mother."

He nodded. "But I was lost in the grand shuffle. They shipped me away to boarding school. My father dropped me off at the gate and drove on to some appointment he had. I walked into the school office by myself, carrying my suitcases, one in each hand, and introduced myself to the headmaster. 'I'm Rogan McCullough,' I said. The man looked at me and smirked. From that moment on, I decided that *I* was going to be the one in charge. *I* was going to have the power. I'd never let myself feel helpless again."

"And you succeeded."

"Of course not. Not then. My mother waltzed through a string of marriages — each one a bigger disaster than the one before. Gossip rags carried every juicy detail. My father got tired of the showgirl and found a model from L.A. Then it was a Dallas stewardess. I lost track after a while.

My mother occasionally seemed to recall I was alive. She would send me a new suit of clothes — usually too small. Once, nobody remembered to pick me up for Thanksgiving, so I spent the holiday with the dormitory cook. And let me tell you something, Fiona — I didn't want any pity like I see in your eyes right now. I felt rage. Mad and determined not to live my life being manipulated and controlled by other people. The minute I was old enough to take command of my own destiny, I never looked back. I moved forward and upward. I became the one giving orders. Anyone tried to push me into a mold, I fought them — because I didn't want to feel like a loser. Not ever again."

"But you feel that way now?"

"What am I going to do about a bunch of elephants? I'm not God. I can't control the weather. I can't force everything to be okay out here."

"And you're angry about it."

"That's right."

"Good." She smiled. "Now, how about lunch?"

She was reaching over the seat when he caught her arm and drew her toward him. "Fiona, what are you —"

"I'm glad you've figured out you're not

God, Rogan. Neither am I. If we're going to submit to Him, that's what we have to admit to ourselves."

"Submit to God, yes. But not to this situation!"

"All right, I'm glad you're angry," she said. The dark clouds in her eyes sent a shiver down his spine. "Your anger means you care, Rogan. And . . . like I've told you . . . when you care about something, you can change —"

"I can't change anything out here."

"Yes, you can." She kissed his cheek and leaned over the seat again. Frustrated, Rogan threw open the door and stomped out of the Land Rover, slamming the door behind him. Standing stock-still, arms crossed over his chest, he stared at the elephants as they began to wander away from the acacias. He wiped a hand across the bridge of his nose.

Dear God, he prayed, not caring that his cheeks were damp. *Help us out here. Please. We're only humans, and we can't fix this. I feel like a little boy again — so frustrated. I need You now . . . right now.*

A flock of superb starlings swooped to the grass nearby and began to feed, their metallic green-blue backs and chestnut bellies shimmering in the sunlight. In the distance, a pair of secretary birds minced through the scrubby growth with apparent distaste in every step. They studied Rogan now and again, their red-rimmed eyes staring and their wispy feather head crests raised.

He didn't move while all the elephants slowly disappeared into the brush. Even after they were gone, he stood rigid, unfazed by the approach of a small herd of zebras as he continued begging God for answers.

He ached to go back to Fiona and take her in his arms. But she might not welcome his longing for her. Worse, he wasn't sure he could allow himself to touch her again. He raked a hand through his hair and turned finally, walking across the withered grass toward her. His face was emotionless, grim.

"Rogan —" Fiona had spread out a worn blue blanket in the shade of the Land Rover and had unpacked the picnic basket.

"Looks like the eggs took a hit," he said, his voice dull.

"Rogan, please. Let's talk about this."

"There's nothing to say." He sat beside her and picked up an egg. He wondered whether there would ever be a time in his life when God would heal all the pain inside him. He wondered if he would always feel as fragmented as the cracked eggshell in his hand.

How could he look into this woman's eyes and tell her everything he was feeling? Could he ever confide all the pain in his past? the healing that her presence brought into his life? the anger and frustration he felt when confronted with a situation he felt powerless to change? Where once he had held himself together so rigidly, he now felt as though he were coming apart again.

He didn't want the life he had worked so hard to build for himself. It was empty. But he also knew he was impotent to matter here — to Fiona and to her work. He wanted to reach out and grab on to something, but there was only empty air within his grasp.

"It doesn't matter, Rogan," she said.

"Yes, it does."

"Not really," she went on. "You just loosen the cracked part, and it peels right off. See?" She took the egg from his hand and deftly removed the crackled shell from the white. Dabbing the egg in a bit of salt, she presented it to him.

Her smile was as bright as the sunshine. He couldn't hold back a grin as he took the egg. Turning it in his hand, he gave a little laugh. "You're beautiful, you know that?" he said.

"Did I ever tell you that when I was a little girl I had freckles everywhere? Zillions of them. My face looked just like an ostrich egg — milky pale but scattered with tiny freckles. And my hair was positively orange. Mama Hannah used to tease me and say that I was part Maasai. You know how the warriors ocher their hair until it's a gleaming orange-red? Well, that was just how I looked."

She was giggling as she sliced a sandwich in half. Rogan imagined her as a child, all freckly and cute. Long, gangly legs. Bright hair in a pair of thick braids. He wished he'd known her then. They would have had great fun exploring the brush, building forts, collecting feathers and snakeskins and unusual stones.

"I thought I'd never look like my mother," she was saying, her voice wistful. "But somewhere during the years after elementary school, the red in my hair began to mellow a little. The gold came out. The freckles faded. And I realized that my wish had come true. I did look like her."

"She must have been stunning."

"But my wish didn't have anything to do with beauty. I wanted to look like my mother so I could remember her better. I felt it would bring her memory closer and somehow prove that I really had been a part of her once."

"You loved her a lot."

She sighed. "You know what's so strange? I can't figure this out, but it was only after I met you that I started being able to remember her. It began in Nairobi, I think. Memories flooding in. And ever since, it's been the same. The one thing I remember most about her is her smile. She used to smile all the time — so happy and light. Her laughter hung around our house in all the corners. We lost it after she died." She paused and smoothed the napkin on her lap. "Do you know what, Rogan?"

"Tell me."

"This morning, I was standing in front of the little mirror on the tree by the shower. I was brushing my hair like I always do. Suddenly I realized I was smiling. Not just a little smile, but a great big ear-to-ear grin. It was my mother's smile. And I was wearing it."

"Fiona." He started to reach for her, but she put her hand on his shoulder.

"You brought that smile to me, Rogan," she whispered, tears glistening in her eyes. "Thank you."

"Fiona, let me hold you."

"I can't, Rogan. Please." She crossed her arms over her stomach. "It hurt too much when you went away before. I can't go through that again."

"What did you miss?" He genuinely wondered. After all, she had found him so annoying.

"You, Rogan — all of you. Your grand ideas, your boldness, your tenderness, your big hands holding that milk bottle for the baby elephants, your nose burned red by the sun. I missed our talks by the campfire. You made me feel human for the first time in years. It was just you. All of you."

"If it was all of me you missed, then it's going to hurt you again if I leave. It's going to hurt both of us."

"I know. I know that."

"Let me hold you now. Please, Fiona. I've needed to touch you. I've been living in a prison without you."

She came into his arms then. The picnic went forgotten as they kissed. His hands slid through her hair, and a release of pent-up tension came from his chest in a deep, male sigh.

"I can't believe how good this feels," he said.

She buried her nose in his neck. "I know

this can't last," she murmured. "There's no way to make it work. It's just that I've felt so much loss in my life . . . loss that has never healed. And so have you. We're like those injured elephants, outwardly whole and complete but bearing a festering, life-threatening wound inside our hearts."

She was right, Rogan realized. They were so alike. Each had faced a childhood loss that had maimed them. How could they be so foolish as to allow a second loss in their lives?

"I can't, Rogan," she whispered, pushing against his chest. "I can't be near you."

"Fiona." Unable to obey, he drew her closer. Didn't she understand that he would do anything to overcome the obstacles separating them? He had asked her to marry him. It might seem impossible, but he was more than willing to work through every barrier to create a future with this woman.

"Fiona, I don't have to leave again," he said. "We can make this happen."

"But listen to me, Rogan. Listen."

The sound of gunfire was all he heard. Screaming blasts that echoed through the ravines and along the valley. And then the shrieks of elephants. Bellows of pain.

Trumpets of fear and panic.

"Rogan!" Fiona screamed. She sat up, her eyes wide and her nostrils flared.

"What's going on?"

"Poachers. Someone's shooting the elephants!"

It took less than a second for him to mobilize. He yanked Fiona to her feet and flung open the Land Rover door. She was still crawling onto the seat when the vehicle roared to life and leapt forward across the plain. Zebras scattered. Birds fluttered into the air with screeches of alarm.

"Where's it coming from?" he shouted.

"There." She pointed to a dry riverbed and the stand of acacias that lined it.

"Dear God," he muttered. "God, please . . . please . . ."

The vehicle flew over a mound of rocks and bottomed out against the hard earth. Thorny scrub scratched at the metal chassis. Tires slammed in and out of holes. Dust flew.

"There they are. Oh no!" Fiona covered her face as the Land Rover slid in a half circle and came to a stop.

The machine-gun fire halted at the sound of the vehicle. A half-dozen Africans scattered, their weapons slung over their backs. The clearing fell silent for a moment before erupting in panic again.

Rogan stared, frozen in his seat. "Margaret," he mouthed.

The venerable matriarch lay dead on the ground, one tusk and half her face hacked away by a chain saw. A dozen bullet holes in her side streamed with blood. The calves ran frantically around her, screaming and trumpeting. Mick stared at his mother's trunk, detached and limp on the ground near her.

Moira, three bullet wounds gushing, staggered across the clearing, bubbly red foam dripping from her mouth. Megan, Mallory, and Mitchell had vanished. Madeline was attempting to corner her baby, but the tiny creature couldn't be calmed. Matilda knelt on the ground. Her tusks were dug deeply into the dirt. She breathed in and out, wheezing with pain.

"Dear God in heaven, help us," Rogan breathed.

Fiona sat immobilized with horror.

For a moment Rogan couldn't make his mind work. But then he saw a white tusk lying in the brush not far from Margaret's body. The killers would be back.

He turned on the ignition and stomped the gas pedal to the floor. The Land Rover blasted out of the clearing and lifted into the air across the dry streambed. In moments it was barreling toward Fiona's camp.

"Mama Hannah!" Rogan shouted as he braked the vehicle next to the kitchen. The little African woman emerged through the cloud of red dust.

"Bwana?"

"Where's Sentero?"

"Not here, bwana."

"Where is he?"

"A message came for him. He went to the lodge at Lake Naivasha."

Rogan thumped his hand on the Land Rover's hood. "Okay, look. I want you to radio the game wardens. Poachers have slaughtered the M family over in . . ."

"D-5," Fiona whispered.

"Tell them D-5. Tell them to get over there. I'm going after the poachers with my plane."

"Yes, bwana."

Rogan slammed the door and started across the clearing at a dead run. Fiona raced after him. "Rogan!"

"Stay here. I'll be back."

"I'm going with you, Rogan." She sprinted back to the Land Rover, flipped open the metal trunk, and took out her rifle. Grabbing a box of bullets, she took off toward the plane.

In minutes they were lifting over the camp in a roar that bent the tops of the acacias and scattered the monkeys. Fiona gripped the rifle between her knees.

"Someone knew where they were," she said. "Someone had to know."

"Yeah, and I know who it was."

"Who?" she stared at him, her face white and her eyes wide with fear.

"Who's been keeping tabs on the elephants for months, Fiona? Who knows where they are every single day? Who has access to a radio? Who belongs to a tribe that thinks nothing of killing elephants?"

Her mouth dropped open. "Not Sentero."

"That's right — Sentero."

"You can't mean it, Rogan. He would never . . ."

"Where is he right now, then? Off at the lodge? No way. He's probably out reconnoitering his troops after their massacre."

"No."

"Wasn't he supposed to stay in camp and feed the calves? Wasn't he supposed to work on the research while you went out in the field?"

"Yes, but Mama Hannah said he got a message."

"Fiona, try to look at this clearly. Who was the last person to spot Margaret and her family?"

She swallowed. "Sentero. But Rogan, he cares for the elephants as much as I do. He's done so much work to ensure their future."

"Did he want you to keep the calves in camp?"

"Well, not really, but —"

"I'm telling you, Fiona —"

"He took his turn at the feedings after Moses ran off. Rogan, Sentero felt just like I did. The babies had to be saved, that's true — but their care threw our primary work into chaos. I resented them at first too. You know that."

He brought the plane down over the treetops as they sped toward the acacia clearing. "You told me yourself, you felt someone was tracking the elephants."

She shook her head. "It can't be Sentero. It just can't be. I couldn't stand it."

He glanced at her ashen face and realized that he should have kept his theory to himself. Her sense of betrayal was absolute. Devastating. Yet he felt certain the dark-eyed Maasai who showed so little empathy was the mastermind behind the systematic poaching in the Rift Valley Game

Park. And the elephant research project was the perfect cover.

"There!" She was pointing toward the clearing. "There they are! Oh, look at Moira. Look what they're doing to her. Rogan . . ."

He watched in horror as the men hacked the elephant's head with huge machete-like pangas and gas-powered saws. Blood reddened the dried grass. As the plane swooped over the clearing, the men turned their automatic rifles to the sky. Flashes sparked from the barrels.

"They're shooting at us!" Fiona cried.

Rogan pulled the plane into a climb. "We're going to keep them here until the wardens arrive. Get the rifle ready. I'm going in for another dip over the site."

"Rogan, this is only a .22! They'll shoot us down."

"Just have it handy, okay?"

For the next half hour the plane buzzed the clearing. When a few rounds from Fiona's .22 let the men on the ground know they were armed, the poachers became more interested in taking cover than in firing back. The gang had finished its grisly harvest, but Rogan made sure they kept to cover. The living elephants had vanished, and only the three gray bodies remained — Margaret, Moira, and Matilda.

"We've got to find Moira's baby," Rogan said through clenched teeth as he frightened a poacher back into the clearing by zooming straight at him. "When we're done here, we've got to get the calf to our camp. She was already weak, and this will kill her."

Fiona didn't speak. Rogan's thoughts spun with every swoop of the plane. *Sentero . . . Margaret . . . blood . . . tusks . . . calves screaming in panic and terror . . . pangas hacking . . . saws snarling . . .*

"There." He pointed. "Thank God. Here come the game wardens. Good work, Mama Hannah. All right, Fiona. Off we go."

He circled the plane around the clearing while the wardens' vehicles roared up. A gun battle ensued, but the poachers had used most of their ammunition on the elephants and Rogan's plane. As the scraggly men — hands on their heads — were herded into a group by the wardens, Rogan landed the plane on a nearby road.

"Well done, Mr. McCullough," one beaming African warden greeted them, his hand extended. "We've been after these chaps for months."

"They killed three elephants," Fiona said.

"We have the tusks in possession. And we will transport the poachers immediately to Nairobi for incarceration. They will be dealt with harshly, Dr. Thornton. You can be sure of it."

"I want to talk to them, Mr. Wambua. May I do that?" Fiona asked.

"They've been disarmed. Go ahead." He turned to Rogan. "We'll need a report from you, sir."

"Of course." Rogan watched Fiona walk to where the poachers lay, stomachs flat on the ground and arms behind their backs as the game wardens handcuffed them. "But if you'll excuse me for a moment, I'd like to go with her."

"Yes."

Rogan followed Fiona to the men. They didn't look so fearsome, really. Just poor, dirty fellows with frightened eyes.

"Which of them is the leader?" Fiona asked one of the wardens. He translated the question into Kikamba, their native language.

There was a moment's silence, until the warden began beating time with his baton on the palm of his hand. Clearly aware that he would not hesitate to use it on them, the prisoners all began to give the same name. The warden prodded the young leader with his baton until he sat up. He stared at Fiona, terror written across his face as she approached.

"I want you to ask this man something," she said to the warden. "Ask him the name of the person who told him where to find the elephants."

The warden spoke rapidly. When the leader refused to answer, the warden wrenched his arm behind him. Rogan watched Fiona's face, but she showed no emotion.

"Who is giving him the information about where to find the elephants?" she repeated. "Ask him again."

The warden spoke once more. When the man shook his head again, the officer forced his arm into an even more unnatural angle. Rogan pulled Fiona close. "Let's go find Sentero," he said. "We'll confront him."

"No. I want to hear it from this man. He knows the truth."

She turned away while the warden exchanged heated words with the man. Finally crying out, he began to blabber.

"Who is it?" Fiona demanded. "What is the name of their leader?"

"The name of the man who betrayed the elephants is Clive Willetts," the warden said. "A pilot for Air-Tours Safaris."

FIFTEEN

While Rogan flew the Air-Tours plane toward Nairobi, he answered questions for the chief game warden who accompanied him. Fiona couldn't hear their voices from her position in the rear lounge. The poachers lay roped and manacled on the floor in the plane's midsection. Their guards kept watch with rifles ready.

Fiona, paralyzed with grief over the deaths of Margaret and the others and stunned by the implication of Willetts's involvement, curled into a seat. As she stared out the bubble-shaped blister window into the cloudless blue, it seemed that she was as separated from Rogan now as the earth was from the sky. How could what they felt — simple human emotion — overcome the innumerable obstacles between them?

Rogan's employee was an accessory in the poaching of elephants. There would surely be an investigation by the Kenyan government. Fiona had given Clive his information. Week after week, she had plotted the elephants' movements on the grid map for him. For his tourists. Clive could accuse her as a coconspirator. Then what?

Even if those issues were resolved somehow, she knew Rogan had already planned to sell Air-Tours. He told her he had an offer — a good one. He had made plans to return to his position as head of McCullough Enterprises. It was only their telegram misunderstanding that had brought him back to her.

No doubt with this new scandalous uproar in his life, Rogan would back away from Africa forever. He would probably sell or abandon the old house and give up his idea for an elephant orphanage. He wouldn't want to stay involved in something that brought him only pain and frustration. Why should he, after all? He was a success in every other area of his life. Why take on something saddled with so many problems?

And the elephants were doomed. Somehow deep inside her heart, Fiona sensed that the elephants could not survive. Not in the wild. What chance did they have? Poachers, drought, disease, or Maasai warriors would inevitably drive the species to extinction. Oh, she could fight for their lives. And she would. But Rogan had been right. What could one person do against such overwhelming odds?

Governments would continue to trade in poached ivory. Oriental carvers would keep creating their gruesome masterpieces. And collectors around the world would buy the piano keys, necklaces, earrings, bracelets, trinket boxes, statues, and mounted tusks that could only mean more deaths, more slaughter, and, finally, the end.

She pushed a tear against her cheek and bit her lower lip. It wasn't like her to focus on the negative in life. But what good could possibly come of all this?

Turning her head, she gazed at the miserable African men huddled on the floor. She could hardly hate the poachers. They were hungry. And men like Clive Willetts promised them untold riches in exchange for the tusks. Could she hate Clive then? He had grown up in Kenya back when hunting was part of life. Perhaps he still saw elephants as game animals. That way he could justify profiting from their slaughter. Where did it all stop? Who, ultimately, was responsible?

She shut her eyes and rested her chin on her arm. All she wanted was to stop feeling. She wanted her old self back — the woman who could turn away from a baby elephant being tormented by hyenas. The woman who dispassionately recorded elephant births and deaths alike. The woman who didn't speak, didn't laugh, didn't cry.

No. What she wanted was Rogan. She ached for him. And she knew her emptiness would take years to fill.

Fiona moved into the background, clenching her hands inside the pockets of her shorts, as Rogan strode across the concrete floor at the Nairobi airport. Clive Willetts had been taken into custody. A pair of ebony-skinned policemen, handsome in their gray uniforms and shiny black boots, marched him toward the emerging passengers.

Willetts appeared relieved to see his boss. "Mr. McCullough —"

"Give me the keys."

"Keys, sir?" The lanky blond man squinted in discomfort.

"The keys to the office. To the desk you keep locked up. You would be wise to cooperate, Willetts."

"Mr. McCullough, sir. This is a misunderstanding. Someone is trying to —"

"I heard what the head poacher said, Willetts. He put the finger on you. I saw the massacre of the elephants. And you're going to pay. Now hand over those keys."

He grabbed the brass key ring from the pilot's hand as the policemen led their suspect away. Marching through the hangar, Rogan led other waiting policemen and the game wardens into the Air-Tours office. From a distance Fiona watched through the large glass window as he opened drawers, pulled out files, ransacked the place. He picked up the telephone and made call after call, speaking with such intensity that the others in the room stood back in silence.

Finally the group of men emerged. They marched through the hangar toward waiting police cars.

Rogan stopped beside Fiona. "I've got to take care of this business," he said.

She nodded.

He glanced at the waiting officers; then his eyes returned to her. "I've been on the phone with Frankfurt and London. And I have messages waiting for me from New York. I'll have to sort everything out."

"Yes," she said. "I understand, Rogan." *I don't understand,* she wanted to cry. *Please, Rogan. Please don't let it all end like this.*

"I'm sorry, Fiona," he said. "I'm sorry about everything."

"No, please . . ."

He took her hand for a moment and squeezed tightly. Then he walked away. She watched him go, his shoulders bent. He spoke briefly to his limousine driver, then followed the policemen toward the waiting cars. As they sped away, she saw him turn and gaze at her. Then the squad car rolled from her sight.

"Dr. Thornton." The limousine driver gave her a courteous nod. "Mr. McCullough has asked me to take you to the hotel."

She stood in silence for a moment, watching the last of the police cars disappear through the airport gate. She supposed she could go to the Nairobi hotel and wait for Rogan. But what would that bring? Only a longer good-bye. And she'd never been good at letting go.

"Take me to the station," she said finally. "I'll ride the bus to Naivasha, and my assistant can pick me up there."

"But Mr. McCullough —"

"He'll understand."

The driver pondered a moment. "Yes, madam."

As she climbed into the long white car, she glanced at the Air-Tours plane. Images of Rogan flooded her mind. His tanned arm waving as he approached with the first case of soy-based formula from Nairobi. His scowl as they droned around and around the scene of the massacre. His emptiness as he climbed from the aircraft this last time.

Rogan was a part of her now. She could read every nuance in his face. She could feel his feelings as clearly as she felt her own. And oh, it was going to be hard to let go of Rogan McCullough.

As each day passed without word from Rogan, Fiona knew she had assessed the situation correctly. She made a valiant effort to carry on with her normal work. The message that had come for Sentero on the day of the massacre had been from the veterinarian, who had arranged to arrive at the lodge in Naivasha and needed to be driven to the camp.

The young African, Dr. Mboya, spent hours examining each of the three elephant calves. He pronounced them fit and growing at a normal rate. Later Fiona took him into the bush, and they were able to find Moira's newborn. The baby was near death by the time they got it to the camp. The rest of the elephants in the Rift Valley park, the vet confirmed, were in as bad a condition as Fiona had suspected. He tried to prepare her for the inevitable deaths.

The poaching had eased off to some extent with the arrest of Clive Willetts and the others. Yet Fiona knew it was only a matter of time before other small gangs of poachers stepped up their work again. They would grow still bolder, realizing how poorly equipped the game wardens were. The authorities lacked sufficient officers, vehicles, and weaponry. And so the slaughter would continue.

Mr. Ngozi with the Wildlife Federation drove to the camp one day and took a look at the four little elephants. By now Mama Hannah had practically given up cooking. She spent most of her time tending to the babies, trying to keep them from escaping their enclosure and making a vain attempt to fill their huge tummies. The elephants adored her, and her initial fear had faded quickly under the loving caresses of rubbery gray trunks and moonstruck gazes from big brown eyes.

"I have made a spice cake for you, *toto*," Mama Hannah said one evening as Fiona sat beside the fire. "But it has fallen down in the middle like an old volcano."

The first smile in many days crossed Fiona's face. Mama Hannah's cakes *never* fell. "It's all right," she said softly. "I'm sure your cake will taste as good as it always does."

Mama Hannah beamed. "The air feels different today. Windy. Perhaps that is the cause of my fallen cake. And with four *tembos*, I do not have much time to cook. It is like raising four little Thorntons."

"Oh, Mama Hannah, you are truly a blessing."

"I will sit down with you now, *toto*."

Fiona patted the arm of the camp chair. "Please do. Shall I make us some tea?"

The little woman shook her head as she settled into the chair and placed her worn dark hands on her lap. "Perhaps you would like chicken tomorrow, *toto*."

Fiona smiled at the term of endearment. "Chicken would be wonderful. But you won't need to make so much food now, with Dr. Mboya and Mr. Ngozi both back in Nairobi."

"A casserole then? With rice?"

"Wonderful. And a salad. Do we have lettuce?"

"No lettuce. I'll make a fruit salad."

For some reason Fiona found that her vision had blurred. The firelight had changed into bright sparkles, and Mama Hannah's face had blended away into the night altogether. She sniffed and tried to stop the trickle that started in the corner of her eye.

"A message came on the radio today for Sentero," Mama Hannah said, her voice gentle. "He has been approved for schooling in London."

"London?" She knew the gifted Maasai had been looking into various options for his doctoral work. But London? It seemed so far away.

"Perhaps you will find another assistant," Mama Hannah commented.

"I don't know. The elephants aren't doing well, and the funds are short, Mama Hannah. I may have to end the project here."

The older woman regarded the younger. "You will stay, *toto*."

"Perhaps not."

"You are Matalai Shamsi. This is your home."

She nodded. "Yes. It is my home."

"Good night, Matalai Shamsi."

"Good night, Mama Hannah."

It was a long time before Fiona left the fire.

Fiona lay in her tent, Sukari snoring against her stomach. She stroked his head, wondering whether other cats snored — or if she had the only one in the world with such a talent. A chill crept through the thin tent walls, so she pulled her blanket over her shoulders and snuggled deeper into the bedding. Closing her eyes, she drifted for a while, memories playing through her mind, plans for the future darting in and out, sadness mingling with determination.

When a sudden boom shook the tent, Sukari bolted onto Fiona's head, claws tangling in her hair. Adrenaline flooded her veins, and she jerked upright. For a moment she was certain the deep sound had come from an airplane. Then a flash of lightning preceded a crash of thunder.

"Rain," Fiona breathed. "Rain! Thank You, God!"

With sudden intensity the western sky exploded. Bursts of jagged light and deafening peals sent Sukari diving under the blanket to curl against Fiona's bare feet. A branch broke and smacked onto the tent roof. Then the even patter of water droplets began to pepper the canvas.

Raising her hands into the air, she lifted her head and breathed deeply. A familiar smell of damp muskiness filled her nostrils. The tap of raindrops increased to a drumming beat. The tent roof shook and began to leak. Water trickled onto the desk. Fiona sat immobile, chin raised, eyes shut, and a smile spreading across her face.

"Rain!" she said again. "Thank You."

"Toto! Toto!"

It was Mama Hannah's voice. The tone of alarm sent a chill through Fiona's bones. She sprang out of bed and yanked back the door flap. The little woman took her wrist and began to pull.

"Mama Hannah — what is it? What's wrong?"

"It is Sentero! Come, *toto.*"

Grabbing her blanket and throwing it over her shoulders, Fiona dashed barefoot into the driving rain. Mama Hannah pulled her across the clearing, past the hissing, smoky fire pit, and down the slope toward the streambed. As her heart pounded with the intensity of the thunder across the plains, Fiona could see nothing but sheets of water illuminated by lightning. Mud sucked at her toes and splashed onto the hem of her nightgown.

"Mama Hannah!" she shouted over the roar. "Where is Sentero? Is it the babies?"

"Come, *toto!*" The older woman said nothing more as she steered Fiona through the last stand of acacias and onto the stream bank. In the midst of a torrent of water sat the Land Rover, headlights faint against the rain as all four tires spun helplessly in the mud.

"Sentero!" Fiona called. "What on earth —"

The Maasai's head emerged from the window. "Look!" He extended a long arm and pointed into the sky.

Amid the curtain of rain and the brilliant flashes of lightning, Fiona caught sight of a silver wing.

"It's the bwana," Sentero yelled. "I heard the plane fly over the camp, and I knew he would need a light to land. But the Land Rover is stuck!"

Fiona pulled the soggy blanket about herself as she stared at the circling plane. Rogan? Rain streamed from the end of her nose and trickled through her parted lips.

"Mama Hannah, you must help too!" Sentero shouted.

The sound of his voice brought Fiona back to reality. With the unspoken communication so familiar between them, she knew what must be done. As Sentero climbed out of the Land Rover and into the knee-deep water, Fiona and Mama Hannah waded in. The older woman hefted herself into the seat and grabbed the wheel. Sentero and Fiona set their shoulders against the vehicle's metal frame.

"*Moja!*" Sentero shouted. "*Mbili! Tatu!*"

At the signal they began to push. Mama Hannah stepped on the gas. The Land Rover slid forward slightly, tires spewing water and mud. Sentero and Fiona climbed onto the rear bumper, creating enough traction for Mama Hannah to steer the heavy car up the bank and onto the firm ground. As the riders jumped off, the driver gunned forward to the edge of the soggy airstrip, now visible in the head-lights.

As Mama Hannah set the brake and stepped down, Sentero and Fiona joined her. They watched in drenched silence, arms linked, while the plane banked, de-scended, skimmed over treetops. Lightning backlit its wings, making them shimmer and blaze. And still the plane came. Lower. Lower. Finally one wheel touched the ground. Then the other. The plane slid to an ungainly stop in the mud. The door flew open.

"Fiona!" Rogan's voice overpowered the thunder. His body emerged from the plane, dark as a shadow, running, arms spread.

She ran toward him, her wet nightgown

sticking to her legs. Her damp hair clung to her shoulders. Water streamed across her face. She blinked, not knowing whether tears or rain clouded her vision. Her feet slipped, but before she fell she was lifted up in arms as strong as the branches of the baobab and crushed against a chest as solid as the mountains of Africa.

"Rogan," she sobbed as he set her down.

"Fiona, why did you go?" He caught her face in his hands. "Why did you leave me alone? I expected to find you at the hotel in Nairobi. They told me you'd come back here. Why, Fiona? Tell me why you left me."

"I didn't want to say good-bye again. You don't need me, Rogan. My way of life . . . the elephants . . . it's been nothing but trouble for you. You don't want —"

"I want *you*, Fiona."

"But the poaching . . . and Clive . . . and your company . . ."

"I worked that out. I thought you knew I could." Taking her shoulders and squeezing them, he stared into her face with such emotion it was all she could do to meet his gaze. "I love you. Don't you realize that? What I feel for you is stronger than anything else that's been trying to get in the way. Do you understand what I'm saying, Fiona? I'm telling you I love you. I'm telling you I want to marry you. I want to make you and me work. Forever."

The onslaught of words numbed her. She searched his face and tried to read his eyes. "Rogan," she whispered.

"Fiona, don't turn me away again. Trust me with your heart. I'll trust you with mine."

She tried to make herself breathe. "Rogan . . ."

"Tell me, Fiona."

"Rogan, I love you."

He caught her in his arms again, and his mouth crushed hers. The African rain caressed their faces, a baptism of love, hope, promise.

EPILOGUE

Bird-of-Paradise blossoms stretched their orange-and-purple petals toward the sun as it slanted across the stone verandah of the old house. Pink frangipani flowers from a nearby tree scented the air with a heady sweet perfume. Red hibiscus flourished trumpets and silken tassels for the bees that hummed an evening tune. Crimson poinsettias nestled against a lace-curtained window, while the mauve, cream, and white flowers of yesterday-today-and-tomorrow shrubs lined the stone walkway.

From inside the house drifted the melodic notes of a bamboo xylophone. In a moment Mama Hannah emerged onto the verandah. Lifting one hand to her brow to shade her eyes from the low orange sunlight, she looked out on the grounds. Near the water hole she saw a row of small gray bodies. Heads lowered to drink, they looked like praying pilgrims in a mosque. She counted. *Twelve. Yes, good. Thank You, Jesus.*

She turned to the airstrip beyond the

steel fence and saw the safari plane lift slowly into the sky. The faces of tourists pressed against glass windows, their eyes eager for a last glimpse of the little elephants.

A lone figure walked from the water hole toward the gate. Tall and handsome, he blended with the landscape in his khaki shirt and shorts, suede boots, tan socks. Three elephants saw the man's movement and bolted after him, ears flopping, wobbly trunks raised in alarm. He stopped, turned, and bent to stroke their gray skin, his face softening into a gentle smile. In a moment, three Africans clothed in the green uniform coats of the Rift Valley Elephant Preserve emerged from the brush to lead the calves back to the water hole.

As the man started up the long path to the stone house, a Land Rover sped over a rise. Bumping and lurching, it rolled through long green grass and swerved to miss hidden antbear holes. Mama Hannah saw the walking man's face break into an expectant grin as he quickened his steps toward the house.

"Rogan!" Fiona's long tanned arm emerged from the vehicle's window as she parked beneath an old baobab tree. "Rogan, you'll never guess!"

The man was running now, his face alight. She leapt down from the Land Rover, her red-gold hair bouncing around her shoulders. In a moment he had caught her up in his arms and she was laughing — a sound that filled Mama Hannah's heart and silenced every other noise in the clearing.

"Oh, Rogan, you just won't believe this! Maggie has adopted William and Amy!"

"You're kidding? Just like that?"

They were walking up the drive now, arm in arm. Mama Hannah watched them come, her eyes moving over the beloved forms of the woman whose hair shone like the sunrise and the man whose eyes were as blue as a rainwashed sky.

"I'm serious." Fiona stopped on the stone walk. One hand, fingers splayed, pressed against her chest as she spoke. "I was worried sick over Maggie, because she just wouldn't join any of the other families. It wasn't as though some of them didn't want her. She didn't want to be with them!"

"Not even the Ms would take her? The M family has dwindled so much, I can't believe they would reject a young female."

"I guess Mallory isn't feeling comfortable enough with her new position as leader. Every time Maggie tried to come near, Mallory ran her off."

Mama Hannah cleared her throat and moved to the edge of the verandah. "Dinner is ready."

"Oh, Mama Hannah — you've got to hear this." Fiona took the man's arm and pulled him toward the house. "I was just telling Rogan about Maggie — remember the half-grown female we had here for a couple of months? Well, after the Ms rejected her, she grew really listless. But then Naikosiai and I decided to see what would happen if we put William and Amy with Maggie."

"She's old enough to look after them," Rogan put in. "And they were sure ready to try life in the bush."

"When the three of them saw each other, it was probably the most intense greeting ceremony I've ever witnessed. Rumbling, flapping, backing into each other, fondling, the whole bit. And the next thing we knew, the three of them were wandering off together, happy as larks. Naikosiai and I followed them for two days and they stuck together the whole time."

"Where's Naikosiai, anyway?"

"I dropped him off at his village on the way home. He wanted to spend the weekend with his family. What a blessing he has turned out to be."

"*Toto,* the roast will be growing cool," Mama Hannah chided her.

"I'm famished," Fiona said, laughing. She leaned her head against Rogan's shoulder as he drew his arm around her, and they walked together into the cool depths of the house.

The parquet floor shone with a waxed gleam as they moved through the large foyer and into the dining room. There, deep maroon curtains blocked the remains of the sunlight, leaving the room bathed in the glow of long candles burning on a white tablecloth.

"How have things been going here?" Fiona asked Rogan. Mama Hannah sat sipping a cup of after-dinner tea with her *toto*s. Though it was her custom to retreat to the special room they had prepared for her in their home, on this night they had asked her to stay.

Rogan leaned back in his chair and gazed at his wife. "I missed you," he told her.

"I missed you too. I wish you could go with me next week."

"Maybe I will," he said.

"Really? The days I work at my old camp seem so long without you."

"I'm hoping that the demands of your fieldwork will taper off a little, since Naikosiai is working out so well and Sentero has decided to take a short sabbatical from his studies."

Fiona nodded. "You'll be so happy to see Maggie out there acting like a regular matriarch," she said. "In some ways she reminds me of Margaret. She's getting very bossy."

Rogan smiled. "Fiona," he said, touching a strand of hair on her shoulder, "I want to talk to you about something that came up today with the tourists. A fellow by the name of Blundell was in the group. Dr. Henry Blundell."

"From Yale?"

"You've heard of him?"

"Of course. He's a brilliant biologist. I wish I'd known he was going to be here. I would have loved to talk with him."

"He was very impressed with the preserve. Said he'd never seen anything like it."

Mama Hannah smiled at the glow on her *toto*'s face. How it pleased her to witness the joy that God had brought into the lives of both of these precious ones.

Rogan went on. "Fiona, Dr. Blundell would like to bring a group out here to study. Students and professionals."

"Great! They'd learn so much from the calves. I could tell them all about Maggie and how she's forming her own herd of orphans."

"How about *showing* them Maggie?" He watched her face for a reaction. "Dr. Blundell wants to work with you, Fiona. He'd like to take a few students — two or three at the most — into the bush. He's proposing to work with you for a period of time. Take notes. Photograph the elephants. Help compile your data. He thinks he could be of service to you, and his students would benefit greatly. Sort of a symbiotic relationship."

He waited in silence, and Mama Hannah could feel his tension. She was aware that this turn of events could bring on the first serious problem since the wedding six months before. The idea of people overrunning the camp had been a very big problem at the beginning — and Mama Hannah knew Rogan would never want to endanger what he and her *toto* had worked so hard to build.

"So it would just be students?" Fiona asked.

"And professors. People in your field."

She tucked a lock of hair behind one ear and traced the rim of her plate. "Well, there's something I've been wanting to talk to you about too, Rogan."

"Okay."

She cleared her throat. "It has to do with babies."

Mama Hannah smiled. At last her *toto* would speak of that which was even more important than her beloved elephants.

"We can take on another seven or eight, no problem," Rogan was saying. "Fiona, I'm telling you, the people coming in here to see the babies are leaving with a new attitude. They are buying those T-shirts we had made up — Only Elephants Should Wear Ivory. They're buying bumper stickers for their cars back in the States and Europe. And most of them are donating. One fellow wrote out a check for five hundred bucks today. I feel like this thing is really going well."

"I'm glad. It's just that —"

"Every bit of the money is going back into saving the elephants, Fiona. And I don't mind taking on as many more babies as you find. I've got the workers to handle them. Two international airlines have made good on their promise to bring in the soy-based formula free of charge. I got a letter from the wildlife service today. They say the automatic rifles and the two helicopter gunships have the poachers on the run."

She smiled and took his hand.

"The letter mentioned that two decades ago, Kenya had a hundred forty thousand elephants. A few years back there were maybe sixteen thousand. But the killing is beginning to level off now. Some of the credit is being given to the funds that come from our project, Fiona. I think there's hope."

"Yes," she said. "There's hope again. Thanks to God . . . thanks to you."

Mama Hannah watched as Rogan studied Fiona's face. "We can't save the world by ourselves, honey. But we can do our part."

"I love you, Rogan." Fiona moistened her lips. "Now . . . about babies . . ."

"Yes?" Rogan asked.

"Human babies."

"Oh."

"I was thinking . . . well, if Dr. Blundell and his groups come out to work in the field . . . there might be a bit more spare time for me around here . . . and I've been thinking about babies. . . ."

"Me too."

They looked at each other. Fiona glanced at Mama Hannah and smiled shyly.

"I believe you will wish to be alone now," Mama Hannah said.

Fiona took her hand. "No, I want you to share this special moment." She turned to Rogan. "Mama Hannah knew even before I did that God has blessed us with a gift — a miracle — something I never dreamed possible in my own life. Rogan, I'm going to have our baby."

Rogan's eyes filled with a depth of love that Mama Hannah had rarely seen. He rose from his chair and lifted his wife into his arms.

Fiona's head fell back as she gazed at him, and Mama Hannah knew she was no longer in their special world.

"Care to sit by the campfire with me, Mr. McCullough?" Fiona asked.

"There's no fire."

"Does it matter?"

Mama Hannah heard the noisy silence of the African night as they opened the door and drifted out onto the verandah. The green grass nearby no longer wept, for within it the crickets began to sing, and across the distant savannah the elephants rumbled to one another — reassurances of companionship, of family, of tomorrow.

Lost in magic, Rogan and Fiona held each other close, their love a promise for the future as they stood beneath the baobab tree and its rare white blossoms.

A Note from the Author

Dear Friend,

I've had so many letters asking, "Are we ever going to get to meet Fiona Thornton?" You'll know about her if you've read the Treasures of the Heart series, which tells the stories of Fiona's siblings: Tillie, Jessica, and Grant. The books in that series are *A Kiss of Adventure*, *A Whisper of Danger*, and *A Touch of Betrayal*.

All four books, including *Sunrise Song*, have led interesting lives. *A Kiss of Adventure* was originally titled *The Treasure of Timbuktu*, and *A Whisper of Danger* was titled *The Treasure of Zanzibar*. Tyndale House chose to repackage and retitle these books to help them fit better into the HeartQuest line of Christian romances. Caught in the midst of these changes, *A Touch of Betrayal* languished for several years as an unpublished manuscript. When it finally was released in 2000, it came out with a bang, winning the 2001 Christy Award!

So Tillie, Jessica, and Grant finally had

their stories in print. But what about poor Fiona? She'd actually had a previous existence too. Long ago, I wrote about her for the general market under a different title. A Tyndale editor read that old book and wanted to build a whole series around it for the Christian market. We had to wait many years for the book's copyright to become free, but finally I have the great privilege of giving Fiona a fresh breath of life. Her story now reflects my true beliefs about God, love, marriage, and of course, the created world for which we Christians have been given responsibility.

Although the Rift Valley Game Park, the Rift Valley Elephant Project, and the Rift Valley Elephant Preserve are products of my imagination, I would like to thank the many organizations in Kenya and worldwide that are helping to preserve the African elephant, whose very real plight has been detailed in *Sunrise Song*. Among these organizations are the David Sheldrick Wildlife Trust, whose work with elephant orphans inspired this book; the East African Wild Life Society; the African Wildlife Foundation; the Kenya Wildlife Service; and the World Wildlife Fund. Researchers whose work allowed me to portray elephant behavior with accuracy include Iain Douglas-Hamilton, Cynthia Moss, Joyce Poole, Katharine Payne, and William Langbauer. It is through the support of these people and organizations — and through our determination never to buy ivory — that the African elephant may have hope for survival.

If you enjoyed *Sunrise Song*, be sure to check out the other three books in my Treasures of the Heart series. Thanks to God, every person who is in Christ is a new creation — and if it is His will, even old books can have new lives!

Blessings,
Catherine Palmer

About the Author

Catherine Palmer's first book was published in 1988, and since then she has published more than 30 books. Her books number nearly one million copies sold.

Catherine's novels *The Happy Room* and *A Dangerous Silence* are CBA best-sellers, and her HeartQuest book *A Touch of Betrayal* won the 2001 Christy Award (Romance category). Her novella "Under His Wings," which appears in the anthology *A Victorian Christmas Cottage*, was named Northern Lights Best Novella of 1999 (Historical category) by Midwest Fiction Writers. Her numerous other awards include Best Historical Romance, Best Contemporary Romance, Best of Romance from the Southwest Writers Workshop; Most Exotic Historical Romance Novel from *Romantic Times* magazine; and Best Historical Romance Novel from Romance Writers of the Panhandle.

Catherine lives in Missouri with her husband, Tim, and sons, Geoffrey and Andrei. She has degrees from Baylor University and Southwest Baptist University.